BIRCH WILLOW

BIRCH WILLOW
THE RUTHLESS ROOT

VINCE HENNESSY

Charleston, SC
www.PalmettoPublishing.com

Birch Willow: The Ruthless Root
Copyright © 2021 by Vince Hennessy

All rights reserved
No portion of this book may be reproduced, stored in a retrieval system, or transmitted in any form by any means—electronic, mechanical, photocopy, recording, or other—except for brief quotations in printed reviews, without prior permission of the author.

First Edition

Paperback ISBN: 978-1-64990-794-3
Hardcover ISBN: 978-1-64990-795-0
eBook ISBN: 978-1-64990-796-7

TABLE OF CONTENTS

Chapter 1: Not The Only Ones	1
Chapter 2: The Daily Life Of A Giant	26
Chapter 3: The World's Strongest Human	54
Chapter 4: Helpful, Humble, And Hurt	78
Chapter 5: The Presentation	117
Chapter 6: The Secret Breakthrough	138
Chapter 7: Meeting The Competition	155
Chapter 8: Analysis And New Rival Scientist	187
Chapter 9: Recovery And Revenge	213

CHAPTER 1
NOT THE ONLY ONES
(Somewhere in, England. April 11, 2022)

Kronos was frantically pacing around the hidden basement he had created at the Primary Laboratory, every inch of his sinister person shaking violently. Each step he took was a kick against the ground, and he breathed unsteadily. He was losing his mind, literally, and he had to save it. He muttered to himself as he often did when theorizing over anything, and his yellowish teeth seemed to glow in the pale light from overhead as they moved up and down with each mumbled word.

"Given the uncertainty of when the disease will return, there's not enough time to pursue The Immortalizer," Kronos muttered to himself. "It's completely useless, as far as I can try and recall. Birch Willow! That superhuman might be able to help me, though. He's the embodiment of health and life, which is exactly what I need to save my disintegrating body," Kronos growled as he checked his hands to make sure he was not falling apart atomically. "But how? What's his scientific discovery? Is he more than human? I-" Kronos quickly looked up like a spooked animal with rabies whose territory was being invaded as he jumped and turned around in response to a sound of mechanical parts moving and concrete blocks sliding.

Sir Thomas entered the room, walking from the secret entrance above with darkness behind him and then down the stone staircase into the palely-lit room. He descended each step like he was a great performer making his debut on stage. There was an almost smugness to his character as if he knew exactly what was going on. It was all a part of his act to purposefully agitate Kronos and get him to confess his plans because he knew that Kronos failed to keep secrets when he was angry.

"You know, Kronos, such actions will give away your secret hideout. At least that's how I discovered its whereabouts. More or less, anyway. You've always been a loud talker. You're yelling before did alert me to your location, and even muttering to yourself, you were still audible. What troubles you so much? Hmm? I haven't seen you this mad since that accident, which shall not be named again."

"Leave me to my vital work," Kronos snapped. "As always, I am rather occupied with the future, Thomas. Disturbing the founder of the future is strictly forbidden, so see yourself out. I happen to have a lot on my mind, given recent circumstances. Can't you understand that I'm *dying*? Death doesn't terrify me in the least bit, but I am terrified over how the world will manage to function with me, their greatest asset, no longer around. The increased possibility of death changes everything I've ever worked for." Kronos continued to pace around in frustration, unable to stop his hands from moving with one another. One could almost feel electricity in the air from the massive amounts of energy his complex brain was exuding.

"My apologies, Kronos, but I'm afraid I can't leave you alone. Not now, and certainly not for a while. From now on, you'll be under my supervision more strictly than before due to your recent incidents. It's clear to me that even as the world's smartest person and a full-grown man, you're not at all mature or responsible for yourself. I'm rather gutted to hear that you're still self-centered after such a life-threatening experience. I thought that the great figure of death would manage to make you realize how insignificant such pride is, but, apparently, even death is no match for you. Now, you seem to be even crazier than you were before, which I had personally thought impossible. I suppose having that weird brain of yours get even more messed up would do just the trick. And I am well aware of what's going on with you, seeing as I'm the one who saved you. What I'm inquiring about doesn't concern that but rather what you're scheming about, and why you were teleporting before."

Sir Thomas paced around the basement space with observant eyes, as this was his first time in the recently constructed room. The stone staircase led down to a smooth yellow sandstone floor. The walls, however, were standard bricks. *Why construct a room using several different types of rocks and materials? It's rather odd. Is there a reason for that, or am I overthinking his complicated mind?* There was a large oaken table in the center of the room. *Looks like Kronos made that. I can tell by the craftsmanship.* On the center of the table was a single manila folder that seemed to have papers in it. There were three chairs on either side of the table, and then one throne-like chair at the end of the table across the room from Sir Thomas. *A team? Why so many chairs? Working with others isn't like Kronos at all... unless he feels so cornered that he needs help. That's extremely concerning, given how prideful he is. Who would he even contact, though? Not Robert or the servants. Arctic Arsemonger and Drunk Diver? I don't think those three get along that well.* There were shelves along the left wall, stocked with all kinds of experimental creations and advanced technology. On the wall opposite to that one, tools were hung up above a countertop covered with a toolbox and some miscellaneous parts.

A map of the world covered the wall straight across from the stairs, and it caught Sir Thomas' attention. *His teleportation locations?* The map had pins marked at various locations. Minnesota, Massachusetts, and West Virginia were clearly marked with an exact location. A circle was drawn around the midwest of America, enclosing around Nebraska and Kansas. The southern end of Florida had a circle around it as well. There were a few pins in Russia as well, but no other countries seemed to be marked.

More curious and suspecting than before, Sir Thomas was about to turn his attention back to Kronos when he realized that there was still more to the secret room than he had initially thought. There were chests filled with non-perishable foods and gallons of water. Blueprints were scattered across the floor, and there was an overflowing wastebasket in one corner of the room. There was also a small flatscreen television mounted in the other corner of the room, but the screen was static appearing, although silent. Everywhere he looked, Sir Thomas noted more and more items and storage units.

Up until now, Sir Thomas had not been in the hidden basement, although he had been suspicious of the room's existence for a few weeks now. Sir Thomas, a man of his word, had not gone through any of Kronos' belongings or any of the videos on the camera. As of now, he still had no idea what was going on with Kronos or what all the markings on the map stood for. He had seen the manilla folder in Kronos' room, but he had not looked at the papers inside it. He wanted answers. Kronos had kept a lot of secrets, but Sir Thomas would not allow this one as he had the others.

Kronos was leaning on the table with his hands, breathing angrily. He had not spoken another word to either Sir Thomas or himself but had retreated into the chaotic realm of his inner mind.

Sir Thomas asked Kronos the question again, this time as a command rather than a request, as even his undying patience was beginning to thin with each second. "Well? What's wrong, Kronos? You better answer my question before I actually lose my temper, and I haven't been truly angry for a *long* time."

"Well, besides my body devouring my own mind, I'm perfectly fine, Thomas!" Kronos yelled out with an unholy rage, his chest rising powerfully. He sat down in one of the rolly chairs along the left side of the table before he covered his face with his hands and sighed as he let his arms fall to either side of himself. "I never thought my greatest creation would be my greatest destruction. It's the first obstacle I've had to overcome in such a long time. My past-self has left me several messages, but none of them make any sense. How could I have been wrong? I'm never wrong, Thomas. Never. If I was wrong on purpose, I still don't know why I messed up, and that means we're all in serious trouble."

"I won't say that you're being too harsh on yourself since you did cause a lot of trouble, but do know that we all make mistakes, Kronos, and the world of the unknown is the easiest place to make those." Sir Thomas now turned to Kronos, having finished looking at everything in the room. His heart almost leaped out of his chest as he actually looked at Kronos for the first time since his recovery. "What in bloody Hell is that? When did you make such a horrid thing?" Sir Thomas asked shockingly, pointing to a thing in the center of Kronos' torso with straps that led around to a black container on his back.

"It's clearly the work of the world's smartest person to have ever existed. Don't get worked up and ruin your fancy suit. What does it look like, Thomas?" Kronos asked as if it were obvious.

"What does it look like?" Sir Thomas asked in hysteria. "It looks like a bloody bomb to me! One set to destroy parliament!"

"Relax yourself before you have another heart attack. I literally just warned you a moment ago about getting worked up. The last one almost killed you, and it wasn't easy to save you that time. This grand invention of pure evil intellect happens to be a mobile version of our teleportation process, which you've probably been suspicious of since I first started disappearing. I call it the R.N.T. Suit."

"The R.N.T. Suit?" Sir Thomas raised an eyebrow. "You're mucking about in treacherous waters. I don't like where this is going."

"Correct. That's what I just said," Kronos retorted. "The letter *R*, then *N*, then *T*. It's quite simple to understand."

"Ah, I see that your sarcasm and arrogance weren't consumed along with your brain cells. How unfortunate for me and anyone within a kilometer of your current location. I'm more than familiar with how letters and acronyms work considering our company name, Kronos. Now, given your condition and recovery, I'm trying my best to work with you, so please put in the same effort. I wasn't questioning the functionality or legitimacy of the R.N.T. Suit. I simply want to know what it stands for."

Kronos' bloodshot eyes shifted from side to side in a nervous manner. His face twisted and his head bobbled around as if he were trying to recall something. "I... I don't actually remember. My memories were eaten by my own immune system, and for some reason, I forgot to explain it in the document regarding the machine. It's a brilliant name, though. That's one of my strongest talents, after all. Naming things and people."

"A brilliant name? Are you serious, Kronos? I think your brain was damaged worse than I thought." Kronos rolled his eyes. "After all, you're horrible when it comes to naming things, and *everyone* knows that. Anyway, what does it do? As your caretaker," he hesitated a moment, "as your father... I do not approve of this. You look like a bloody terrorist."

"Well, if you must know, *Thomas*, it does a lot of things. It's an advanced machine of complicated processes beyond the average person's comprehension! Even the highest-ranking scientists of the modern world wouldn't be able to fathom how it works. I'll explain it as simply as I can, however. This button," Kronos gestured to the button on his torso, "once pushed, will send a signal through the omnidirectional antenna to automatically activate a device in the library to start emitting and receiving the frequency wave." Kronos stood up and turned around to show what was on his back. A black rectangular box was covering his back like a backpack would, although much larger. The top featured a dome and an antenna. Four straps looped around to the button in front of his torso. "Then, whoosh, I'm back at the library, safe and sound."

"Ah, I see. That *was* the simplest explanation. So it only performs *one* complicated process, not many," Sir Thomas replied in a challenging manner with a smirk.

"You are terribly mistaken, old man. Your ignorance is physically sickening to me, and my immune system is still relatively weak. It is a scientific work of ingenious technological innovations, and there's a lot more than just one thing," Kronos shot back. "The teleportation is just one feature of the R.N.T. Suit.

"Oh, yes, of course. My sincerest apologies," Sir Thomas replied sarcastically. "I was greatly mistaken. How *dare* I think otherwise. Let me ask you then, *Dr.* Kronos Nephus amazing egotistic genius of all things science and he who stands above all humans as their future leader-"

"Get on with it!"

"If I threw something at you right now, and it accidentally hit that button, and you got teleported to the library, how genius is that?" Sir Thomas smiled proudly to himself at finding a flaw in the machine that had been created behind his back.

"Very genius since I already thought of that and took care of that problem," Kronos retorted. Sir Thomas put his hands up in a joking manner as a sign of backing off. "That's what I thought, Thomas. You know that I associate for every variable. I'm always several steps ahead, and you should know that by now. The button is protected through the use of fingerprint I.D. so that it can't just be hit by someone else or by any old object during combat."

"Combat? What in bloody Hell are you talking about? Has the capital fallen already? Should I alert the Queen's men?" Before Kronos could even reply, Sir Thomas raised his hand in a gesture to stop. "I don't even want to know what combat you're talking about. We'll save that discussion for later."

"If you insist," Kronos said with a shrug of his shoulders. "It's bound to come up in a few minutes anyway."

"Now, I assume in the future this R.N.T. Suit will go to more than just our library since someone might be able to track such movements, therefore leading them straight to our location!"

"I'm not really trying to keep it a secret or anything, considering that nobody should be able to trace it. And I doubt that anyone is trying to track a teleporting man. Unfortunately, society still doubts many of the fantastic possibilities of science. Besides, it's a castle. Just let the moat do its work. There are alligators in it, I believe."

"We don't own a moat," Sir Thomas replied, shaking his head and sighing. He then walked over to Kronos to carefully inspect the backside of the R.N.T. Suit. Two rods were vertically parallel in the box, slightly bulging through the back of it. Sir Thomas pointed at them with curiosity as he tried to figure out the purpose for them. "And might I ask what those two cylinders are? I'm almost afraid to ask. I assume they're part of the power source?"

"Those are nuclear control rods used to help the powering process of the module, but of course, I've made sure that radiation isn't a problem in this box. I've determined that the time it takes to deconstruct and reconstruct is proportional to the amount of energy given to the electrical current that performs the task. The more power fueling this baby, the faster the teleportation process, and, of course, we want it to be as fast as possible. This little half-sphere here on top of the box," Kronos pointed to the dome on top of the box, "is a container for the brain cells. A syringe comes out as soon as I press the button, and it sucks out my brain cells. Then, with the nuclear power, I teleport away almost instantly. Although non-living, the module can be broken down and rebuilt just the same, and as soon as it's rebuilt, the program is activated to reinject my brain cells. All through the omnidirectional antennae that projects out from inside the center of the sphere."

Sir Thomas shook his head in utter disbelief at such statements while also going over the science behind it all. An angry sigh of frustration escaped his old lungs. He had begun pacing back and forth across the room. "Well, that's about the damn bloodiest idea I've ever heard you say, and there's been a lot of those! You really have gone mad, Kronos! I thought you'd never be able to be more of an eccentric madman then you were, but you've surpassed it in every way possible! Perhaps your immune system isn't the problem, but this radiation is what's going to your head," Sir Thomas said, tapping his own head for emphasis.

"You know *what*, Thomas? Thank you *sooooo* much!" Kronos was starting to get even more sarcastic as well. "You're sarcasm is really helping everything! It's far more helpful than my endless intellect. Really, it is. I *applaud* you for it," Kronos yelled as he began to clap quickly.

"There's no need to clap. I'm well aware of how helpful my sarcasm is since you're the one who always makes me sarcastic."

"If you *must* know," Kronos turned around and pointed right underneath the dome to a series of small panels, "it's also solar-powered. It's a green and clean power source with no radiation to rot my brain since you think it has! Not that radiation could ever harm my glorious brain, but precautions never hurt. See, *this* right here," Kronos gestured between the two of them, "is why I'm not even going to tell you how the R.N.T. Suit keeps my brain intact while teleporting since you clearly don't support me."

"As if I care! My apologies for being rude, but there are more pressing matters at hand." Sir Thomas, who was a man of patience and sympathy, was now a bit angered by Kronos' tone and failure to realize the seriousness of the situation they were in. "You are very immature for a man with such a high intellect! I suppose the smarter you are, the dumber you behave. Is that it? Is it that intelligence leads to entitlement and laziness, and those lead to not caring about how you act or what you do? It's my love and concern that makes me speak in such a sarcastic tone to you since you never listen to anyone but yourself. Your situation is a dangerous one, and as your guardian, I'm concerned for your wellbeing, as I should be. First of all, let's ignore the fact that you completely did all of this behind my back. That alone is disgraceful, besides everything else you've done."

Kronos should have looked ashamed of his actions of betraying his almost-father and friends in the way he had, but his greed drove him beyond that, and perhaps, a secret scheme was even more so the cause for his actions. There was only resentment in his eyes as if he was the one being betrayed. "As if you would have approved. I-"

"I'm not quite done yet," Sir Thomas bellowed, his voice echoing throughout the room. It grew silent. "I was giving you a moment to reflect to yourself on your behavior, but I still have much to say." Kronos plopped down into his throne at the end of the table, pouting in anger but respectful of his caretaker. "What you're doing is completely reckless. This machine you're wearing is entirely experimental, and even as brilliant a man as you are, no first-time creation should ever be tested like this! That goes against the moral code of real-life scientists. You should never experiment on yourself or on people like we have. Does it restrain science? Yes, but some things are meant to be restrained and for good reasons!" Sir Thomas started moving his arms as he spoke, getting angrier with each word. His heart pounded in his chest. "After years and years of raising you, this is the treatment I get? I'm worried, Kronos. You've always been secretive and crafty, but this is on a whole other level than that. What corrupts you so? I believe in the justification of actions, but I can't understand your actions if you won't tell me the motive behind them. I trust you with my life and have been with you for years, Kronos, so I know that something is really concerning you to cause such a mess."

"When a threat larger than anything is looming in the distance but approaching fast, it's necessary to cut the restraints so that you can fight it. Fighting restrained certainly proves how powerful you are, but it will be your downfall when facing a threat that is far greater than anything you've ever seen before. Science must be unleashed. It has been controlled and restrained for far too long. The world could have been changed countless times by now, but everyone wants to say no for some reason."

"I have no idea what large threat in the distance you're talking about, but if you defeat something by sacrificing your morals, then you've lost yourself. You'll be left with nothing but guilt, shame, and possibly regret. I assure you that it isn't the kind of noble self-sacrifice that you're making it up to be."

"It is, Thomas," Kronos stated bitterly with a pondering mind. He was serious now, and Thomas knew it. "Some threats require the shedding of morals. They're too powerful to defeat while holding back, and that's something you've never understood. I admire you, Thomas. You've taken care of me and put up with me when everyone else would've left a long time ago. I admire that you're determined to do good and that you're a gentleman, but it's always held you back. Do gentlemen win in the end? Do the good people win in the end? Perhaps in the fairytales, romance movies, and the Bible, but not in the real world. They always suffer more than anyone else, and I've witnessed it with my own lives. We always end up questioning whether someone is a good person because their life sucks so much or if their life sucks so much because they're a good person. The answer is simple: just don't be a gentleman or lady like the world used to have, because it clearly doesn't accept them anymore."

"I don't believe that, Kronos, and I never will. I'm not even as much of a gentleman as I'd like to be, as the path to being one is filled with many obstacles, and they aren't easy ones to overcome. Nevermind all that rubbish! That has absolutely nothing to do with you and your behavior, and you're just changing the topic. What even is this threat that you're talking about?"

"All I have is a vague idea. My past-self knew what was coming, or he at least knew that something greater than himself was coming. He had everything planned out, but he had to erase his memories to intentionally trick whatever threat he was worried about, which is exactly why you shall tell absolutely no one that I lost my memories on purpose."

"Are you sure that it was purposeful?"

"No. I'm uncertain about it all now. I know everything, but it's all random ideas and goals that don't make any sense. For the first time in forever… I'm completely lost." Kronos' gaze fell to the table as he held up his head with his hand. "I don't know what to do. If I fail, then the sacrifices and plans that my past-self made will have been in vain."

A bitter frown formed on Sir Thomas' face as he realized how grave all of this was. He sighed depressingly. "I haven't seen you this gutted in a long, long time, Kronos. This really is bad, isn't it? I can't say that I'm not mad at you anymore, but I forgive you for the scare you gave all of us. Clearly, you were doing it for the right reasons, and it was imperative to everything, but that doesn't excuse your actions." Realizing that Kronos needed to be comforted, Sir Thomas slowly began to make his way over to Kronos, who seemed to be sobbing. His body, which was half-hunched over the table, appeared to have a heavy burden upon it.

Kronos sighed aggressively. "The truth is that I just want to save humanity and be the single leader of the world," Kronos stated in the bitterest voice. There was a slight hint of heroism to his words, although his looks and attitude appeared villainous. "To unite all of its people and places would only be logical. Why be the smartest person to have ever existed if you don't do something good for the world. Creating inventions isn't enough anymore. Something horrible is coming to destroy society as we know it, and it is amongst ourselves that it is created. I can't save the world from a threat I don't know about."

"You're not meant to save the world, Kronos. Nobody is. I'm glad that you finally understand the good morals I tried to raise you to have, but no single man or woman could ever save everyone. We can all pitch in a bit, but that's really it. Some of us contribute more than others, but this doesn't seem like you. I know you better than this sappy talk. I mean, I'm sure you do want to save humanity, but you only want to do that so they'll worship you and so you'll be number one and have all the power that would come with such a position and fame. Why, Kronos? Why are you so greedy?"

"Incorrect. You can get the fuck out of here if you've come to doubt and judge me," Kronos retorted as he raised his head and looked at Sir Thomas, his eyes almost glaring at the old man. He licked his upper lip quickly, his sharp yellowish teeth flashing. There was something unholy in his eyes, and their existence almost seemed to be impossible. "Besides, you're also incorrect about helping the world. If everyone keeps saying that no single person is meant to save it and that all we can do is pitch in small bits of help, then no one will ever help because they'll leave it to others. Having one prominent person step forward and contribute more than all the leaders of the past would be the spark needed to light a blazing fire of change." Kronos fidgeted his fingers around, his mind concocting something undeterminable behind his scheming face. "If you had the power to manipulate reality through the technological ability to manipulate any and all atoms down to the scale of a single atom at a time, what would you do?"

Sir Thomas looked over at Kronos and met his eyes, trembling internally at what seemed to be lurking within them. "I don't quite understand what you're asking, Kronos? I suppose I would try my best to help everyone while trying to prevent the technology from falling into the wrong hands. Where is this coming from? What do you mean?"

"That's what we've created, Thomas!" Kronos cried out with a bang of his fist against the table. "We could list my goals as creating teleportation or trying to bring back the dead, but those aren't correct. My true goal is ultimate power, Thomas. It always has been. It's in my genes. I can feel it. I've strung you along with various excuses, but if you want the truth, my true goal is ultimate power with control over reality. I have it. I can manipulate atoms any way I want, and since reality, as we know it, is just made up of atoms, that means I'm in charge now. I can take any atoms and force them together to make anything I want. I can rip atoms apart wherever I want. I, **King Kronos**, can turn mountains into dust or liquids into solids on my command through my technology. With a push of a button, I can teleport to almost anywhere. I am a god! I have truly bent science to my will, just as I shall do to the world. With control over reality, I will be king of the world. I'll be able to fix everything. I'll be able to create a utopia. It's a fictional idea, but it will become real, just as I have made control over atoms real!"

There were tears in Sir Thomas' eyes, although they might have been ones of utter horror and fear. The shock of what he heard rang throughout his body as his chest clenched up. "No! Bloody Hell!" He took a step backward as if afraid, almost shaking with disbelief. "That isn't how it's meant to be done," he desperately cried out. "The utter madness of your goals and ideas has exceeded what I thought it could! A utopia is formed with a foundation of democracy, not tyranny or dictatorship. It's meant to be made by men and women, not an unholy being forged by unethical scientific practices!"

"I know," Kronos said as he hung his head in defeat. "I tried to change reality too fast. Now, the universe is resisting my rule. It's not ready to be tamed, so it has stuck me down with a sickness that's unlike any other. Now we must go on a quest for a permanent cure, and to get more powers for me so that I become greater than any god of any religion. Control over reality isn't enough to rule this world. It's clear to me now that expanding my powers and drastically enhancing my body is absolutely necessary."

"Expand your powers? Enhance your body? What hogwash and rubbish are you spewing from the foul mouth of yours? It's horrifying because you believe every word of it. The distortion between fiction and reality seems to have completely warped your mind. The world didn't strike you down with a sickness! You brought that disease upon yourself, and it was a fitting punishment. A permanent cure? There's no need for that, Kronos. You're healthy and fixed, as long as you don't try any more experimental processes on yourself," Sir Thomas stated desperately. "The fact that you need a permanent cure means you plan on continuing what you were doing instead of learning your lesson from the consequences. I healed you. Leave all of this behind. Just live a normal life. You must cast aside these delusional ideas! There is no threat to humanity! You are safe. *We* are safe. You're just trying to use your sickness as an excuse to get more power through whatever means necessary!"

Kronos smirked. *Exactly so, my caretaker. I'm afraid you're not supposed to know that, though.* He shook his head. "Incorrect! Cured? Yes, I am cured, but I live in constant fear that at any second, my immune system might eat me from the inside out or that my body will fall apart atomically. It's absolutely terrifying and horrific. I can't just leave everything I've discovered behind and then try to live a normal life. I've never had a normal life, and I'll never be able to. It's far too late for me. My life was ruined decades ago, but the future generations," Kronos looked up with hope, an insane glow in his eyes, "they can live normal lives. With my powers, I shall create a better world for them."

"How, Kronos? You can teleport, but that's it! You can't actually control reality or the universe! That's not what our goal was. That isn't what we created. You aren't some superpowered person. You're a brilliant man, but just a man when all is actually taken into account." A grave expression sprang onto Sir Thomas' face from the depth of his soul, and he clutched his chest. "No. It can't be… you've gone delusional with brain damage from your sickness. I-"

"Old man, noooooo!"

※ ※ ※

Sir Thomas awoke with a sense of panic as he looked around, unaware of where he was. He stopped when he spotted Kronos still sitting in the throne-like chair at the end of the table, the map just behind him on the wall. Both his mind and vision were fuzzy, but Sir Thomas recovered rather quickly and came to his senses. "Kronos? What happened? Where are we?"

"I'm afraid you passed out and were unconsciousness for a few minutes, old friend. Luckily, you're very healthy for your age. At first, I thought you were having a stroke. I suppose my inner heart was too vile for a heart as pure as yours to look at. I don't blame you. Such ambition and raw power in a single man can be intimidating to many. The knowledge of the **Empirical Emperor** is overwhelming."

"I remember everything that happened. Unlike you, I actually keep my memories." Sir Thomas sighed in frustration. He took a moment as he thought over everything that had been said. "I still don't understand you, Kronos. I've spent decades trying to, but I never will. If I didn't feel like I owed your parents my life, and if I didn't have good morals and a sense of duty, I would have *never* stayed with you. Every time I see you, you're a bigger disgrace and dishonor to them." Sir Thomas sat back more comfortably in his chair. "You're also a reflection on me, and it is one that I am greatly ashamed of. This is all my fault. Granted, you were constantly off on your own or hiding away, but I failed at raising you."

"Incorrect. Don't be too harsh on yourself, old man. *Nobody* could have raised a more-than-human such as myself. A king has an advisor and those who take care of him, but at the end of the day, the way he rules and makes decisions is of his own accord. At least for kings who are powerful and strong-willed. Considering all of that, along with my complex brain and twisted heart, you've done an excellent job. Such intellect and visions are hard for any person to handle, including me. If I understood my brain, I'd have already become the true ruler of the world. So take an easy on blaming yourself. I do respect you enough and have enough good morals left in me to accept my own faults and know that the man I am is purely a result of me. It is no reflection of you, and your sacrifices are greatly appreciated."

The two men sat in silence for a long time. The whole room seemed to be depressed. The walls appeared blander, the lights seemed dimmer, and the air felt thicker, but Sir Thomas knew it was all just his senses attaching his sorrow to everything. He took deep breaths and slowly exhaled as he thought over the past few decades, starting with the day he first took Kronos under his supervision. Then, Sir Thomas looked over at present-day Kronos, who was deep in thought, planning out every second to come for the next few weeks. His heart almost stopped as his tongue hesitated, but he had come to his final decision. He wanted to do what was best for everyone. "Bloody Hell. I truly wish I could have done more. I *should* have done more. I hate myself for being a failure. This aches my heart, but it is what must be done." Sir Thomas shook his head, shame and regret resonating with each slow movement to the side. "I think this is where we finally part ways, son," he said bitterly with as best a smile as he could summon, though he was clearly torn over the decision he was making.

Kronos slowly looked up at Sir Thomas indifferently. "What are you talking about?"

"You already know what I mean, Kronos. It's time for us to go our separate ways," Sir Thomas stated, his voice truly regretful.

"Incorrect. You say that, but I know you don't mean it. I account for all variables, and you are a pattern that's easy to understand. You always say that, but you never act upon it because you always forgive, and you're a push-over. Of course, there's nothing wrong with that, but because of it, I know you're not serious."

Sir Thomas sighed a breath filled with sorrowful determination, and it hurt him to do so. "That's true, but I'm afraid it's different this time," he stated, his voice sounding far older than it was. "Everything has a limit, Kronos, and I'm at mine. It's taken a long time and a lot of horrible actions, but you've finally managed to push me to my limit of patience, forgiveness, and tolerance. You, of all people, should understand that patterns aren't necessarily absolute or permanent. I blame myself, but I also accept that some people can't be helped. I hate to say that, as I think we should attempt to help everyone, but some people truly are beyond our help or even their own help. You're actually delusional, and there's nothing I can do to help you. Just try and think about how a regular person would respond to everything you said today. You've gone far beyond the madness of the past, and it's not healthy."

Kronos rolled his eyes in denial. "Incorrect. You can't possibly mean that. You know that I'm good at heart. You've seen me at my worst, but you've also seen me at my best. My greatness is a blessing to all."

"You are good at heart, but you don't use it. I have raised and loved you like a son, but you are an unappreciative ambitious man with delusional visions of a future that will never exist. I cannot support you or your experimental work any longer." Kronos jerked back as if he had been shot in the chest. "It would be wrong to fill your head with hope for these false dreams of yours. It would be wrong of me to help you achieve such villainous things, even if you think they're right and even if they will save society. You don't know what's coming, and that's what scares you, but Kronos… the truth is that none of us know what's coming. I think you're scared because you've been humbled by your illness, and you finally see yourself and feel like a human. Even geniuses don't know everything, and you should realize that." Sir Thomas pushed his chair back and stood up. "Don't devote your life to save people for your own selfish reasons. They don't want your help, Kronos. You could save a lot of people through your science and technology, but not like this," Sir Thomas said with a gesture to everything in the room. "You can't enforce your will on everyone through power. You have to know that by now. Honestly, I could go on and on about why I'm leaving, but I think that somewhere in that pitiful heart of yours, you know how worthless of a human being you are. Have your wish. You can officially be Mr. Monatomic. Goodbye, Kronos. It has almost been an honor. I am proud of you despite all of this." He walked away, headed toward the only entrance and exit of the room.

An entire wave of mixed emotions washed over Kronos, and he almost physically convulsed. A clashing battle of rage and melancholy warred within him as he watched Sir Thomas start to leave. *You think I'm lying? You think I'm delusional? This is the thanks I get for trying to stop the threat that is coming? I knew that I'd have to sacrifice a lot in order to achieve all of my goals, but I didn't think those sacrifices included losing you. The truth is, I can't handle that.* Before Sir Thomas could escape, Kronos jumped out of his throne, reaching forward like a savage animal. "Wait! Please don't leave, Thomas. I have all of these glorious inventions, but the truth is that you're the only thing I have in my life. I don't say I love you or call you my father, but I admire and respect you, Thomas. You're an intelligent and caring man, and that's something I've always desired to be, but my fate is to be something far different. There's something much larger at play here, and I need you to trust me on this one. I don't remember what's coming, but I have a few details. I need you to believe that I know what I'm doing and that when everything's over with you'll realize that I was right. You have to trust me!"

"*Trust* you? You're a damn *liar*! You're not a backstabber, but you are a *cruel, selfish* man, Kronos! You keep too many secrets to be trusted! I can never believe you or understand what's going on. You never trust me, yet you expect complete trust all the time despite all the reasons that say otherwise." Sir Thomas stopped and stood firmly where he was, just a few feet away from the staircase. He wiped the tears from his eyes. "I've lost a lot because of you. More than you'd ever know, and for what? Most people like me, but I feel like I'm a failure. I'm supposed to be a gentleman, a religious man, and the good-hearted neighbor, but you've ruined me. Not that I can blame only you. Much of it is my fault as well. I've spent so much time on you that I forgot about me and everyone else. I've devoted my *whole* life to you. I've been a faithful and caring guardian through all of the struggles and trouble we've had to face."

"You're wrong, Thomas. You *are* a good man, and being associated with a horrible person like me doesn't take away from that. In fact, it adds to it. You could have gone off and lived a life of your own while I suffered in underfunded orphanages, but you chose to raise me. I am forever thankful for that. It proves how selfless you are. You blame yourself for how I turned out to be and the choices I make, but you and I both know that I practically raised myself. You tried your best, old man, but I'm a truly unique case. Despite all of the negative traits I have, you can trust me, Thomas. There are things beyond my comprehension, but I know what must be done for everyone. You've spent your whole life devoted to me. Allow my final experiment to be devoted to you, old man."

"Final experiment? Hmm. I don't believe that part at all, but then I can retire, and we'll all live happily ever after?"

"Correct."

Sir Thomas let out a huge sigh of defeat. "Then I suppose a few more months wouldn't hurt," Sir Thomas grumbled. He glanced at his expensive watch. "Bloody Hell." He turned around and slowly started walking back to the table. He stopped. "Were… were you crying, Kronos?"

There was a single tear in Kronos' right eye. He crushed it into atoms with a blink of his eyelid, leaving no liquid trace of the physical emotion visible on his face. "Of course not. How impudent of you to assume such a thing. Besides, it'd be a reflection on your part if I had been upset. After all, what kind of gentleman makes others cry? Anyway, that sounds like a plan," Kronos said wickedly as he shook Sir Thomas' hand.

"Bollocks. I'm going to regret this," Sir Thomas commented as he shook his head. He let go of Kronos' rough hand. "You'll have to fill me in on all the details, though. Like, what in bloody Hell is this?" Sir Thomas asked as he picked up an experimental gun that was displayed on a rack on the shelf that stood against the left wall.

"Be careful with that! It's called the D.O.O.M. Shooter, and it's a highly dangerous weapon." Just like that, they were back to how they always were. It was as if nothing had happened or changed, although there was a growing doubt in Sir Thomas' heart that he wished was not there.

"DOOM Shooter! Your brain really has been destroyed by your own body! Your names for things are getting worse and worse."

"It's doom as in D-O-O-M. It's an acronym, which you *should* have known. It stands for Deconstructor of Organic Matter! As expected, I found a way to weaponize the atomic current. I created a way to rip apart atoms at will." Kronos was proud of himself and his creation. He was actually a bit relieved to be talking to Sir Thomas and telling him everything now. It was as if a weight had been lifted off of him a bit, and although it was still there, it felt much lighter than before. Kronos had wanted to tell of everything that had happened, preferably on his own terms, but this would work just as well. Finding a way to confess a secret life was hard for everyone and anyone, and that even included a perfect planner and strategist like Kronos.

"Is that a weaponized gauntlet over there?" Sir Thomas asked with a point to a ledge one higher than the one the D.O.O.M. Shooter had been displayed on. "Why would you ever need that?" He noticed a chainsaw on the ground to the left of the shelf. "My God! A chainsaw? What are all of these weapons and tools for? The price for making these is far too expensive to be able to resell on the market at a price that even the richest person alive could afford, and that's you!"

"That's exactly why I only made one of each thing, except for a few of the smaller tools that aren't as complicated. There's something I've been putting together for some time now. At least I think so, but my memories are gone, so it's hard to tell. Unfortunately, I had mostly been working on it for the past few months. Here are the files." Treating it like a priceless possession, Kronos handed the manila folder containing the weapon blueprints and profiles in it to Sir Thomas. "Read those. This is all part of what I think is coming, and you deserve to know everything that's going on. Those are the enemies and allies of our future quest."

Sir Thomas gently put the D.O.O.M. Shooter back in its place, and he took a seat in a chair at the table. He began to look through all of the files and papers. A self-proclaimed lord of literature, Sir Thomas was an extremely fast reader, while still absorbing all the information he read entirely. He had just finished looking over one of the blueprints when he felt Kronos looming behind him. "Do you *mind*?" Sir Thomas asked as he turned around and glared at Kronos. "How many times do I have to tell you that it's very rude to read over someone's shoulder unless given permission to do so?"

"Sorry for looking at my own files and blueprints," Kronos replied sarcastically while rolling his eyes.

"That's precisely why you don't need to be reading them right now. You already know what's on them. Now shoo."

After Kronos had stormed away, Sir Thomas resumed quickly reading over everything carefully, making subtle humming noises of understanding and muttering things to himself. After some time had passed, he sighed as he closed the manila folder. He looked up at Kronos, who was staring him down with eager eyes. "So this is what you've been doing? Chasing myths? You make fun of me for reading the Bible every night before bed, but here you are researching fairytales." Sir Thomas shook his head in disbelief. "Bloody Hell. This is worse than anything I could have possibly imagined. We don't even know if any of these people are real. Why are you wasting your time with this? Wasted time is something a man like you would absolutely despise. Half of them don't even sound real!"

"Except they are real! Just take a look at *us*, Thomas! At *me*. Do you think normal people would think that we're real if told the truth? You said something similar earlier! To them, R.O.M.A.B.A. Industries is simply a company that sells furniture, phones, vehicles, gizmos and gadgets, and some artwork. Yet we've created not only teleportation, but we've actually created a current that allows us to manipulate atoms on a scale down to one atom at a time. That's *remarkable*. These people must be geniuses like us! Why would you believe in an invisible ruler of the universe but doubt the existence of advanced people like ourselves?"

"Blimey, Kronos. Don't bring religion into this, and these people aren't like ourselves at all. A *telekinetic* man? Superhumans and the complete transformation of cells? Invisibility and large-scale magnetic manipulations? Are you actually kidding me right now? I was *so* worried about you. I suppose it was for nothing because this is all hogwash and rubbish. Our research and breakthroughs have boosted my faith in what is possible, but most of these are too fictional to be true."

Kronos sighed frustratedly because Sir Thomas was missing the point, although his doubts were understandable. "There are logical explanations to these people's real-life powers. If something can be backed by logic and science, then the chances of it being real are much higher" Kronos looked at Sir Thomas, a cold and serious expression on his face. "Listen to me. If we can tear apart cells, send them out on waves, and then rebuild them, then why can't these people do similar things? Science is the absolute answer to a lot of questions, and it is the key to creating everything. They could help us, Thomas."

"Help us with what? Your illness? You think that this man you nicknamed The Immortalizer can help us prevent this new disease or restore your youth? Looking for him is probably why your symptoms have worsened. He's just as much of a myth as time travel is. He's probably just direct lineage or something of the sort. You couldn't even find him, as far as we know." Sir Thomas was trying to talk sense into Kronos, but he had a feeling that it would not work. This was not the first time that something like this had happened, and he knew that Kronos was stubborn. It was already too late. "Please…"

"We don't have to find him, Thomas. You don't hunt myths. When it comes to things like that, you set a trap using some bait. He wasn't entirely a dead end." Kronos smirked at Sir Thomas, a crafty look in his eyes.

Sir Thomas sighed and shook his head. "I agreed to help you, but this is already too much. Blimey and bollocks." He was filled with disbelief and frustration. "What do you mean? What have you done this time?"

"I'm not entirely sure, but I believe I left a trail for him to follow. I think. There was a video of me in Cape Cod, and in the background, there seems to be a man spying on me. I identified the man using our custom technology. It was a local man named Steve something or other. He most likely told The Immortalizer about what happened since he probably saw me teleport away. Now, this immortal man knows that I was looking for him, and he'll either want answers or our technology. We don't have to find him. His curiosity and greed are all we need to help us. He's going to find us, just as I had planned. Well, the backup plan, anyway. The real goal was to find him."

"No! He probably doesn't want to be found, and now he might just go into further hiding. Besides, you're a coding genius, aren't you? After all, you made that program that goes through the internet that uses all of its data to predict every move of your specified target or whatever. Why not track these people using technology, so that we don't actually have to do anything?"

"Incorrect. It's not that easy, Thomas. These are people who don't want to be found."

"Exactly! Just retire already, Kronos! We're rich, and we don't need all of this crap in our lives." Sir Thomas had raised his voice by this time and was now waving his hands around and pointing. "Your disease doesn't need a cure. It's gone! It was fixed by me who did everything I could to take care of you." He started to violently point at himself as he took credit for the cure. "Oh, and that's even if this is about finding a permanent cure, which I doubt it is. R.O.M.A.B.A. Industries is a huge success. You want more power and money? Fine! We can reinvent the world with just what we have now. We can teleport nonliving things. Every big business would bow to us and acknowledge us as the new dominant shipping company. The world would be changed forever. There are hundreds of possible things we could invent using our ability to manipulate atoms."

"Correct, but that's not what I want. The world doesn't need another shipping company. It needs *us*. It needs *me*. Some of these people are criminals. Only we can stop them. Plus, I want their technology and science… *all* of it."

Sir Thomas sighed and took a deep breath to calm himself down. He already knew that Kronos' mind could not be dissuaded, but he figured he would try anyway. "It's not our job to stop them, Kronos. Even if they are real and they are criminals. I'm growing weary from my years of service. You're almost forty-five, and only growing older. I'm turning sixty years old in less than a month. Granted, I'm in excellent shape and quite healthy, but this adventure is a bit too much for me. We don't even know where to start. These could just be rumors for all we know, and we *don't* know."

Kronos began to smirk at Sir Thomas again. He had a mischievous look in his amber-yellow eyes. "Check again, old man," Kronos said smugly with an evil grin. "*We do know* who exists, and I know exactly what we need. Not all of them are rumors. It is only fitting that they be our first target." Kronos took one of the papers out of the manilla folder and slid it across the table to Sir Thomas, who was not thrilled at all. As a caretaker, though, he knew it would be good to go along with

Kronos. Someone had to keep his reckless actions in check. Sir Thomas skimmed the file as Kronos got up from where he was sitting. "Pack your bags, we're going on an adventure of new discoveries, Thomas," Kronos declared with a pump of his fist into the air.

His eyes closed with dread, Sir Thomas slowly shook his head in a combination of disbelief and regret before massaging his temples. This was a suicidal mission, and he knew that meeting all of these people would end up with either one or both of them dead. "I really can't stand you, Kronos, but I'll tag along. This guy doesn't seem too bad. All of this *better* turn out okay, though." Sir Thomas forced a smile as he put his arm around Kronos, and the two of them laughed everything off. The risks were understood, but what else did they have to do? They were family, after all, and one last scientific trip before a peaceful lifestyle of luxurious retirement sounded harmless enough.

CHAPTER 2

THE DAILY LIFE OF A GIANT

(Charleston, West Virginia. The Next Day: April 12, 2022)

After the screeching cry of his rooster pierced the silence of the night, Birch Willow woke up groggily from his restless night of sleep as usual. He arose slowly and then shuffled his way down the old stairs of the antique house. After a large glass of water, which was mixed with lemon juice, and a swig of apple cider vinegar, Birch hopped into a cold shower to help stimulate the start of the day. In the semi-darkness of dawn, Birch left the lights off in his house as he slowly ate two bland bowls of grits with various fruits mixed in. He glanced over at the old grandfather clock he had kept in the house from when he had bequeathed it, noticing that it was a bit past 5:30 in the morning. The gym he owned did not open until 8:00 in the morning, but there were a few things on his to-do list to complete before he could open up, and he knew the ride usually took him about half an hour.

After a peaceful stroll down the dirt path that led to where he parked it, Birch got into his custom-made convertible, which had been made to accommodate his monstrous size. The large and expensive red vehicle stood out in contrast to the humble rural setting of the farm he lived on. The noise of the powerful engine sent a flock of geese flapping away to a small pond on the property, although one could barely call it a pond. The natural water source was more like a puddle on steroids that supported only a small amount of life. He slowly pulled onto the road before driving off, ready to begin his day with a positive attitude.

The golden rays of the sun were slowly waking up like everyone else as the beams of light started to break through the dark morning dawn. The grass, trees, and leaves were still slick with the dewdrops of the rainfall that had occurred yesterday. It was slightly humid, but Birch drove fast so that the breeze would cool him. The wind comfortably flowed over his bald head and his muscular arms, which bulged out of his custom-made black muscle-tee as if they were entire tree trunks. On the back of the muscle-tee was a white silhouette of a muscular man, snapping a barbell in half on the backside of his neck. The gym name, The Heaviest Lifters, formed a half-circle around the man, each end of the name stopping at the horizontal sentence: **Healthier. Stronger. Better.** Below the tight muscle-tee, Birch wore grey cargo shorts that stopped just before his knees, and his giant legs had goosebumps from the morning, but he knew that once the sun came out, it would be a hot day. The long and unpopulated road leading from his house and farm was barren, so he happily sang aloud to himself to pass the time. They were all upbeat and clean songs from three decades back.

Birch soon arrived into the town, which was quiet except for the birds that hopped around looking for something to eat. A few people on their way to work waved to him, but besides them, the city was scarce of life during that hour of the morning. Birch arrived at his gym, slowly pulling into the large parking lot before driving around to the backside of the building. He covered up the convertible with a grey tarp and, with a gentle click of the keys with his giant thumb, locked it. Walking to the front of the enormous gym, Birch sipped at water from one of the gym's merchandise thermoses as the gravel crunched underneath his feet. He had been waking up early for a few years now, but Birch was still tired as he rubbed his eyes a bit. He swung his arms in small circles, getting ready for the day to start.

A man and a woman in spunky neon clothes were jogging across the street. "**Morning, Birch**," they yelled in unison as they both slowly came to a stop.

Birch smiled warmly as he walked to the curb on his side of the street. "Mornin', Austin! Mornin', Melanie! It's been uh while! Looks like it'll be lovely weather out tuhday." Birch looked at the sky, which was starting to turn blue as the sun slashed more and more of the clouds away with its rays of light. "I'm glad tuh bump into the both of ya. I haven't seen y'all in uh while now. How's everything been?"

"Pretty good," Austin replied. "*Busy* but good. Mel wanted to go for a run today, and she dragged me outta bed early, so here I am." He chuckled. "Just a light jog though, since we're goin' white river rafting later on today. What about you? Anything exciting planned for the day?"

Birch shook his head casually. "Nah, just the usual routine up until the late afternoon when I have the fighting-"

"I forgot all about that!" Melanie cried out. "We would've gone and watched, but we're not gonna be here. Sorry, Birch. Holy crap! I can't believe that we're going to miss it. Son of a bitch. An international event that'll probably be on every news channel, and we completely forgot about it. It's because we're friends with you that we sometimes forget how much of a celebrity you are."

"Shit. You're right, Mel," Austin said with a shake of his head. "I can't believe we're going to miss it, but I forgot about it too. It's not like you didn't remind us either." Austin rubbed the back of his neck. "We're both complete idiots, but we've been swamped."

"Eh, it's no big deal. Don't even worry 'bout it. You don't just have tuh come because you're friends with me or because it's gonna be on the news. Honestly, I don't want tuh have the fighting tournament. Ya know I hate the idea o' violence and the glorification o' it. At least when it comes tuh me, since I can accidentally hurt people quite easily. It's going to raise uh lot o' money, though, and I think it'll end up being muh biggest charity event yet. That said," Birch reached into his pocket and pulled out a half-dollar coin, "I don't want tuh leave ya feelin' disappointed all day. This is uh party trick for kids mostly, but I'm sure you two will find it entertainin' as well."

Austin and Mel walked across the street and met up with Birch, studying the coin in his hand. He had his right hand curled up in a fist with the thumb sticking up as if he were going to thumb-wrestle. The large coin rested on his curled index finger, one-third of the top hanging in the air past his finger. Pressing into the top half with his thumb, Birch bent the coin over his finger, stopping just before the point where any more force would have snapped the coin into two.

A wide grin on his face like a little kid on his birthday, Austin laughed as Birch handed him the deformed coin. "Man! Your grip strength is absolutely incredible! The strength you have in your fingers and hand alone is almost unnatural. It's jaw-dropping!"

Mel laughed. "So, do you always just keep a half-dollar coin in your pocket at all times?"

"I've had uh few people on the street ask me tuh do uh trick like this fuh them, and I've also used it tuh escape some awkward or boring situations. Also, it really impresses the kids I teach at muh gym, and inspiring them is something that's really important tuh me. So, I do keep one on me at all times. Although," Birch scratched the back of his bald head, "I am runnin' out of half-dollar coins. They're not that easy tuh get, and most probably consider me uh felon for what I do tuh these precious items." Birch shrugged his shoulders. "Oh well. They can always come tuh me if they find one, and I'll bend it back for them as best as I can."

"Oh, wow! Do you have any other cool tricks on you right now? I want to see something else. Don't you want to see something else, Austin? This is so cool! Not that we haven't seen you do some amazing things before, but I never realized that your hands and fingers were so strong too."

"The man has a fighting tournament to prepare for," Austin pointed out. "We shouldn't keep him any longer."

Birch stopped them both with a raise of his hand. "I've got plenty o' time. It's no bother at all. I'm used tuh stuff like this by now. When you're almost uh literal giant in the world, your schedule tends tuh get sidetracked on uh daily basis." Birch reached into his other pocket and pulled out a standard golf ball. Resting it in the palm of his right hand, Birch then closed his fist and squeezed his hand tightly before opening his fist back up and displaying his palm upward. As easily as a strong person could impressively crush an apple in their hand, Birch had crushed the entire golf ball into pieces.

Austin and Mel were speechless once again. They had been friends with Birch for a few years, and they had seen his phenomenal strength in action before but never compressed to a scale that small.

Laughing, Austin shook his head in disbelief. "Damn. You made that look so easy. I almost want to think that it was a ping-pong ball and not a golf ball. I wish I was as strong as you!"

"Everyone always says that, but trust me, it's not the glorious life you think it is. Still, I get how ya feel. Not many can place uh soda can between their thumb and index finger and then flatten it into uh pancake just by pressing them together. Regardless of your size, one thing is always true about gettin' strong, and it's somethin' that people don't always realize. The time, sacrifice, and devotion required of ya tuh put in tuh get strong are uh lot more than y'all know. It'll take over your life, and all your other hobbies will be thrown away. Unless, of course, you don't have tuh work all day at uh job. Then you've got plenty o' time. Most of us, though, got uh lot of stuff tuh do, including work, so makin' time for trainin' isn't always that easy. Speaking of, I gotta go get 'er ready for the day," Birch said with a point of his thumb over his back at the gym.

"That and I'm too lazy to work that hard," Austin added with a laugh. "It was a struggle to get me just to go for a run this morning. Sorry again that we won't be there today, but we'll be cheering for ya, bud," Austin said with a nod of his head as he took off.

"Buh-bye, Birch," Mel said with a wave as she took off running as well. "Kick some ass today, and thanks for the coin!"

"No problem. Y'all have uh good one and have fun rafting," Birch said with a hearty wave and smile before turning around. "Firs' things first, though," Birch said to himself as he walked around the other side of the building to the track. He twisted to the left and to the right, stretching his back and cracking his spine. "Time for muh warmup."

After running six miles around the track while almost accidentally breaking a few records with his remarkable speed, large stride, and strong legs, Birch cooled down for five minutes, sweating a bit. He wiped his bald head with a towel and took a swig of a plant shake he had with him before making his way to the front of the building. Birch pulled a large key out of his pockets, unlocked the front doors, which were made to accommodate his staggering height, and walked in.

Except for the golden sunlight seeping in through the front windows, the building was dark inside, so Birch turned on the overhead lights and fans. Whistling to himself, he swept all of the floors, even performing a song or two with the broom as his partner. Birch reset the weight on all of the lifting machines to their lightest weights, as not everyone was courteous enough to reset the weight when they were done using the machine. He even had to remove weights from bars that people had not returned, but he was used to it by now. Then he went and sanitized everything with a disinfecting wipe to ensure that everything was properly cleaned since not all of his members had absolute integrity. Birch even made sure to test the several water fountains in the building to make sure they were working. After going through the locker rooms and checking for lost items, Birch decided that everything was ready for the day. He preferred to do all of this in the morning before opening, as to do it after the gym closed would have had him up far later than he liked.

Birch's gym was top of the line and featured a lot more amenities than most gyms. It filled him with great pride every morning to look at all that his gym had to offer. He stood in the middle of the building and looked around, a feeling of hope and happiness swelling in his giant chest. Everything in the massive building represented his American

Dream and all that he had accomplished. The gym had plenty of free space, weights, machines, equipment, and a huge separate room with a fighting ring. The fighting room alone was large enough to host one-thousand adoring fans watching the fights. Not to mention the bar area that also served as a healthy restaurant, the lounge, basketball courts, an indoor tennis court, two indoor volleyball courts, and then the stage setup for presentations. The second floor alone was dedicated to all the classes, such as the Zumba and yoga programs. The third floor had various different types of rooms and an indoor track. Then, on the first floor, there was a large room with the indoor pool, which featured a glass ceiling. The place had cost every cent he had ever earned, but it had all been worth it.

Birch had decided on naming the building The Heaviest Lifters since the gym mainly concentrated on healthy people who lifted immensely and trained vigorously or people who were absolutely determined to get to that point. However, the force of time had softened Birch, and so the gym was slowly becoming less strict about who they took in. Birch himself was 8'2" tall and 310 pounds of pure muscle, the other thirty pounds being everything else. That was why the gym had been so specific at first, but Birch was a genuine guy, and he tried his best to make everyone happy. So, now the gym was almost open to everyone.

Nobody ever messed with Birch, but not because they feared the supernaturally muscular giant. Everyone in the town praised Birch as a hero and a celebrity. He had helped them out a lot. It was his passion to help others. His gym drew in a lot of people, brought the community together, and provided many unique services that people enjoyed. Birch frequently donated to charities and would give out loans when people asked without ever charging interest. He also visited local hospitals to talk to sick children, spoke at meetings regarding mental health and suicide awareness, volunteered at the local nursing homes for events, and even visited the prisons to speak with the prisoners. By doing so, Birch had actually managed to change the perspectives and lives of several criminals. They respected him, whether they were locked away or out on the streets committing a crime. He had stopped multiple crimes from happening by talking the situation out, though his presence alone was enough to make even an experienced criminal piss themself.

When the church had burnt down in a horrible fire a few years ago, Birch rebuilt it in a matter of just a few days for free using his own bare hands. His greatest contributions to the city, however, came about when the remnants of a huge hurricane brought heavy rain and powerful winds to Charleston. He helped rebuild and clean more than most of the locals combined, and he was a fast and diligent worker besides.

Birch was so loved by the locals that they had decided to give him a special name. After all, everyone had watched Birch grow up or had grown up along with him. They were all one large family, and Birch was the centerpiece of it all. The nickname he had received over the years of living there, Charleston Crusher, was one of praise and admiration, not intimidation. The original suggestion had been Charleston Crusader, but people felt that it was too similar to the rumored vigilante from decades ago in Cape Cod. Besides that, everyone felt that Birch was not a crusader but a large force of positivity that tanked through everything. He crushed negativity. He crushed stereotypes, sexism, and racism. He crushed his goals.

Birch had arrived in Charleston decades ago and stayed there ever since. He was just sixteen when he had arrived back in 1996, but by that time, he looked more like a professional fighter who had trained for years at the gym than a teenager in high school. People considered Birch to be superhuman, and they always had. He was not, though, and as far as everyone knew or was concerned, he was like any other person but was just born big- *really* big. They assumed so anyway, as nobody really knew too much about his past or personal life. Out of respect, nobody had ever tried looking into it to find out. All anyone knew was that Birch had been a runaway orphan who stumbled upon Charleston after backpacking through the wilderness for some time.

A middle-aged couple who owned a farm right outside of the city had been asking God for a child since they could not have kids of their own, and that was when Birch happened to show up. The rest was just vague tales of his farm life and struggle at school until 2007 when his parents died. After that, Birch changed a bit, and for the better, as everyone had agreed upon. He bequeathed the farm, house, and the many acres of land that surrounded it. Birch worked alone for a few years on that farm, but by 2012, he had begun working on his new project: The Heaviest Lifters. His life needed a purpose, and so he found it one.

After buying a plot of land in the city of Charleston, only about half an hour away from the farm, Birch began to build his gym. It had stayed open ever since, for a total of ten years already. Here, he promoted his unique experiment. At least the public part of it, as he kept the experimental part of it to himself and would continue to do so until he knew that it could be safely publicized. His experiment, as he called it, was nothing more than a plant smoothie that was packed with more micronutrients than any other of its kind. As of now, that was all the public would be getting, which was nothing special to anyone, but when combined with his scientific discovery, it was completely life-changing.

Birch drank at least three plant-shakes a day, along with almost a gallon of water. The shake was neither a smoothie nor a juice but rather a blend of various plants chosen specifically for his physiology, mostly consisting of green plants. He needed the energy and nutrients, however, as he was a personal trainer, taught multiple classes, sparred and wrestled, swam, and he was continually working throughout the gym, all after his daily run before work. That was just his morning routine, however, and most of his days were packed with events after he left the gym. Though the amount of food he ate would seem shockingly low to people based on how large he was, Birch burnt through a lot of calories, and his experiment, combined with the plant shakes, was vital to maintaining the balanced diet and energy he needed to live such a busy lifestyle devoted to others.

A warm but flat smile came across Birch's face, and he subtly nodded his head, having made up his mind. He glanced over at the analog clock hanging above the tall front doors of the building. "There's enough time," he said to himself with a slight hint of excitement. "I think I'll treat muhself tuh the sauna."

Birch disappeared into the men's locker room before emerging naked, a large towel meant for a family trip to the beach wrapped around his waist and ripped upper thighs. He entered the large sauna room and sat down leisurely, making himself comfortable. "Now *this* is niiiiice," he sighed out as he relaxed. What relaxed Birch the most was knowing that the steam from the sauna room helped create a surplus of power through a turbine system. The entire gym was eco-friendly, in fact. Everything was energy efficient and conservative, including the saltwater pool. The whole place, including the lights that kept the track lit all night long, were powered by advanced bladeless-turbines and solar panels, which were only sold by R.O.M.A.B.A. Industries. The solar panels were strong enough to use just the energy reflected off of the moon's surface at night if needed, and the bladeless-turbines only required a small amount of wind. When days were absolutely dark, windless, or the power went out, Birch had a whole kinetic energy generator in place. It was similar to a portable radio with a crank that someone had to keep turning in order to give it power. The task of keeping the gym powered by turning a whole system of gears would have been extremely tiring and difficult for ordinary people, but for Birch, it was nothing harder than a simple workout. It was an energy source that only he could power.

Despite the advance technology, turning the gym into a green energy user was not as expensive as people thought, and Birch had made up for it already. He was an expert in finances and business, after all. The gym did not require a membership, but people had to meet certain requirements. A test of lifting, running, and other various challenges would have to be completed in order to join, and that was where he charged people. Once you were qualified, the gym was essentially free, except for the classes and having a personal trainer. Birch had a smaller program where he trained people who can handle the required challenges on a slightly smaller scale and were almost ready for the big test. That too was income. On top of that, Birch sold diet plans, clothes, books, DVDs, gym merchandise, and the like. He also charged for seminars on health and fitness. Besides all of that, the bar area of the gym made income off of the shakes they sold, as well as healthy meals.

The gym had never been about money, however. Birch created the gym to be the embodiment of his good nature. It was a way to get involved with the community, help people, and give back. He did not take his size for granted, and he knew how hard some people were trying to get in shape, and he wanted to help them as best as he could.

Birch was just flipping the open-closed-sign when a man strolled into the gym, a 5'o'clock shadow on his face, and his jet black hair flipped up neatly on his head. The man was exuding energy as a wide grin decked his face, his dark eyes shining with knowledge and determination. It was Michael Kellson, the co-owner of the gym, and Birch's childhood best friend. His weekdays were spent at the local high school teaching several science courses, and convincing his adoring students that he was not going to run for president. His weekends were devoted to the gym, and he was pumped for today.

"Happy Saturday, everyone!" Michael exclaimed as he looked around the neatly swept building, a disappointing smile growing across his face as he noticed that nobody was in the gym yet. Even in such excited speech, he sounded professional and intelligent. Michael was always composed, and that was important for both the school and the gym. "Or just happy Saturday to *us*, I guess. The downside of being the first ones here. Of course, nothing beats the sight of the gym when it is so freshly neat and clean."

Birch turned his attention to Michael. "What on Earth are ya wearing, Michael?" Birch could not contain his laughter as he looked over and down at Michael, who was just the size of an average man. His arms were muscular, slightly bulging out of the black muscle-tee he wore, which was the same one as Birch. He had a red sweatband around the top of his head, and two green stripes of paint under each of his eyes. "Dude, why are ya dressed like that? Ya look like you weren't drafted into the army, but you decided you were gonna go and fight anyway."

Michael pulled his hands out of the pockets of his army-patterned cargo shorts. "Well, today is the big fight, isn't it? That's today, right?"

"Yeah, but not until 'round two-in-the-afternoon."

"But you gotta be gettin' ready, big man," Michael said excitedly as he threw a couple punches at Birch's giant arm, which was almost the size of Michael.

"Aww, no! There's uh bee in here!"

Michael's head quickly whipped in each direction as he searched for it. "Where is it, man?"

"I'm talking 'bout you and those little punches of yours," Birch said with a teasing laugh and smile.

"That's not even funny, man," Michael replied, trying not to laugh or smile. "I go out of my way to get dressed and act pumped for this big fight, and you're going to say stuff like that?"

"I'm only messin' with ya, little man," Birch said with a friendly slap to Michael's back that almost knocked him over. "Yaknow that I'm never mean tuh nobody."

"I know, man. You're a big softie. But seriously, why aren't you getting ready for the fight? Should we even have the gym open today?"

"Today is just like any other day, Michael. There's no reason tuh cheat our members out of uh day of training. I'm running the gym until noon, and then I have tuh go get ready, which shouldn't take long. It's just uh quick meal and uh change of clothes. It's not like anyone could beat me anyway, and even if somebody did, I don't care. I'm uh humble man, and this is about the money we raise for the charity. Everyone considers me tuh be the strongest human alive, and they want tuh know if I'm also the best fighter alive or if I can be taken down by someone smaller. It is what it is. There's no need tuh do anything special in preparation."

Michael nodded his head. "I have full confidence in you, but I sent out an invitation for the biggest, toughest, most ripped guys to come and challenge you for the title of the world's strongest man. I would've invited women too, but you didn't want to fight them since you believe in not harming women even if it's for sport. I respect that. I'm honestly worried about you not killing these guys by accident. You're definitely going to have some work cut out for you. There are going to be Olympians and giant powerlifters for sure. Those are the strong ones, but the real threat will be the trained fighters who have devoted their lives to trying to be an unstoppable force."

Birch cracked his knuckles and punched his deadly fist into the palm of his other hand, the air around him almost flying back. "Ain't no problem for Charleston Crusher. Let's get tuh work, Michael. We'll close up at noon, and then be back here like forty-five minutes or so before the fight. It'll be fun."

After what seemed like a normal day at the gym, Birch quickly headed home to prepare for the fight. The wind had picked up a bit, especially in the red convertible, so Birch turned the radio off and thought to himself, despite knowing that it would be a negative conversation. *The biggest and the toughest, huh? I'm sure a few really big guys'll show up tuh-day. Yaknow, that might be muh ticket out o' the spotlight. To lose on purpose and hand over the title to somebody else, though? I mean... I could live uh life without everybody botherin' me about who I am and what I should do. Not that anybody ever says nothin' tuh me, but still. I just wanna be uh normal man. Everyone's got uh choice 'cept for me. I have one, but tuh not live up tuh everyone's expectations would disappoint uh lot of people. I don't want tuh be uh celebrity, but I'm helping so many people. My fame allows me tuh help others, so why do I want tuh get rid of it?* Birch shook his head, hoping to shake his thoughts out through his ears. "I *am* uh normal man," he said firmly to himself. *But would everything I've done*

have been noticed or as praised if I were the size of uh regular man? Would muh actions mean any more or any less?

The rest of the car ride was filled with thoughts of insecurity and questions about everything, but all of that quickly left Birch's mind as he arrived at the farm to find the place a bit chaotic. Old-Spike, the largest cow on the farm, was loose and running around savagely, seemingly in a mad frenzy of some sort. The other animals in the outside pens, in turn, were going crazy with jealousy over the loose animal.

Birch looked at the cow running around just a few yards away, trying to think of the best course of action to take against the wild creature. *Rabies? Nah. That don't add up. How'd ya get out?* Birch looked over at the enclosure where all the other cows were. *The fence ain't broken, but there's no way ya jumped over that thing. That's suspicious fuh sure. I just got tuh get ya back in.* Birch started to cautiously walk toward Old-Spike, one hand in front of him, palm outward. "Eaaaaaasy there...." Old-Spike looked over at Birch, his animal eyes wide and glassy. "Yeah, I'm talking tuh you, pal," Birch said with a point at the animal. "You usually keep tuh yaself and don't bother no one. This ain't like you, Old-Spike. How'd you get out o' your pen?"

Old-Spike had been named after the massive horns that decked its head, which were facing toward Birch. The cow's name had originally been Spike, but now it was getting old, and so Birch had added the age to the name in a playful insult to the cow. Birch had raised it from a young calf almost twenty years ago. The cow had grown up to become the prime specimen of the farm, almost twice the size of the others. However, Birch kept the animals on the farm as pets and not livestock, so he never sold Old-Spike despite the offers he got from a few local butchers. He had grown especially attached to the large cow, although he insisted that he did not have any favorites among his farm animals.

After stomping its foot into the ground, Old-Spike came charging full-speed at Birch with no intention of stopping.

"Well, that's not good," Birch muttered to himself. The giant braced himself by flexing his enormous arm muscles as he tightened his ripped thighs and calves and planted his legs firmly against the ground like they were sturdy trees. Old-Spike was almost at him when Birch jabbed both of his arms out and grabbed the cow by its massive horns, stopping the cow's charge instantly, causing a dust cloud to form from the ground below it as the cow's back end went into the air before dropping back down from the collision with a seemingly unmovable man. "That's what I thought, tough guy."

Quickly moving to the side, Birch reached under the cow and wrapped his arms around the creature, carrying it sideways to the pen, keeping an eye on the horns, which were just to the right of his arm. He dropped Old-Spike into the enclosure as gently as he was able to, making sure the cow was placed on its hooves. Birch brushed his hands against one another before rubbing his back. "Granted, I'm really strong, but I'm not really supposed tuh be liftin' up cows as heavy as you," Birch said to Old-Spike. "You're lucky that I didn't hurt muh back before the big fight today. Otherwise, I would've been chopping ya up for uh nice meal," Birch said heartily with a playful laugh.

Old-Spike ignored the humorous threat. The cow quickly looked around for a short moment before letting out an aggressive cry.

Birch's face hardened. He had never heard the cow make a noise like that before. "What's wrong, Old-Spike? That ain't natural."

The cow did not respond but instead went on a wild rampage, stomping around the pen and attacking the other cows in the enclosure like it was a Texas bull with rabies. Birch watched in absolute horror as Old-Spike charged into a baby calf and stabbed it. The animal continued its frenzy, attacking the other cows in the pen, using it's hooves and horns in a way that a cow never would.

With a vertical jump straight up, Birch launched himself over the four-foot-tall fence through a strong burst of power from his muscular legs. He landed on the other side of the pen, the ground shaking as he did. Like a speeding freight train, Birch instantly dashed over to Old-Spike. He quickly wrapped his arms around the cow in an attempt to hold it still and subdue it, but the cow was unnaturally wild. Using its back right hoof, the cow stomped powerfully on Birch's foot, which was bare, as Birch never wore socks or shoes due to how large his feet were. Despite his thick and trained skin, the unexpected attack was enough of a distraction for the cow to escape from Birch and continue its unexplained rampage.

The other cows were running around the enclosure to avoid the wild cow, adding to the chaos. Several had already been injured. A firm expression with deep pain in it came over Birch's face as his chest swelled up against the burden of a hard choice already made as he avoided getting hit by the other fleeing cows. There was no hesitation. He knew what he had to do for the sake of multiple lives over one. Quickly catching up to the cow, Birch grabbed Old-Spike and suplexed the cow into the ground, snapping its back.

Old-Spike struggled and cried out in pain, kicking the air. Large tears streamed down Birch's face, his mouth unable to stay closed as he sobbed. "I won't let you suffer, best friend," Birch cried out, choking on the words. "Old-Spike... *forgive* me," Birch screamed as he snapped the cow's neck. The large, old cow grew lifeless and still, thick saliva pooling out of its mouth. Birch fell to his knees in the dusty pen, crying.

Birch set off, traveling back down the road toward the city, his eyes puffy and red from crying. He had the radio on as a distraction, but his mind kept going back to the pile of dirt with the small home-made cross that stood next to the farm now. Then, he pictured the calf being taken away by the local vet. Birch had washed his dangerous hands and scrubbed them until they were sore and red, but he kept picturing Old-Spike's blood on them, even though he had never even had the animal's blood on his hands.

Fifteen minutes passed by in grief as Birch's mind destroyed itself with guilt and remorse. The radio had failed to distract Birch, but rather it crept along his nerves in agitation, and he ended up smashing it with a single blow from his giant fist. He had contemplated canceling the fight, as he was not in the mood for a big show, but he knew it was too late to do that. Everyone was looking forward to his appearance, so he knew he would have to fake a smile and act happy. If he, the inspiration for so many, was unable to fight through sorrow with joy, then how could those who looked up to him do the same?

Birch rubbed his eyes and looked up just in time to slow his convertible to a stop. A police car was parked across the road with its lights flashing. An officer, who had been standing in the street looking down the road, started walking toward Birch.

Birch studied the cop, not recognizing the guy. *That must be the rookie everyone told me about. I hope he don't give me uh hard time.* Birch craned his neck to try and see what was going on down the road, but he was unable to see past the car and the flashing lights. "What seems tuh be the problem, officer?" Birch shouted from his car.

"A dead tree fell across the road, and then two others fell down with it. The road will be closed until we can get it cleaned up."

"Mind if I take uh look? I'm in uh bit of uh hurry."

The cop eyed Birch suspiciously as he continued approaching the custom-made vehicle. From where he was, Birch looked like a regular bald guy sitting in a car, probably going to the gym. "There's not much to see, but you're welcome to check it out if you feel like you have to," he answered reluctantly. "I don't think looking at them will do much. It'll be some time until everything is cleaned up. To be completely honest, any plans you had will either be delayed or canceled." Getting closer, the cop looked through the windshield and noticed the smashed radio, marking it as a red flag that perhaps the man he was approaching was aggressive or had road rage.

Birch got out of his convertible, a staggering giant of masculinity as his bare feet kissed the hot asphalt without flinching. The cop looked up at Birch and gulped, almost shaking, his hand reaching for his gun. Birch ignored the man and closed the door on his car. "I understand, but I gotta get goin' to an important event, and this is the only way intuh town unless I go back and around, which'll take me too long. Can't be late tuh hostin' uh fightin' tournament that'll have some news channels there recordin' it all. I worked in landscapin' for uh while, and I know uh thing or two 'bout movin' trees."

"You're Mr. Willow? I'm sorry, but I-" The cop abruptly excused himself, as a car pulled behind Birch's red convertible, and he went over to inform the lady about what was going on. He wanted to stop Birch, but he had gotten a lot of advice from people since he joined the force two weeks ago, and the biggest tip of advice he had been given was to respect and listen to Charleston Crusher.

Walking past the police car, Birch stopped and placed his hands on his sturdy hips as he surveyed the road. Three trees had fallen across the road, and they were relatively large. The first two seemed manageable for a giant such as Birch to move on his own, but the third tree, which was the dead tree, was far larger than the other two, and it seemed to be decades old.

Birch made his way over to the end of the first tree, which consisted of thick roots that had latched themselves onto a large rock. Gripping the roots and rock on either side, Birch's muscular arms flexed, and his veins bulged as he summoned his strength, his back and shoulder muscles visible through the black muscle-tee. Lifting the fallen tree about a foot off the ground, Birch thrust the tree into the air with a powerful extension of his arms. The tree almost went straight up, but it began to fall back down. Before this could happen, Birch charged into the tree and pressing his large hands against it, pushed with his ripped calves, thighs, and back. The tree stood straight up before falling the opposite way from where it had been lying on the road as he jumped back. He repeated the process of extraordinary strength with the second tree. Despite the ends of the trees resting on part of the left side of the road, Birch had cleared the road enough for cars to pass by, one at a time.

The only tree left was the third one, which, despite being dead, was too heavy for even Birch to move. However, he was in no mood to be inconvenienced. Dropping down to his left knee, Birch brought his right arm straight up, his fingers together like a karate hand, although his entire limb was more like the giant sword a fictional character would wield that was bigger than themself. Bringing it down with incredible force, Birch broke the tree into two halves, fragments of wood scattering as his thick flesh broke through the ancient tree without a scratch. He repeated the process a few more times, breaking the tree into several pieces that he then chucked into the woods.

Birch was beginning to drip with sweat, his hands covered with small pieces of bark and wood-dust. The rookie cop looked on, absolutely in awe at Birch's astounding feats of human strength. The woman in the car looked on in fear and admiration. Neither of them spoke, and they seemed frozen in place. Noticing that the cop was seemingly frozen in place, Birch took the liberty of pushing his police car across the road into the grass so that the road was clear. He apologized for doing that and then quickly hopped into his convertible and sped off, the two bystanders left looking after him, their mouths agape.

❅ ❅ ❅

Michael was waiting outside the back of the gym, pacing around the gravel in the hot sun, dressed just as fashionably as he had been earlier in the day. "You're late," he yelled lightly to Birch. "You're never late! Did people stop you for autographs again?" He laughed at first, but Michael dropped his light-hearted tone when he looked at Birch. "Oh, shit. Man… what happened?"

"Is it *that* obvious?" Birch asked somberly, his eyes and mouth still drooping with grief. Combined with his sweat, the dust, and the remnants of wood, Birch looked as though he had just fought through a battlefield and slain countless enemies as his allies died on either side of him. It was a look that only Michael had ever seen on Birch before, and it had been only once during all their years of friendship. Other than that, Birch was always smiling and positive. The man before him now, however, was far different.

"Birch, *what* happened? I haven't seen you this upset in a long time."

"Old-Spike, he... died today," Birch said with a low exhale, his voice barely audible.

Michael hung his head in a grave gesture, understanding the situation. "A great life has been taken from us today. I know that cow was basically your pet and that you two were close. I mean, I practically grew up with Old-Spike too. But it's part of life, I guess. You've spent more time with nature than anyone I know, so I'm sure you understand. He was getting old and-"

"No," Birch stated bitterly, tightening his hands into fists. "It wasn't old age." His gaze focused on the gravel below, Birch was unable to look his best friend in the eyes. "*I* killed him, Michael." He glanced at his giant fists, hating them. "It wasn't his age. He still had plenty o' time left."

"*What?*" Michael looked up with shock at Birch, whose head was still lowered, his gaze studying the individual pieces of gravel. Michael quickly thought over everything he knew, trying to understand what might have happened, but he could not figure it out. "Birch, what do you mean? Why... why would you kill him?"

"It was uh decision made on the spot. There wasn't time tuh think everything over. Somehow, he escaped his pen while I was at the gym this morning, and luckily, he hadn't gone far. There's no tellin' how long he was loose for, but he was loose and buckin' around when I got back. He charged at me, and I stopped his attack before pickin' 'im up and returnin' 'im tuh the pen. I thought that was the end o' the problem, but he started attackin' the other cows. He stabbed one of the calves, and 'e grazed the sides of uh few o' the others. I had tuh stop him in order tuh save the others. I ended up snappin' his spine with uh suplex, but..." Birch's voice fell as his eyes leaked out more tears, and Michael almost shook at the sight of the gentle giant crying. "He was still alive and strugglin' in pain. I had tuh end his life. I couldn't just stand there and watch 'im die uh slow and painful death. Nor could

I let him live and be paralyzed. He deserved so much more than that. He deserved tuh live for uh few more years like 'e was supposed tuh." Birch's giant fists shook unsteadily. "I feel like this is all muh fault. How'd he even get out?"

"I've known you for a long time, Birch. Every year, I teach new kids. I work with them and try to find their potential, so I can help them succeed in life. I've traveled across the country to conventions and everything. Never, and I mean *never* before have I met a more determined, a more humble, or a kinder man than you, Birch Willow. I know life wasn't easy for you growing up. I was there alongside you as your best friend, and so was Rose. Never did you let your anger overcome you. Never did you crush any of those bullies or destroy the envious ones. Never did you take advantage of your size or strength."

"Michael, what does any o' that have tuh do-"

"I'm not finished yet," Michael stated firmly. "Birch, I've never even seen you step on a spider! Everyone looks up to you for inspiration. They see you as the unofficial symbol of peace, and the greatest human there is. To them, they think that you have it all: money, family, peace, success, strength, good health, love, fame, and everything a person could ever need or want. Sure, they don't know about the failed dates that left you heartbroken or the fact that you had no friends growing up. They don't know about your troubles at the orphanages or how much of a curse your size is. But, they all know who you are," Michael said with a point at Birch's heart. "They know how gentle you are and how helping others is what brings you joy." He patted Birch's arm as he was unable to reach his shoulder. "The point is, you're a good man. You would never kill someone or something without good cause. You respect all life, and you don't consider anything a pest. You don't have to justify or defend your actions, nor doubt that they were the right choice. You've always done what is right, and we all trust that you always will, unlike everyone else in this world."

Birch raised his head up and looked at Michael with the faintest attempt at a bitter smile. "I know you're right, and I really appreciate it, brutha, but I'm still terribly upset. Even if it was for the greater good, it still hurt tuh have tuh kill muh companion. Old-Spike deserved tuh die in peace. He had always behaved and been friendly." Birch looked up at the beautiful sky. "So, I'll miss him uh lot, but, hopefully, he's up there now, hanging out with Rose."

Michael looked at his friend's somber face, wishing he could help out more. There was unimaginable pain and sorrow in Birch's eyes. "It's not just Old-Spike's death that has you upset, is it? You're thinking about how much it hurts that you didn't get to say goodbye to Rose or tell her how you felt, right?"

"Is it *that* obvious?" Birch softly chuckled. "Yup. Sayin' goodbye tuh Old-Spike hurt, but part of me is grateful that I was there when he went because I know just how much it hurts tuh not be able tuh say goodbye. It don't make it any less painful, but it doesn't hurt as much as it did when she died. There's not all o' that regret. Still, it reminded me of how I wasn't there fuh her when she did die." Birch wiped the tears away from his eyes as he turned his head and looked at the gym. "His death'll be an emotional burden I have tuh carry for the rest of my life now. Right alongside hers, in fact. It's different because his death was actually one that could've been prevented, but what happened in the past cannot be changed. I'm uh religious man, and if it's time fuh Old-Spike tuh go, then I won't stop him from goin' tuh where he needs tuh go. That, and we have uh fighting tournament tuh host. If muh smile is what keeps everyone inspired, then I better cheer up."

"That's the spirit." Michael studied the pain visible on Birch's face and in his gentle eyes. He sighed internally. "Just make sure you don't put too much pressure and responsibility on yourself, man. You have a big heart, Birch, but let's not overload it. I'm here for you if you want to talk about it more, later on, but we do have a tournament to host." Michael noticed the dirt and small pieces of wood on Birch's hands. "What happened with that?"

Birch noticed that Michael was looking at the small pieces of natural debris that had stuck to his hands. "Oh. Yep, the troubles o' the day didn't end with Old-Spike's escape. Three trees had fallen 'cross the road as well on muh way over here. I had tuh move 'em muhself. Otherwise, I would've never made it over here in time for the fight. Normally, I have plenty o' patience, but I couldn't afford tuh miss today's event. It's goin' tuh raise uh lot o' money for uh lot o' people."

"Quite the strenuous day, then. Fighting cattle and moving trees are certainly part of the formula for a bad day. Not that those tasks were a problem for you, but it's still a drain on your energy and muscles, and now you have to go fight people determined to beat you."

Reaching into the convertible parked right next to him, Birch pulled out a see-through thermos, which featured the gym name, filled with a green liquid. "Thank God for our scientific breakthrough then. Well, thank *you*, actually. Today has made me all the more apprec'ativ' of your work." Birch took a huge chug of the green mixture before shaking and throwing some shadow punches. "Ah, much better. Besides, I wasn't expectin' tuh fight 'em at uh hundred percent anyway. It never works out that way."

Michael's face hardened with a mixture of disapproval and concern, his eyes growing darker, and a seldom-seen frown appeared on his face. "Don't do that," he commanded as he gestured to Birch and the drink.

"Do what? Have uh drink of uh plant-shake so soon before the fight? It's not the worst thing tuh do. I'll digest it quickly."

"*Don't*, Birch. You know *exactly* what I mean," Michael stated coldly with a disapproving shake of his head. "That isn't some kind of a miracle in a bottle or a super-soldier serum, and you know that! You act all happy and cheery now, drinking that plant-shake and pretending like everything is alright, but it's not. You used my research while I was gone and changed your body with untested theories," Michael hissed seriously. "There is nothing right about that at all. Don't you get it, Birch? We don't even know if there are side effects to what you've done to your body, and I've told you that, but you keep acting like everything is perfectly okay. Then, on top of it, you're pushing yourself instead of living a normal life, even though a normal life is all you want."

Birch nodded his head, his face now matching the grave expression on Michael's. "I understand, Michael. While I understand your concern, you don't have tuh lecture me, though. I know it's not uh miracle in uh bottle, but with what I did, it's certainly uh life-changing thing. Your research could help benefit the lives of millions of people, Michael! You should be proud of that. I know what I did was wrong, but think of it like I'm enduring the trial for the world so that other people won't have tuh. We're testin' your research out on me because I volunteered tuh do it, and I'll accept death as uh result if I have tuh. That way, no one who is innocent has to endure this or deal with the consequences." Birch shook his head in shame and frustration. "Look, I'm takin' care of muhself. I'll be alright. I get headaches every now and then, and I don't feel a hundred percent, but I'm fine. I have intestinal and stomach pains here and there, but nothin' I wouldn't expect from what I did. Heck, we don't even know if it's from what I did to my body. It could all just be uh coincidence."

"See, that's exactly the problem, Birch. That attitude of optimism and denial is unacceptable, given the circumstances. Out in the world, it's great, and I love it, but when it comes to experimental science and the unknown, we have to expect and prepare for the worst. We can't just chalk it up to coincidence or something. You experimented on your body to the point that it could naturally produce the enzyme cellulase. You think there aren't going to be negative effects because of that? The disruption of the balance of your body's chemicals and enzymes alone is enough to concern me. Don't just casually say that you have some pain here and there. Now I've been extremely tolerant, but after a certain point, it's not good enough. It just isn't." Michael sighed aggressively in frustration. "None of this is safe. This isn't scientifically proven, but honestly, if you weren't a gargantuan-of-a-person when you used my research on yourself, I don't think you would've survived. Nobody else probably would have. You're lucky, Birch. You stand at the pinnacle of health, and that's why you survived the experiment."

"You're uh genius, Michael. Please, don't say inaccurate things about the research just because you're upset. My body size has nothin' tuh do with it, and we both know that. You're just sayin' that tuh scare me, and I respect your feelings. Either way, I'm lucky I survived, and I'm lucky to have uh forgiving friend who is concerned for me. I'm very grateful for everything I have. Uh lot of my life is thanks tuh you stickin' beside me and helping me out with the gym and school back in the day."

The strong bond of friendship between the two of them helped Michael's frustration with Birch to dissipate, as they had been through a lot together over the years. He also knew that Birch always did everything with good intentions, so his friend meant no harm at all by what he had done, but Michael could never understand why Birch had experimented on himself the way he had. "We don't have time to talk about all of this right now, but we *will* resume this conversation later. Have you at least gone to a doctor to check it out and make sure that it's not something seriously wrong?"

Birch looked around before turning his attention back to Michael, fearful someone might overhear his secret. "You know I get anxiety attacks at medicinal places. I can't stand hospitals or doctors, let alone needles and bloodwork. My arms go completely numb just thinkin' about gettin' blood drawn. It'd be uh suicide mission tuh even attempt tuh go there. I'll freak out, and someone will end up gettin' hurt if muh survival instincts take over and muh body moves on its own."

"I know, but this is extremely important, Birch. It could decide between life and death for you."

"I'll just look up muh symptoms online."

Michael quickly shook his head and sighed. "*No!* That's the worst thing to do, Birch. Do you want a false death sentence? Searching your symptoms up online will inevitably lead to a placebo effect with negative consequences. Plus, there won't be anything online since we're the first people to do this, and you don't even have a computer! You have to go to the doctors." Michael took a deep breath to brace himself.

He's going to freak out, but you need to, Birch. Michael looked up at Birch, whose hand was already trembling as it gripped the convertible. "Besides, this isn't just something simple like that. You not only have to go to a doctor, but you have to get everything done: blood pressure, heart tests, cholesterol levels, colonoscopy, endoscopy, bloodwork, urine sample, a whole physical checkup, and a load of other tests too. We have to check everything."

Birch was beginning to drip with sweat, and his massive chest was heaving up and down in quick breaths. He bobbed his head around as if he were dizzy, and his body seemed to tremble. He crushed the top edge of the convertible driver's side door, where his hand had been gripping. "I can't. Michael, that's too much. That's-" Birch stopped talking, his breathing almost reaching a state of hyperventilating. He wiped the sweat off his brow with the back of his other hand, while the hand on the convertible gripped the car even tighter. He was on the brink of passing out from dread and fear.

"Hey, it's okay, buddy. You're fine." Michael put his right hand out toward Birch as if he were approaching a scared child. *There it is. Just the idea is enough to scare him. I hope nobody's around to see this.* Michael scanned the area before taking a step toward Birch, who had backed up against the convertible. "I know. We all have our fears and phobias. I'm asking a lot, but you owe me that much, Birch. I hate to use that card, but you owe me. You stole my research and experimented on yourself. I forgave you, though. Most people wouldn't have been so forgiving. The least you can do in return is to make sure that you're not sick or dying. Can you do that for me? Can you do that for yourself? For everyone counting on you to stay around for a while? It'll be alright. The needles are difficult to get through your packed muscle fibers, but they shouldn't hurt too much, and the other tests aren't too invasive or scary. In fact, I'll make sure they knock you out so you won't feel a thing."

"They'll knock me out and test me and experiment on me and take me away," Birch said quickly, rambling to himself, his eyes skimming the gravel below him back and forth, his eyes almost popping out of his skull. "They want me knocked out! That's exactly what they're waitin' for. I have tuh be alert at all times!" He zoned out, muttering to himself at a speed almost too fast to understand. "It'd be easy tuh kill me that way and eliminate me as uh potential threat. The government will take me away or some pharmaceutical company will do it. It's not often that ya find uh man who grows up tuh be over eight feet tall and is so muscular. Granted, I have myostatin-related muscular hypertrophy, but they'll try tuh take muh D.N.A. for that tuh make clones or an army. It's so rare, and they'll want it for themselves. Greedy agents. If they discover muh ability tuh naturally produce cellulase, both of us will be in fuh it. That's all those medical people ever care about. Pokin' an' proddin' me as uh unique specimen. I-"

"Hey! Birch!" Michael yelled as he slapped one of Birch's giant arms. "Snap out of it, man. I know how hard it is. You're not the only person with anxiety. You're a celebrity, though. Everyone knows better than to get rid of you because it would have rippling effects throughout society. Your traits may lure exploiters, but they're also the same things that protect you. On the other hand, I understand why you're paranoid. You're a human miracle, and people want to exploit that, but you have to get looked at. It was hard enough losing Rose from our small group of friends. I know it was even harder for you. Don't you think she'd want you to live for as long as you can and enjoy life? We'll get a trustworthy doctor from right here in town. We're not going to have any random quack look at you. I'll get a person I truly trust. I promise you that it'll be fine. If you're not going to do it for me or you, at least do it for her."

Birch calmed down, and he let go of the convertible, although the damage had already been done to the vehicle. He had tears in his eyes from anxiety missed with grief. He took in a deep breath before slowly exhaling. "I guess you're right, Michael. You almost always are. Those kids you teach at the high school are real lucky tuh have such uh great man as their teacher. I owe you the reassurance that I'll be fine, so as soon as I have the chance, I'll set up some appointments with your help."

"Thank you. Just say the word, and I'll take over the gym for the day if you need me to. I've got plenty of sick-days stored up, and your health is a priority. Now, let's get ready to kick some major ass!" Michael pounded his fist into his hand a couple of times as he and Birch headed into the gym to set everything up for the tournament.

CHAPTER 3

THE WORLD'S STRONGEST HUMAN
(Charleston, West Virginia. The Same Day: April 12, 2022)

After half an hour had passed, the fighting room was filled to its max capacity as people flooded the gym. The energy was through the roof as everyone screamed and cheered with excitement. The fighting ring was larger than a typical one, and it stood as the centerpiece of the room. The walls were lined with bleachers, the edges of the room dark, as all of the light in the giant room was focused on the fighting ring. Michael stood in the middle of it all as the announcer of the fights that would be taking place. He was not shaken at all, but rather he took the crowd's energy and adoring eyes all in, loving every moment of it as he maintained his constant composure of calm authority. He and Birch had been planning the fight for over a year after a smaller version they had hosted.

Michael cleared his throat and deepened his voice to sound just like an announcer at a fight. "Laaaaaadies and gentlemeeeeen, thank you all for being here today!" Everyone broke out into applause and cheering, screaming at the top of their lungs. "Don't forget that we have our own rules here. In a moment, I will be leaving the ring and taking my seat with the judges at the table, who will be determining a winner if a fighter is not knocked out or if the time runs out. Fighters will have twenty seconds total to recover. Each match will consist of two ten-minute-long rounds, giving more than enough time for Birch's opponents to try and win the title of the strongest and greatest fighter in the *entire* world," Michael yelled with an enthusiastic fist pump that created a chain reaction of excited screaming from the bleachers. He exited the ring and took a seat at the table with the judges. There were four judges in total. "I'll be commentating alongside Matthew Johnson from American News 50, who is well-known for reporting on all major fights. We're happy to have him here with us once again. He did a great job at the smaller tournament we hosted a year ago, and he's excited to be here, so give him a round of applause."

Matthew, an African-American man of sturdy build, stood up and waved at everyone with a big smile that was decorated by his bushy mustache. "Thank you, and yes, I'm thrilled to be here. It's been a while, but I'm glad to be back and here today. I am more than hyped for this fighting tournament, and I can't believe I get to see it all happen right in front of me." Matthew turned and looked straight ahead at the camera in front of the judge's table that was focused on him and Michael. "We're streaming the entire fight live on our channel as well as on our website, and I hope that all of you at home can hear and see the energy here. It is unbelievable! Everyone is so excited about the fights we have lined up today, and with that said, I think we should get straight into introducing our first opponent. Don't you agree, Michael?"

"That's right. Without further ado, folks, we're going to get this show on the road. It's fighting time! We're going to start the tournament off with a man who is our largest contestant, and perhaps one of our most determined fighters. Matthew, I'll let you have the honor of explaining the rest since you had the pleasure of interviewing him beforehand."

"That's right, Michael, and you can watch the whole exclusive interview on our website or visit one of our social media platforms, but here is what you need to know. Our first opponent certainly is a big man, weighing in at 460 pounds and standing a whopping 7'6" tall.

He's not quite as tall as Birch is, but he's definitely up there with the tallest in the world. I spoke with him for a while, and you had mentioned that he is one of our most determined fighters, and I have to agree with that. His determination actually comes from meeting Birch years ago, isn't that right, Michael?"

"Indeed, it is, Matthew. A few years ago, Birch went on a charity trip to the Samoan Islands. It wasn't meant to be anything newsworthy, but then a baby humpback whale got beached, and Birch actually rescued it all on his own. It's probably one of his greatest feats of strengths- pushing that baby whale through the sand and back into the water all by himself. He made the rest of the trip a vacation after that, and I don't blame him. It was during this time that Anaru Loane witnessed Birch's inhuman strength right before his very own eyes and decided that he would begin a journey of weight loss and muscle gain. He was over six-hundred pounds at the time. He's been training for years in the hopes of being on an equal level with Birch, if not surpass him. He believes he's worked and trained harder than anyone else fighting tonight, and he apologized for missing the last tournament."

"After interviewing him, I have to agree. Anaru is a humble man and very grateful, but he is truly determined to win tonight. He was only twenty when he saw Birch, and that was five years ago. Whether he wins or loses tonight, he said that he is forever grateful for seeing Birch that day, because he has no doubt that his obesity would have killed him. Now, after training every day for five years, he believes his body is in the best shape it can be, and he's looking forward to tonight. During our interview, we went over pictures of his progress over the past five years, and the transformation is absolutely incredible! Anaru is hoping to inspire and motivate some people tonight, and I believe he can do just that. His book, called *Pushing The Whale*, is all about his journey and struggles, and the title represents himself as well as the miracle he saw that inspired him. But that's enough about him. Let's get fighting!"

"That's right! It's time to get fightinnnnng!" Michael stood up, almost jumping out of his chair. He held the microphone in his hand

and turned from left to right. "Ladies and gentlemen, turn your attention to the red corner! Here comes Anaru Loane!"

Everyone either gasped or grew silent, but they were all in awe at the man that exited the backroom and headed toward the red corner of the ring. Like an ancient golem from an old folktale, Anaru came walking forward with a presence of strength and strong willpower. His humbleness and quietness matched his golem-like stride. He was wearing nothing but small green shorts. He was almost as much of a giant as Birch was, and one could easily believe that they might have secretly been brothers. Unlike Birch, however, Anaru's large muscles were also combined with some leftover fat from his previous lifestyle, and it made him seem all the more unbreakable. Then, there were his islander tattoos, which spanned his back and covered both of his arms. Down to his shoulders was black curly hair. His eyes were dark and focused. His breathing was steady. Every part of his body, which had been forged into a fighting machine, was ready to take on Charleston Crusher. He carefully stepped over the ropes and entered the fighting ring, taking his place in the red corner.

Michael smirked and nodded to himself with satisfaction. It was going to be a historical fight. "Then, in the blue corner we have the hometown hero and undisputed world champion, Birch Willow! Also known as Charleston Crusherrrrrr!"

Upon hearing his nickname called, Birch, dressed in his grey cargo shorts and black muscle-tee, ran into the fighting room, the ground shaking with each thunderous step. The crowd went berserk with screaming and cheering. In a single mighty leap, Birch launched himself over the ropes, and he landed in the blue corner with a thud that shook the entire ring. The viewers at home must have thought that an earthquake had occurred as the cameraman grabbed the camera to stop it from shaking. Slowly standing up erect, Birch was a towering giant that even seemed to loom over Anaru, who was already a mountain himself, from across the ring. The size difference was not that noticeable, however, because it was concealed by the thick tension between the two men. It was a fighter's tension, uniquely different from aggression or what occurs out on the streets. It was a tension comprised of respect, willpower, and an understanding that nothing was personal.

The audience stopped screaming and cheering, and everyone sat down. The judges were silent, and even Micahel and Matthew had nothing to say. It was clear that the two fighters had words to exchange with each other, and no one was going to dare to stop them.

Anaru seemed emotionless as he looked up at Birch and gazed into his eyes. He spoke with an accent, but his English was clear. "Here, you are called Charleston Crusher, but back on my island, we say **'le tamaloa e fagatua tafola'** when referring to you. I started that, and I have taught it to many of the children there. The English translation can be heard as 'the man who wrestles whales.' That is how I came to know that such humans existed. That is how I came to know that people were capable of extraordinary things like the tales of the island I heard growing up. You are my inspiration, Mr. Willow. It is because of you that I am not dead, and it is because of you that I have become one of the strongest in the world. Perhaps it is strange, but this is my way of showing my gratitude and paying my respects to you." Anaru dropped to one knee and bowed down before Birch, and then he slowly got up and looked at Birch again, determination and respect in his eyes.

Birch bowed his head down with closed eyes. "I thank you, Anaru, for your deep respect. It is somethin' I greatly admire. My life is devoted tuh helping others, but an even greater feelin' fills me when I help others indirectly, such as your case. I was merely saving uh baby whale that day, but muh actions inspired ya tuh take the initiative tuh change your life. Now, you've come all this way tuh show me your progress as well as tuh inspire others, and I respect that. Your journey *will* inspire many, and all I have tuh say is good luck to ya today." Birch walked forward and extended his hand toward Anaru. "I'm glad ya came out all this way just tuh fight me, brutha."

Anaru, the emotionless golem, could not help but smile at the kindness Birch always showed. "Likewise. May the most determined man win." He grabbed Birch's hand, which was larger than his, and shook it firmly. "Don't hold back on me. I've heard many rumors that you keep your strength a great secret because you are too powerful. Nothing would be a greater insult to me than for you to not give it your all as I shall. So, do not worry about hurting me too much. You are a kind man, but remember that this fight is what I have trained for, Mr. Willow."

Nodding his head firmly, Birch turned around and walked toward his corner as Anaru did the same.

It was entirely silent.

All that was left was for the bell to sound.

The referee, cautious of how close he was to the two giants, waited a moment, and then he rang the bell. The second the metal clang rang out, the audience went wild again.

Anaru wanted to finish the fight as quickly as possible, as he knew that his stamina was nothing compared to Birch's seemingly endless endurance. With a burst of speed, the islander rushed forward at Birch and then spun left, getting to Birch's right side. Before the giant could respond, Anaru sent a powerful kick to the back of Birch's right knee, which had been combined with the momentum of his spin. Birch's massive leg buckled slightly in response, but he was still standing, so Anaru quickly followed his attack with another powerful kick, managing to get Birch onto one knee. The whole ring shook as Birch thudded onto his right knee, seemingly caught by surprise by the attack to his leg. Using this to his advantage, Anaru got behind Birch and then jumped onto him, getting Birch into a rear naked choke that looked unbreakable.

"Holy crap! I can't believe it. Anaru has already gotten Birch down and is attempting to choke him out," Matthew announced excitedly as the crowd screamed. "It's an underdog story! Will this fight be over before it even starts?"

"Not at all," Birch shouted in response to the rhetorical question, silencing everyone as he stood up, appearing like an entire mountain rising out of the ocean. As he stood up and began to flex, Anaru almost lost some of his grip, but he still clung around the neck of the giant, trying to choke him into submission. Now, he seemed like a mere koala holding on desperately to the predator before him, however. "After all, Anaru asked me tuh not hold anything back. I'd hate tuh insult 'im by doing so." Everyone, including Anaru, gulped at the statement. "Y'all came tuh see an excitin' show, didn't ya? Isn't that what ya wanted?"

Roaring with anxiety and excitement, the crowd responded like the sadistic patrons of a Roman colosseum fight.

Anaru tuned out the noise as he tried to tighten his hold on Birch's neck. His forearms struggled as they slipped against the giant traps that kept pressing up against him, and the skin around Birch's neck almost seemed too thick to choke. The monstrous muscles of Birch's back were pressing into Anaru more and more, almost pushing him off like a wall of pistons. Despite the struggle, Anaru knew changing strategies would be too risky, and he was still hoping to end the fight quickly. He flexed his arms and legs to their fullness as he tightened his grip on his superhuman opponent.

Birch smirked. The weight around his neck and on his back would have been enough to bring any person down, but Birch could squat ten times the amount of weight, and he had easily dragged vehicles that weighed far more. He respected Anaru's strategy, but he wanted his opponent to grow and train a lot more, so he would do as he had promised. His goal was not to completely obliterate Anaru, but he did want to break him down enough that he could grow from the fight afterward. He also wanted to entertain the crowd a bit. So, Birch decided that he would hold back still, but not as much as he had originally planned. No one would be able to tell the difference, though.

Squatting down and charging up power in his legs for a moment, Birch launched up with a jump before spinning forward. He did a front flip, spinning a single time before landing on his back, crushing Anaru, who released his grip as a result.

"Unbelievable! Charleston *Crusher* counters with a *crushing* attack that flattens Anaru right against the ring floor, breaking his grip on the giant," Matthew commented in an enthusiastic yell. "What an amazing display of strength! He did a front flip into a back landing with all of Anaru's weight on his back on top of a diminishing air supply. This day is going to be full of jaw-dropping moments for sure! That's a move you would never see anywhere else!"

If Anaru groaned in pain, it was internally, for he seemed unfazed by the attack other than a wince on his face. Birch had not put any extra force into the landing, so the impact with the ground was more of a fall than an attack, but the weight of Birch and the height had been enough to send pain along Anaru's back and spine. It had been enough to break free of the naked rear hold. Seeing Birch looming over him like the judgment of God, Anaru, despite his massive size, flipped backward and rolled three times before jumping up into a fighting stance. He thought for sure that the giant would have demolished him in a single blow if he had not moved just now, but Birch was not doing anything.

Matthew stroked his chin as he watched on, thrilled inside but composed outside. "Missing his opportunity to defeat Anaru while he was on the ground, the champion seems to be giving the challenger another chance. I would expect nothing less of Birch Willow."

"Let's just hope that his mercy isn't his downfall," Michael added.

Anaru constantly moved in his fighting stance and maintained his defense while he contemplated what to do. He knew he only had a few seconds before someone had to act. Not wanting Birch to take the offensive, Anaru rushed forward again and then spun to his right, which was Birch's left.

"Goin' fuh muh other knee, huh?" Birch said as Anaru quickly spun to Birch's left side, appearing to attempt the same attack from earlier but on the opposite leg.

Birch went to counter this attack with a powerful jab from his left elbow, but Anaru dodged it by agiley ducking, and he ended up right in front of Birch with a big smile. "No, my friend. That is only what I *wanted* you to think," Anaru exclaimed as he hit Birch with a powerful right uppercut that slightly jerked his head back and then an upward jab to the face that sounded like a hammer hitting a coconut. The giant looked like he was going to stumble back a step. "I got past your defe-"

Anaru was instantly cut off as Birch's bald head smashed onto the top of his face. The impact was like a powerlifter smashing a bowling ball right into a human skull at full force. Blood spurted from Anaru's forehead, and his eyes had rolled back into his skull as his mouth involuntarily opened. Had the impact been any lower, his nose would have undoubtedly been broken. The challenger fell straight back as if completely knocked out.

The entire room was silent.

The cameraman switched from the ring to the audience to the judges to Michael and Matthew and then back to the ring.

Everyone's expression was just one of entire shock and horror.

Almost trembling, a woman gulped. "Is he... dead?"

No one answered her.

After a moment's hesitation, the referee started counting. Five. Ten. At fifteen, he heard moans and groans of consciousness from the limp body, but he still counted. Before he reached twenty, he felt a vice grip around his arm. Terrified, he saw Anaru struggling to get up and desperate to stop the count. However, the challenger fell back down silently. Twenty seconds had elapsed. The referee looked over at the judge's table, unsure what to do.

Matthew was almost trembling as he stood up and peered forward, verifying that his eyes were telling the truth. He spoke quietly, matching the tone of the somber and shocked room. He was unsure what to announce. "This is... unexpected. The fight is over after just a few seconds, and Anaru was defeated by a single headbutt from Charleston Crusher. It was like two overpowered characters exchanging their two ultimate moves. That was just like the kind of Japanese shit my children watch all the time." Matthew slowly turned and looked at Michael, who also had a grave expression on his face. "Mi... Michael, what do you think?"

"I'm speechless. I had genuinely believed that Anaru would be setting the bar high tonight, but that was... that was a different fight than what everyone expected to witness here today." Michael slowly shook his head. "It's a shame. I had truly hoped to see Anaru do well. I read his book, and it was very motivational. I mean, you interviewed him, and we all heard what he said before the fight. At the end of the day, either his strength didn't match his heart, or his strength just couldn't match Birch's, and there's nothing that can be done about it."

"Unfortunately, you are completely right, Michael. Now folks, don't worry at all about Anaru. We have medical professionals on standby, and they will be taking care of him. Actually, here they are now," Matthew said with a point at the fighting ring. The cameraman turned around to show the viewers at home medical professionals loading Anaru onto a stretcher. The cameraman turned back around and focused on the judge's table. "Hopefully, there should be no brain damage at all. At most, Anaru might have a fracture or microfracture in his skull, but the extent of his injuries shouldn't be anything worse than a regular concussion."

Birch looked over at Michael, a grim expression on his face, and his humble eyes were disappointed. Through their years of friendship, Michael understood what Birch wanted. "With that said, we are going to take a ten minute break," Michael announced. "Now is the time to use the bathroom or buy food and beverages at the concession stand. As soon as five minutes has elapsed, we will announce the next fighter."

Everyone turned to talk to one another or get up and go where they need to go, hoping that the lines were not too long.

With everyone distracted, as Birch had silently told Michael to do, the champion followed the stretcher out of the building. They stopped right before the back of the ambulance, which was ready to take Anaru over to the hospital. Standing in the late afternoon sun, Birch politely asked the medical professionals to give him a moment alone with

Anaru, and they immediately left. He looked down at Anaru. The blood trickling down his forehead had been wiped away, but the area was swollen.

A subtle groan of pain escaped the mouth of the defeated challenger, and his eyes slowly began to open. His vision was as fuzzy as his head was, but after it had cleared a bit, Anaru turned his head a bit to look up at Birch. "Guess I lost, huh?"

Sad to see the defeated challenger and have to answer him with an unfortunate response, Birch slowly nodded his head. "Yup… it was over relatively quickly. I'm really sorry. I nevuh meant for the fight tuh end like that. I wanted tuh give ya uh chance tuh make your people proud, and more importantly, tuh make yourself proud. I-"

"You insult my pride and honor by apologizing, Mr. Willow. I know you mean very well, but I cannot accept an apology. You defeated me under fair conditions, and I'm glad that you didn't hold back." Anaru closed his eyes. "I still have a far way to go, my friend. My journey seemed like it had been a long one and that today would be its conclusion, but now I realize that my journey is still just in its beginning phase. I am a strong man and a skilled fighter, but your level is still way beyond me. My goal is to be like you one day. It was never to beat you, and I don't think that I ever will. Still, I'm not giving up just yet."

"Hmh." Birch nodded his head and smiled a bit. "I'm glad tuh hear that. Take care, Anaru. I wish ya well, and hopefully, we'll meet again." Birch turned and walked away as Anaru was loaded into the ambulance and then taken away. He was glad that Anaru was optimistic about the outcome of the fight. Still, Birch was bitterly disappointed in himself. He had wanted to give Anaru a few chances to beat him, and he had accidentally ended the fight before it ever truly began.

Disappointed as he was, especially on a day that was already a somber one for him, Birch was not feeling up to fighting anyone else, but he knew that there were still several competitors left. It was his duty to fight them all. He easily forgot just how strong he was, and just how much of a curse his strength was to him. Now reminded of that by his fight with Anaru, Birch decided that he would be holding back for the rest of the day. As he entered the gym and made his way into the room where he prepared for the fights, the ten-minute break was just about to end. Birch could hear the excitement coming from the fighting room. Everyone else had recovered and was ready for the next fight. They had already forgotten about Anaru, his reasons for fighting, and his unfortunate defeat. It angered Birch and made him truly upset, but he did not blame them for their attitudes. He listened to the noise, mentally preparing himself for when they called his name.

Michael checked his watch. "Folks, please take your seats as we get ready to announce our next challenger."

"This is so exciting, and I have no doubt that this match will be *very* exciting." Matthew had recovered from the previous fight, and he was back to being hyped to announce. "Some of you may have known Anaru, but this guy is bound to be known by a lot more of you. Heee's aggressive. Heee's blood-thirsty. Heee's as tough as they get in the entertainment industry. Turn your attention to the red corner. Heee's a brute, known for having more W.W.E. wins than anyone else in the past decade, please welcome, all the way from Dallas, Texas... The Ghooost Outlaaaaaw!"

Screaming with exhilaration, everyone anxiously turned and looked to the red corner of the ring, where an enormous man ran toward it, grabbing onto the ropes and jumping over them while doing several flips. He was well over seven feet tall, and his stage presence was impressive. His build was strong but also lean and athletic. He wore a white cowboy hat, with a fancy white vest-like jacket, his solid six-pack of abs showing through the part down the middle. Then, along with a golden belt with fake diamonds, he wore tight white shorts. Too tight. He grinned menacingly at the crowd, loving the attention he was used to receiving, and absorbing it all as if it powered him. The smile revealed an engraved golden tooth. The man tipped his cowboy hat down before tossing it into the crowd. A group of ladies fought each other to get the hat as the man's dirty-blonde hair swung free, down to his shoulders. He winked at the girl who managed to grab his hat and clutch it close to her chest. Ripping off the vest-like jacket, he flexed, showing massive muscles for an ordinary man. Then again, his opponent was not an ordinary man.

The man had stripped down to nothing except the tight shorts and fancy belt, revealing several Western-themed tattoos. He had the large skull of a bull cow in black and grey ink on his upper back. On his left calf was a sexy cowgirl. His left tricep featured a cactus, and on his right deltoid, the man had a large tattoo of the state of Texas with the inside colored-in with the state's flag.

"Normally, I don't get so macho fuh nobody, but Mistah Willow has mah respect," the man said with a Texas accent and a salute. He took a pause between very few words. "Howevuh, I am here tuh win. Y'all saw what he did tuh that island-boy, but I ain't some rookie like that wannabe. No, sir. I am a professional who's been in this industry fuh over uh decade. Are y'all ready for this?" he asked while throwing his hands in the air to pump up the crowd. They cheered and screamed in response. "Some call me uh cattle wrangla, but do ya want tuh see what I do to men who challenge me?" He let the crowd cheer and go wild with suspense. "I pulverize 'em!" He roared and flexed some more. He beat his chest like a gorilla and stomped his foot like a rhinoceros, roaring like a lion before yelling, "I am The *Ghost* Outlaaaw!" The crowd loved every second of it, and they chanted his fake name with a violent passion.

Matthew laughed heartily, flashing a bright smile. "You *have* to love it! What a competitive spirit, and we're all aware of just how dangerous The Ghost Outlaw can be. *And...* in the blue corner... we have the hometown hero, who has already defeated one challenger out of many, it's Charleston Crusherrrr!"

The crowd was a mixture of cheers and uncertainty that created silence. Some people still wanted to see Birch pulverize every challenger, but the fight with Anaru had converted many over to the underdog side for the remaining fights. They could sense Birch coming, for the ground began to shake with each thundering step he took as he approached. Birch charged into the fighting center, and rather than grab onto the ring ropes and hop over them like his opponent did, Birch super-jumped right over everything, going higher than his entrance for the last match. Birch had managed to make himself appear happy and unfazed, and he almost smirked as he landed in his corner once again. The whole ring shook in response, and The Ghost Outlaw had to balance himself to not fall.

"I appreciate ya makin' an exception and being all macho fuh me and this event," Birch said to his challenger, announcing it for everyone to hear. "It means uh lot tuh know that I have your respect. So, as uh courtesy," Birch stated loudly, almost as a threat, "I'll do the same."

Everyone gulped as the room grew silent. There was no more cheering or yelling. All everyone felt was a thrilling feeling trapped inside of them that they knew would ruin the moment if it were allowed to escape. Some men covered the eyes of their wives or children. The cameraman made sure to focus on Birch. Michael, who knew that Birch was never shirtless in public, gasped in shock, and Matthew was shaking with excitement. Everyone understood that it was almost a historical moment happening in front of them.

Birch ripped his muscle-tee in half to either side of him like it were a piece of paper. Now shirtless, he stood erect, appearing even taller and larger, revealing a body that was unlike any other. It was the pinnacle of masculinity and strength, and there was no doubt that it was the goal humans had biologically been seeking since primal times. His body-fat percentage seemed to be the unattainable perfect amount for survival and cosmetic appearance. He was almost purely muscle, and his muscles were far beyond just intertwined fibers of organic material. He was not a girthy ball of muscle, but instead, his figure was the perfect combination of lean and broad and strong. He had distinct abdominal muscles forming a large eight pack of abs, which were the priceless parts many hoped to attain but failed to. He seemed to be the masterpiece of a humanist and artist project that had been sculpted into steel made soft with flesh. It seemed like no human, animal, or anything else alive could ever challenge Birch.

Everyone's attention, however, was past the phenomenal display of human anatomy. Their eyes were all focused on Birch's left pectoral muscle, as directly over his heart, there were three large scars that appeared to have been the result of an animal attack.

After some hesitation, murmurs and whispers broke out among the crowd before full conversations were being held. Everyone was curious about the scars. They watched as Birch and The Ghost Outlaw exchanged words, an exchange of banter and threats.

"Impressive." Matthew let out a hefty sigh of awe. "This man is a work of art. I think the real reason we never saw Birch shirtless up until now is that he knew how much of our self-esteem would be destroyed after looking at that perfect body. At least to most people, it's perfect. Those scars are rather intriguing, Michael, and I'm guessing it's a story that not many know about either. It was on the news a few years back and kept relatively quiet, correct?"

"That's right, Matthew. There was a town picnic, and the whole town was eating out on blankets with wooden baskets and all. Well, a baby black bear cub wandered out of the woods somewhere and started causing trouble. It went to attack a group of little girls, but Birch went and snapped its neck like it was nothing. He's a peaceful man, but when it comes to protecting people, he'll ensure that everyone is safe. That's just the beginning of the story, however. See, the mother bear came on over, and when she found her cub dead, well... she wasn't happy. Her and Birch had themselves a tussle. It was quite a fight, to say the least. Gave him those scars. He's lucky that only three of her claws snagged him, and the bear was lucky that she even managed to hurt Birch. Anyway, he was bigger and stronger, so putting his hands facing away from each other in her mouth, he ripped the whole thing open. Broke its jaw and tore all the flesh around her mouth apart. Of course, that's not how he wanted things to go, but sometimes survival can get really ugly."

The audience was quiet again after hearing the story that sounded like a tale from Greek literature. "An *amazing* story, but I'm afraid we've wasted enough time talking. Either the testosterone in the ring or the crowd's anticipation is going to blow up, so let's get to the match at hand. It's time to fight!" Matthew yelled out enthusiastically.

The bell rang, and the fighters charged at each other, the two men colliding like triceratopses as their hands interlocked, their arms at ninety-degree angles. They pushed and pulled for a bit, evenly matched for a slight moment, as The Ghost Outlaw used his lower center of gravity to his advantage. The challenger lost his grip, however, and was instantly defenseless. Birch sent him flying back into the ropes with a thrust of his massive arms. Using this to his advantage, The Ghost Outlaw shot himself with remarkable speed from the ropes, his body flying across the ring like a slingshot-projectile. He caught Birch by surprise and smashed him in the waist, right in the soft spot below his eight-pack of abs. It was a mighty blow, and Birch stumbled back a bit, shock in his eyes. As of late, his digestive organs had been in pain, and the power-packed punch had just inflamed his intestines. The man wailed at Birch with a speeding frenzy of punches to the abdomen and sides, even throwing a robust kick while he was at it. That was his mistake. Birch grabbed the man's leg and threw him across the ring with one hand as if the massive man weighed nothing.

An outroar of screams and cheers broke out among the crowd in response as they all jumped out of their seats and threw their arms in the air. They started chanting Birch's nickname as he slowly began to walk thunderingly over to where his opponent was on the ground. He towered over the flashy wrestler, but he was now tuning out the crowd and announcer, busy in his own mind. Bringing his right arm back, Birch lowered down as he swung at his opponent. The Ghost Outlaw rolled over and avoided the punch that could have cracked the ring floor if Birch was actually trying. Quickly getting up and grabbing Birch's head, he jumped up and swung forward, wrapping his legs around

Birch's neck in a variation of a triangle chokehold. He flexed his ripped quads and thighs, trying to choke Birch to knock him unconscious.

The wrestler's strategy was flawed, however, and anyone smart enough to recognize the error either prayed or shook their head in disappointment.

Birch raised his bald head high, the light reflecting off of it, causing the large orb to appear like the sun itself. The Ghost Outlaw instantly realized then what his mistake had been, and he quickly kicked off of Birch before he could be hit with a powerful headbutt that Birch had used to break bricks in the past for shows. After all, he saw what had happened to Anaru, and he regretted setting himself up for such an obvious counter despite his knowledge.

The Ghost Outlaw successfully escaped the would-be headbutt, only to get hit with a quick hook from Birch. Combined with his jump backward, the punch sent the wrestler to the ground. He stood up and shot blood from his left nostril, a smirk on his face that was reflective of his good sportsmanship and fighting spirit.

Ducking down, he quickly tried to throw a strong right hook to the kidneys, but Birch caught the powerful punch with his left hand. The man was not willing to be defeated yet. The Ghost Outlaw quickly used his free hand, backed with all of his force, to uppercut Birch on the underside of his left wrist, immediately followed by a kick straight up to hit the same spot. They were untypical moves for The Ghost Outlaw to use, but he had made sure that he was trained in multiple fighting styles, at least on a basic level.

Birch released his grip on his opponent in response as he held his wrist in pain, shocked that he had been hit there. It was true that his forearms and grip strength were phenomenal, but the underside of the wrist just before the palm was still a vulnerable spot. He cocked his head and smiled at The Ghost Outlaw, suggesting that now it was his turn to hit back. He quickly raised his right knee up and back, and in a burst of strength, Birch shot his leg out at the man, who went flying back again, bruised but not broken.

Throwing the wrestler was like throwing a boomerang, however, and The Ghost Outlaw came flying back at Birch once again. He caught his giant opponent off-guard with a mighty leg sweep, and Birch fell backward to the ground with a heavy thud. The whole ring shook. The cowboy rushed in to make a final series of blows to the face while Birch was on the ground, but to his surprise, Birch backhanded him, sending him flying across the ring. Birch jumped up from the ground without using his arms, the ring shaking again in response as he landed. His flexed thighs began to rip and tear the grey cargo shorts apart. He stormed over to where The Ghost Outlaw was standing, half-dazed. With a raise of his giant fist, Birch went to deliver the final blow, but The Ghost Outlaw threw his two arms up and grabbed the punch, trying to hold the immense force back. Both of his large arms shook violently as his muscles and veins bulged to the point of tearing. It was an admirable resistance against such a phenomenal strength, but the fight was over. Birch looked at his left arm with a smile before knocking out The Ghost Outlaw.

The muscular and previously undefeated professional wrestler fell backward to the ground, unable to claim the title as the world's strongest and best fighter. There was a small clinking noise as his golden tooth went rolling across the fighting ring. An adoring girl quickly snatched it. Birch caught the look of a greedy man behind her who probably would have sold that golden tooth for a nice profit had he gotten his grubby fingers on it. Birch had accidentally broken his opponent's nose, but there was no helping that. Dark blood streamed from the nostrils, spilling onto the floor of the fighting ring.

The crowd grew silent with awe for a moment until Birch pumped a fist into the air. Screaming cheers and applause broke out among everyone. The match had been much more of a show, and while people knew that Birch was practically unbeatable, they still wanted to see a good fight.

As they took The Ghost Outlaw away and everyone got ready for the next match, Birch went back into his preparation room. While it had been a good match, he felt awful. He hated being the final unmovable obstacle standing in the way of all of the people who had come to challenge him. Birch also hated violence, for the most part. What he hated more, however, was the small flame inside of his subconscious that loved violence. It was the part of him that knew how strong and blessed he was, and it just wanted to go on a rampage and display and demonstrate that strength everywhere. That part of him wanted Charleston Crusher to actually crush enemies. He hated that small flame because he feared a fire would spread, fueled by each match. Combined with the fact that he was crushing people's dreams by defending his title, he could be nothing other than utterly bitter. Yet, it was a burden and struggle he gladly faced, as he knew that the fighting tournament had raised more money than any other event he had ever hosted.

After the second ten-minute break had concluded, Birch headed out for the next fight before repeating the process several times. The rest of the fights all resulted in the same result: Birch Willow was the strongest human alive, and no fighter could ever hope to beat him. An enormous sumo wrestler was the only one to almost succeed due to the nature of their match, but Birch even won that battle of strength, however, making a last-minute comeback as he pushed the man across the whole ring into the ropes, which were serving as the out-of-bounds. A lively boxer got a couple of fast punches in, but Birch once again prevailed. After that, all of the matches were against opponents using special styles of martial arts, who hoped that their technique could win against Birch's strength. It was useless.

The most gruesome injury of the night resulted when a karate master tried to spear Birch in the throat. Seeing the attack, Birch jumped up while flexing his eight-pack of abs. The timing aligned so that the spear-hand went straight into Birch's abs, and the karate expert broke his fingers on the wall of abdominal muscles that were almost truly as hard as steel.

After the final fight, Birch sat down on a large stool in his corner and chugged a half-gallon of water, and then he slowly sipped at one of his plant-shakes. He wiped his body down with a white towel, although he was not sweating that much. Due to the sweat, his bald head was shiny under the lights of the ring, and his slimy scars popped vibrantly compared to the beginning of the night. After that, Birch quickly disappeared from the fighting room.

Michael hopped back into the ring with the microphone, a proud smile on his face. "And that, ladies and gentlemen, concludes today's event! Let's give a round of applause for all of today's champion fighters!" The crowd clapped and cheered, appreciative of the effort that all of the contestants had put in. They were sad that there was no underdog story to amaze them, but not many had expected one to occur. "Now, folks, don't worry about them. As we have said time and again, they are being medically treated. We'd love to have them back next year or whenever we decide to host something like this again. They are always welcome back here for a second round, and they are all entitled to free memberships at the gym with no placement test required. I also want to thank Matthew and American News 50 for being here. It was a pleasure working with them." Matthew and the people with him all waved as they exited the room. The judges had ended up not doing anything, and they had left before Michael could even thank them for their time nonetheless. "Now before you all leave, our undefeated champion, Birch Willow, has some things he'd like to say."

Upon hearing his name, Birch reentered the room, now wearing one of his custom-made black muscle tees for the gym again. He felt it was not professional to address his audience shirtless, despite the fact that there were good reasons why he would have been shirtless. It was simply the way he was. At the same time, he felt like his scars scared people, and he hated for people to focus solely on his large muscles. Birch walked over to the fighting ring, everyone cheering and applauding him until he got there. He took a step over the ropes and walked over to Michael, who handed the microphone to Birch, and stepped back as his friend took the spotlight.

Birch glanced around at the waves of faces surrounding him as he cleared his throat. "Michael just said this, but I want tuh say it too because they really deserve the credit and ruhspect that they earned here tuhday. Thank you so much tuh all of our contestants who showed up tuhday. All of 'em fought extremely well, and it was uh pleasure and an honor havin' all of 'em here at The Heaviest Lifters gym. They all have muh praise and muh respect, and they are all the strongest people. It may have looked like they barely did anything, but they were putin' in uh lot more effort and strength than any of y'all could evuh imagine. Everyone, please give uh hearty round o' applause tuh 'em," Birch bellowed. The crowd applauded loudly and for quite a while. "Now, I also want tuh thank y'all for comin' tuh this event. This is uh way huger turnout than I had expected, and fuh that, I am very, very thankful." The crowd broke out into applause again, and people whistled and cheered.

"**We love you, Birch**," some random peeople yelled from somewhere up in the bleachers.

"And I love all of you too!" Birch yelled back with a point as the crowd went wild with admiration. "But there's uh good reason for that... so let's get serious now," he said firmly but in a friendly manner with a calming motion of his hand. The energy of the room dissipated as it turned dead quiet. All eyes and ears turned and focused respectfully on Birch. "This event wasn't free, and I want tuh explain why. I know that the tickets were expensive, but it wasn't for the gym. It's for somethin' much bigger than muh business or me. All o' the money raised tuhday will be donated tuh charity for Wilson's Disease." Birch glanced over at Michael with a solemn look that only the two of them understood. "Michael and I lost one of our closest friends tuh it, and I don't want that tuh ever happen to anyone else. I know it's not typically fatal, but it still makes life very difficult. They didn't catch it in her, but times have gotten better. Yet, research and fundin' aren't the highest since the condition is so rare, considering that it's uh genetic disease. But that doesn't make it any less important!" Everyone applauded Birch's inspiring words, and he held back tears. "Uh lot o' genetic diseases are rare, but those small percents deserve all of our attention too. We are raisin' money for uh personal disease because *we* are personal! We are uh big, loving family, and I don't jus' mean this gym. It goes beyond that. The city, the state, society, the world- each is its own big family, and we should all love and support one another. I will also be dividin' the money up among three of the least funded cancer charities. Why? Because the world is truly an amazin' and beautiful place, and those people deserve tuh live, eat, sleep, and breathe just like we do!" Birch shouted with a mighty pump of his fist into the air, trying not to let his sympathy and empathy overwhelm him.

Yet, when everyone cheered as well, tears escaped Birch's gentle eyes, although they were small ones. Not tears of sorrow or grief, but of overwhelming joy as everyone all shared a moment of reality and hope. He glanced over at Michael, who nodded his head in pride. "She'd be proud," he mouthed to Birch, who nodded his head in agreement as he looked around at the packed bleachers. Everyone was cheering and clapping as loud as they could. Birch smiled bitterly. One man *could* change the world. A small piece at a time, but a piece nonetheless. He truly believed that. He wiped the small tears away with one of his large fingers, and he pulled himself together with a high-rising breath in his chest.

"Thank you! Thank you. Also, I want tuh invite all of ya back tuh the gym tomorrow night at six. I will be hosting an educational session on health awareness, nutrition, working out, and diet. I'll mostly focus on the gym's idea and use of plant-shakes, but I'll be open tuh all questions about health. Please stop by. It's inspirational, and there's uh lot of good information that I hope everyone can benefit from. I hope tuh see some of you there. Again, thank all of you, and have uh wonderful rest of your day!" He waved his hand in the air as he walked triumphantly off of the stage. Everyone gave one last round of applause before they all started to head out, some grabbing flyers for the gym as they left.

By the time Birch got back to the farm after cleaning everything up with Michael, it was a little past 5:00 p.m. He parked his convertible at the end of the long dirt driveway and walked groggily into the house. He threw the keys onto the round wooden table in the kitchen before making his way over to the living room. On a small table on the left side of the couch, Birch set an alarm on an old clock to ensure that he ate dinner and did not sleep to the point that he would not be able to fall back asleep come nightfall. Exhausted from his day of physical exertion on top of a night of poor sleep, Birch sprawled out on the couch and fell asleep. For once, his sleep was not plagued with nightmares, as even his mind was too tired.

An hour and a half later, Birch woke up against his will, his old-fashioned alarm clock making enough noise to arouse a bear in the dead of winter. "Piece o' garbage," Birch muttered as he smashed the clock into pieces with a slam of his giant fist. Lethargically getting off of the couch, Birch stumbled over to the bathroom, holding his stomach in pain as he clenched the inside of his throat. Leaning against the bathroom wall, half bent over the toilet, Birch threw up violently before falling down onto his knees. The putrid mixture of chunky green liquid and blood came projecting out all over the toilet and floor.

Lightheaded from vomiting, Birch decided to take a bath, rather than a shower as he usually did. Getting into his custom-made bathtub, Birch slid into the hot bubbly water, relaxing a bit. He looked up toward the ceiling. "Guess I'm goin' tuh be joinin' ya soon, Rose. Old-Spike too. Somethin' ain't right." He pointed at the ceiling with a bit of a smile. "And I know what you're thinking, but it's not muh fault. They say that bad things happen tuh good people. You proved that when you died of Wilson's disease. That shouldn't have killed ya. I've met uh lot o' people doin' this business. All great folks, but none evuh come close to ya. Ain't never met uh person as good as you. Well, some call ya an angel, but still. You were always kind, caring, helpful, protective, and you were just everythin' to me. Always there fuh me. My best friend. I… I nevuh got tuh tell ya any o' that. Michael says that you knew all along, but still… Worst part is that the kids who made fun of me and who came after me are all still alive. They're laughin' while you're dead.

How is that fair? *Why* did ya have tuh go? I could've used your help uh lot over these past few years."

Birch thought to himself for a moment, staring at his large toes at the other end of the bathtub. He sighed. Glancing at his left wrist, he noticed a small bruise where he had been surprisingly uppercutted by The Ghost Outlaw. There were also a few bruises on his waist.

"But I'm not as good as you were, and I don't think that I ever will be. I'm tryin' tuh be just like ya. That day changed everything. The point is, maybe I did do this tuh myself, but some part of me is sayin' that I didn't. I'm not meant to exist in the first place, so does it really even matter? I know that you would argue yes, just like you always did. I don't know, though." Birch looked over at the clock on the wall. "I best get tuh dinner, and see if I can even handle anything in muh stomach."

CHAPTER 4
HELPFUL, HUMBLE, AND HURT
(Charleston, West Virginia. The Next Day: April 13, 2022)

Birch's giant heart began to pound in his chest as if he were having a heart attack, the muscles around it clenched tight. His whole body was drained of all power and energy, and he felt weighed down by an unmovable force. He summoned all of his superhuman strength and tried to raise his arms and legs, but they were mentally cemented down. He attempted to tense and flex every muscle, but he was utterly powerless. He could not even twitch or roll over onto either side of his body.

Unable to see a single thing in the threatening darkness, Birch assumed that he was in his bedroom, as that was where he had last gone. He scanned his surroundings, but there was nothing visible. In fact, the pitch black of the room seemed to be growing darker with each second and grew closer to Birch, caving in on him. Despite the absence of a clock, Birch heard a ticking noise that grew louder and faster as his breathing quickened. His tongue and glands swelled in his mouth as he attempted to scream, but he was unable to utter a sound, his throat muscles clenched. Then, everything went black as the darkness closed in, his body unable to do anything against the caving force.

Two hours of dreamless sleep later, Birch groggily woke up in extreme frustration when there was knocking at his front door. Hoping he had imagined the unexpected noise, Birch closed his eyes again, as he was tired to the point of almost lifelessness. Reluctantly, he opened them when the sound was repeated again, this time louder than before. Although his room lacked an alarm clock since he had destroyed his only one hours ago, Birch knew that it was in the early morning hours, as his rooster had not yet screeched its morning call. The sun was still tucked away beneath the horizon, although it was slowly beginning to peak out.

Sliding out of his custom-sized bed, Birch made his way down the steep stairs of the old house. Each wooden board creaked under his weight as he descended, and his footsteps were heavy and thudded each time they hit the stairs and then the floor when he reached the lower level of the house.

"On muh way," Birch called out through a huge yawn, his pearly-white teeth the only bright thing in the room. The knocking stopped. *Who could it be at this hour? Can't get no sleep 'round this farm.* He rubbed his eyes, which were crusted over, and after blinking a few times, he was able to make out the outline of everything in the house, although it was still pitch black. After shuffling his way through the darkness, Birch managed to get to the front door. He opened the old wooden door without checking first to see who it was. He was simply too tired to be bothered with performing such a cautionary task.

A young Asian woman was on the other side of the door. She screamed as she looked up at the towering figure of Birch, who loomed in the low doorway in the dark, cramped in its frame.

"Ay, easy wit' the screaming," Birch said with another heavy yawn as he ducked through the doorway and stepped onto the porch. "It's early, and I'm uh farmer, so ya know that means it's really early for me tuh be saying that. We tend tuh rise 'n shine pretty early."

The woman was flustered, and it took her a moment to recompose herself. "I-I-I'm sorry, I just didn't expect to see-"

"An over-eight-foot-tall guy answerin' the door in his gym merch'ndise unduhwear? I bet. I wasn't expectin' tuh be here either."

"Well, yeah... that's part of it. I mean, I *didn't* look at your underwear or notice them, but I'm more surprised by the fact that I'm meeting *the* Birch Willow."

"Hmph," Birch grunted. "You know me?"

"Of course! You're quite popular online, although I thought you might've been some kind of online joke that was photoshopped. No offense or anything. It's just that none of the accounts were like *official* accounts. More like fan-pages and conspiracy theories. Despite that, I've read *all* about you. I'd say you're a famous person, in fact."

"I try not tuh be," Birch muttered. "I don't even have uh phone or social media. Must be other people recording me. Hate that. Privacy ain't uh thing anymore, I guess. The gym does have an account online, I believe. Not my area o' supervision." Birch rubbed his eyes again as he looked at the woman. "If ya came here for an autograph, I'm afraid you'll have tuh come back later at uh more respectful and understandable time. As you can imagine, I need some sleep. Especially tuh keep this behemoth of uh body workin'. I literally fought uh bunch of champion people yesterday and then vomited all over the place. If ya know so much about me, ya know what I'm talkin' about. Either way, sleep is this fella's only goal in life right now," Birch said with a firm point of his thumb at himself. "It's uh thing that far too many take fuh granted."

"*Oh*," the woman said distastefully but with shock. "You fought champion fighters *and* vomited? Well, that's awful. I did see a few clips, but I wasn't sure if they were highlights from the tournament you had a year ago or new ones. Guess they were new ones! Sorry to hear about that, but I need your help."

"My help?" Birch asked, his eyes almost popping out of his big head. "With what? Can't it wait?"

"Unfortunately, I'm afraid it can't wait. See, I'm with some friends. Our pickup truck broke down, and you're the closest house. I didn't know it was yours, but I suppose I'm very lucky now."

"Hmph," Birch grunted in frustration and suspicion, eager to get back to his uncomfortable bed in an effort to sleep. "And why's that?"

"Well, I don't have to call a tow truck now. I came because we don't have phones on us, and so I was hoping to borrow yours. But you're a very generous person, and I'm sure you could pull the truck to the nearest gas station."

"You want me tuh pull the truck?"

"Well, you don't have a phone for me to use, and I'm sure you could do it easily."

"First of all, that's really takin' advantage of me, and I don't like that too much. Secondly, the sun ain't even up in the sky yet. Thirdly, I'm flattered and all, but what makes ya say I could easily pull uh pickup truck?"

"Well, you're the strongest man in the world!"

"I like tuh think I'm one of the strongest men in the world, but certainly not the strongest one of 'em all. That tournament yesterday didn't prove nothing."

"That's overly humble of you, Birch. It's true, though. I've watched all of your lifting videos and read all of the articles online. In that one charity event you hosted, you pushed a few vehicles as if they weighed nothing. I mean, that's crazy! My pickup truck doesn't weigh that much, and you're a lot taller than it besides, so I don't think it would be that difficult. At least I don't think it would be *too* difficult."

"Plenty o' strong men an' women have pushed and pulled cars. It's not that uncommon, and some people have pressed cars into the air with just their legs. I ain't that special or different from anyone else who has trained tuh be strong. Others have even pulled airplanes for uh bit with their bare strength."

"True. I've watched those kinds of competitions before with my dad. But I also read in the newspaper that you helped a small boat that had conked out in the water just by going behind it and kicking your legs. It takes a lot of strength to do that, especially for over a mile. Plus, you never used any machines to get strong due to your size, so bodyweight, dumbbells, and strange lifting methods are how you got strong, which means you're waaaay stronger than anyone else. And, well, look at the size of you," the woman said excitedly with a gesture at Birch.

"*I try not to*," Birch commented gruffly with a hint of annoyance at what he considered an unintentionally rude statement. *Seems tuh know an awful lot about me,* Birch thought to himself as he eyed the woman with suspicion. *Might be uh trap, if she's an agent of The Organization or something. But if that's not the case... then I'm denying help tuh people who need it, and that's no good in my book. I'll have tuh be careful.* Birch quickly scanned the yard before looking back down at the woman. "But yeah, of course, I'll help y'all out with your problem. Just le' me get changed intuh real clothes and grab uh plant-shake real quick. And I'm sorry 'bout not being so hospitable. I had another fit of sleep paralysis just uh few hours ago, and it takes uh toll on me. You disturbin' muh sleep certainly don't make me feel any better after it either." Birch turned around and closed the door before the woman could say anything.

A few minutes later, Birch exited the house dressed in grey cargo shorts and the black muscle-tee, which was for his gym. In fact, it was the same outfit that he wore every day, but not the same article of clothing as the day before. He had a closet full of identical shorts and muscle-tees, as ordering custom-made clothing in bulk was cheaper. Birch had never been one for fashion.

Birch locked the front door and walked past the woman down the wooden porch steps with more energy than before. "Follow me over tuh the barn," he commanded with a wave of his large hand. "I think I have uh chain and hook in there tuh hook up to the truck, so I can pull it. And uh harness tuh strap around muhself tuh attach the chain to."

"Really? I always keep a spare one close by as well," the woman said jokingly.

"Hmph," Birch sounded as he continued on his path to the barn.

"Not a morning person, I guess," the woman mumbled quietly to herself.

"***Oh, I assure ya that I am***," Birch said firmly without turning around, though his tone was not entirely aggressive. The woman was shocked that Birch had heard her muttered remark, and he took note of it. "Yeah, I can hear ya all the way up here at this altitude. Usually, in the morning, I'm drivin' around wavin' and smilin' at everyone. It's just that we're not even in the mornin' hours as of now. We're approachin' mornin' time, but most normal people are uhsleep right now. Everyone within ten miles is probably uhsleep in their beds right now. Even my rooster is asleep! So, combined with muh sleep paralysis, I ain't in the best of moods. Even *I* can get uh bit cranky sometimes. Besides that, I don't really care too much for sarcasm. Ironic compliments and remarks that are meant tuh insult or degrade people ain't muh kind of humor."

The woman, embarrassed that Birch had heard her, hung her head in shame as she reflected on her remark and what Birch had said in response to it. Considering how praised and glorified Birch was on the internet for being a nice guy, she knew that she was at fault. Not to mention, he was already doing her a favor, and at an unreasonable time besides. So, the woman followed Birch silently as he walked over to the farm, which was only a short distance away from the house. It had been there for a few decades.

The first morning rays of the sun were finally just starting to peek out enough so that everything outside was visible, although the landscape was still covered by the darkness left over from the night. The weak rays glinted off of the top of the slightly rusty silo next to the barn, and the newly-installed solar panels that lined the barn roof, which Birch had purchased from R.O.M.A.B.A. Industries.

Birch swung open the massive doors of the old barn. The inside was exactly like a typical barn seen on television or in books. There were piles of hay, wooden beams, and rafters holding everything together, along with a ladder leading up to the second floor of the building. Besides one old tractor that had not been used in years, tools and equipment were piled around on various tables, as Birch used the barn as both a shed and a barn. Along the walls were large sledgehammers, pickaxes, saws, rakes, hoes, pitchforks, a chainsaw, regular axes, and other various tools. There were a few animals inside the stalls, detectable by the smell of the place, although they were hidden away, sleeping and quiet. A few flies buzzed around, but overall, the inside was neat, with the floors well swept, where there was no hay, and the walls and ceilings washed clean.

The woman looked at everything inside the place as she followed the slow-moving person of Birch over to a huge crate of various junk. She looked over at the stalls, which lined both sides of the barn, but was unable to see the animals sleeping inside. "Nice barn. It has a mix of modern and rustic design to it. You have any animals? I can't see them since they must be sleeping in the back."

Birch went to say he wished that he was sleeping in the back, but he bit his tongue. He felt that he had made enough comments about his sleep to get his message across to the woman. "Yeah, but I don't have too many. Just the stereotypical farm animals you'd imagine in uh barn and uh few pests, I s'pose, though they don't bother me none. They're just pests tuh others. I stepped on uh rat once by accident. Poor fella."

The woman cocked her head in confusion as she immediately scanned the floor in paranoia, looking for a rat. "You feel bad about its death? Isn't a rat usually a pest in barns? They're considered an unwanted pest anywhere, actually. They bring diseases and stuff."

Birch stopped in place and turned around to face the woman, a disapproving frown on his face. "Tuh most people, they are, but I value all life. Nothing is uh pest so long as it lives. An animal or plant's life may inconvenience ours, but it's not intentional, and therefore, they are not pests. We, ourselves, often inconvenience the lives of others. Who are we tuh do so and not allow such mercy toward others who do the same? That is known as hypocrisy, which is the dangerous root of most evil and self-destruction. The world is uh natural place of life and empowering spirit. I am no man tuh take any o' that away, whether they be bothersome or not. It is only in the natural and desperate defense of other precious life that one shall be taken, should no other option be at my disposal."

The woman's eyes widened, and her jaw almost dropped open as her face jolted back from the impact of the surprising wisdom. She was almost on the verge of tears, though no water came to the surface of her eyes. "It was just a yes or no question," she commented jokingly. Recalling the incident before with her attempt at humor, she instantly regretted her reply. "That was actually really deep, though. Now I know why everyone says that you're one of the best inspirational speakers out there. That alone was enough to make me respect nature so much more and value all life. It was almost enough to inspire me to become a vegan. That was actually amazing."

"That's overly kind of ya tuh say, and I thank ya for the compliments. Yet, I don't speak as such for inspiration or tuh change people's views. My words weren't meant to be anything life-changing or special. They're simply the philosophies by which I live," Birch stated as he turned back around and headed for the crate. "It's my personal belief that *all* people should live by those philosophies, but humans have the ability tuh make decisions for themselves. At the end o' the day, words and ideas are just those: words and ideas. It is purely up tuh uh person's interpretation whether they actually mean something or not."

The woman closed her eyes and laughed. "Really? Even that was inspirational." She shook her head and smiled. "You are as wise a man as you are a strong one. Perhaps it isn't intentional, but your wise words combined with your deep voice just seem so moving. I admire that you have so pure a heart and so clear a mind. A lot of people lack those traits nowadays. Are you a vegetarian or vegan due to your views on animals and people?"

"Nah. Most people think that I am, but I'm not. Course, it don't have anything tuh do with muh body needin' fuel, as plants can provide that despite what most people think. I respect all life and nature, but that includes respecting and understanding the food chain. I won't go into the whole discussion 'bout hatcheries and treatment of livestock, but of course, it does upset me uh ton. Ain't nothin' I can do about it, though. At least fuh now. There are uh lotta humans on this world, and we gotta eat, don't we? So, yeah, I eat meat, but muh diet is mostly made up o' plants and carbohydrates, considerin' how much energy I need tuh live and function properly. Respectin' animals and tryin' tuh be the savior of 'em all are two entirely different things."

"I see. I'm a bit shocked, but I also understand. You're completely right… *again*." The woman looked into the barn again to try and see the animals, but they were still tucked cozily away amongst the hay. "Anyway, do you breed the animals or sell meat or-"

"None of the above," Birch answered as he lowered himself onto one knee and hunched over as he began to dig through all of the junk in the huge crate. "I don't do anythin' with 'em 'cept let 'em roam around how they please. It keeps the place lively, and they were all left behind from my parents when I inherited the farm. No sense in slaughterin' 'em for uh few bucks that I don't need. Plus, it helps keep the memory of ol' Mom and Pops alive."

"Oh, so you focus more on growing and selling organic crops since that preserves animal life while still supporting you financially," the woman said while tapping a finger against her cheek. "Smart. I get it. What do you grow?"

"Nothing. I don't grow or sell anything," Birch gruffly replied non-attentively as he continued to dig through the crate. "One o' the only things I've ever planted was uh willow tree in front o' the house since muh last name by birth is Willow. I took my adoptive parents' last name as my middle name. Oh, and there's uh birch tree 'round the back o' the house somewhere."

The woman made a confused face as she cocked her head again, unaware that Birch had been adopted. That fact about him had been kept relatively quiet online, and he certainly did not talk about it ever. To him, his parents through adoption were his real parents. "That's nice and all, but why don't you grow crops? Aren't you a farmer?"

"Nope."

"Earlier before, you said you were a farmer!"

"Hmph. My apologies. I did say that. I'm not really an actual farmer. I just happen tuh live on uh farm and take care of the animals and the yard, but not for business. I was an agricultural man growin' up with muh parents, but I stopped after they died. Not 'cause o' the memories attached to 'em and farming, but I switched my focus tuh what I wanted tuh do. Not that I disliked farming, but it had never been my dream."

"Oh. I understand. You started the gym, right?"

"Yup. I started it 'bout ten years ago with muh friend and partner, Michael Kellson. It wasn't easy, but certainly worth it. That place means everything tuh me, and hopefully, it means everything tuh muh members and Michael as well."

"Not to invade your personal finances, but where'd you even get the money for such a huge project?" Birch tensed up for a moment and froze in place with his breath held in before continuing to dig through the crate as the woman kept talking. "I've never actually been to it, but I've seen pictures of your gym, and that place is enormous! It's actually considered one of the top fitness centers in the world, and that's a pretty big accomplishment."

"I s'pose it is, and I'm honored by the fact. Although, that had never been muh intention. For uh couple o' years, I had been doin' various jobs for uh good amount o' money, but it only paid cash. Not that I cared, but it's better tuh have uh balanced combination of on-the-book and off-the-book pay. It was the easiest thing tuh do at the time, though. I would cut down trees, remove stumps, clear fallen trees, move boulders and rocks, move furniture, and uh whole list of other things. Mostly landscapin' stuff, I guess. Usually, the work I did would be relatively costly 'cause it would've required uh machine, but I charged less than the companies would, and I could do it with just muh bare muscles as soon as needed, so it made me uh good enough profit tuh get started with what I truly wanted tuh do."

"All of that money just from doing those jobs? I'm shocked by how much money that would make, but it *is* work that's always needed and always pays. Guess it adds up after time, just like most things. That's pretty smart financial managing. I do that stuff for major companies."

"Oh, nice. I had always wanted tuh enter the business field since I'm good at math and arrangin' everything, but I'm not really meant for an office building. They don't make extra-large cubicles."

"True, but if you're as good of a business and financial expert as I've heard you are, and as you seem to be, you could have worked from home! That would've possibly given you the ability to make your own hours, therefore allowing you to also continue your laborious work and get additional cash."

"Hmm. I admire your brilliant thinking, as that is uh great plan in theory. However, I'm afraid ya didn't account fuh one thing, which is the most vital part of such uh lifestyle."

"I don't… I don't think so," the woman replied defensively as she thought over her idea. "What are you talking about?"

"Tuh work from home as you suggested, I'd need tuh use uh laptop or uh computer. Not only do I not own either o' those, but I also can't use either of 'em. My fingers are too large. Don't even suggest usin' uh pencil or somethin' tuh type with. It ain't as easy as television makes it seem. Plus, uh custom-ordered ginormous computer would be expensive and uh headache."

"Ohhh," the woman exclaimed with a laugh. "I didn't even think of that. I never realized that you can't use computers and stuff. Normal people don't really think about all the restrictions tall and giant people have. That's actually really sad."

"Eh, I guess. It don't bother me none. I can't let that kind o' stuff bother me. Anyway, it wasn't just those jobs," Birch commented as he grabbed the strap, chain, and hook, slinging them all over his right shoulder. He walked out of the barn, the woman following behind him. Birch gestured to the rolling hills and flat land behind the house and farm, various crops across the terrain. "See all o' those acres o' land out there? I rent 'em out tuh some folks nearby, and they pay me monthly in exchange for the land, and they grow and sell crops. It's uh pretty good business."

"Oh, wow! It looks like you have a lot of property back there," the woman said with her hand above her right eye like a salute as she scanned the fields. "How many acres do you own?"

Birch scratched the back of his bald head. "Hmm. I'd say 'bout eighty-two acres or so o' land total. It's not uh lot compared tuh most farms, but it's all I need. Keeps the property manageable. Well, they do most o' the work, but still makes it easier for me."

"That's a lot of income, I assume. Wouldn't it be fairer to take a small percentage of what they make instead of charging them monthly?"

"Nope."

"What if there's a bad harvest?"

"Not muh fault. I don't control the weather. I pay taxes on the land whether I grow crops on it or not. They're payin' for the opportunity, and they owe me the money, whether they're successful or not. Providing them the land and takin' uh small percentage of uh harvest that yielded no vegetables and sold for low prices would be like givin' out uh loan and taking uh few cents back instead o' the hundreds of dollars owed tuh me. So, it's fairer tuh charge for the land. Understand? Plus, they take the land with an idea of what the future holds, and they know it's uh chance."

"I guess that makes sense. I just feel bad for them if they have a bad season and have to pay for the land even though it wasn't good."

"I understand what you're saying, but I'll give you uh relatable example. You buy food at a restaurant without knowin' whether or not it'll be good, and if it's bad, ya still paid for it or have tuh pay for it. Real estate and farming are the exact same way in that sense."

"Is the land any good? Do they make enough money?"

"Accordin' tuh them, the land is so fertile that there are earthworms the size o' snakes, but I'm not sure how true that is. They always bring me uh sample of what they're growing, and I 'preciate it. They're all the same people from the past few years. Other people offer me slightly more money, but I keep the same people each year since I've established uh relationship with 'em. They're all good people," Birch remarked as he turned away from the landscape and headed over to the long dirt driveway that led to the main street.

The woman stared out at the land for a moment before jogging after Birch. "I see. So you don't actually grow anything while still making a profit off of the farmland. Smart, since it saves you all of the hard work and allows you to be at the gym."

"Eh, I guess. I wouldn't care in all honesty. I grew up doin' hard work every day, so I know uh thing or two 'bout farming."

"Really? Can you grow almost anything?"

"I s'pose so. I don't mean tuh sound like uh braggart, but I'm essentially uh botanist, florist, and an arborist considering all of the experience that I have. With no technology in muh life and no close neighbors, time outside in the garden was all I had. I was never the brightest student in school since I moved around uh bit an' such, but I actually understand plants more than anything. Somethin' 'bout 'em that muh brain just seems tuh registuh. Well, I know uh lot 'bout animals too, actually. All uh part of the farm life, I s'pose. It's not just that, though. I've also studied uh lot about 'em. I've always had uh more developed connection tuh nature than most people. If I wanted tuh grow all kinds of crops, I could do so, but I feel no need tuh do such a thing. Plus, I've got the gym. That's muh passion."

"What about those roses just beginning to grow along the front of the house? I noticed them earlier when you went back into the house, and they stand out considering that there are no other plants except for the grass in the yard and that one willow tree."

"My yard must be really ugly if the grass is the most noticeable plant," Birch said with a chuckle to himself.

"It's not that ugly. My eye was just caught by how tall and pretty they are. Obviously, they aren't in full bloom or anything, but they're still really nice."

"Trust me... as pretty as they are, those roses aren't much at all," Birch said with a soft chuckle of nostalgia. "See, uh membuh o' muh gym had moved here from Kansas for uh few months. Back when he had been livin' in the country, he grew sunflowers that almost reached twenty feet tall. I couldn't believe it! He actually won all kinds o' competitions with 'em. About three total, as far as I know."

The woman laughed a bit. "Is your gym secretly all musclemen in the garden?"

"*Warriors* in the garden, tuh be precise. Him and I were both big fans of that concept. He liked it because he was always ready, and I liked it because breaking stereotypes is on muh list o' things tuh do and help teach others about. People shouldn't be shocked that uh muscular man is uh gardener or enjoys growing flowers. Gardenin' is nothin' more than uh hobby that can easily be done by anyone, right? So, why does society, or at least most people, feel the need tuh believe that it's weird and shocking for certain people tuh enjoy gardening, or that gardenin' can only be done by uh select group of people? Why is plantin' flowers feminime but plantin' crops isn't? Ya get what I'm tryin' tuh explain here?"

"I do," the woman replied as she studied the roses, which were in the early stages of blooming. "In fact, it's not limited to just gardening! I believe that the whole stereotype-thing and certain-people-thing are both major problems. We've been trying to fight them, or at least some of us have, but the battle is slow and difficult. Judging a man for growing flowers doesn't benefit anyone! All it does is hurt his pride or make him self-conscious when there's no need to be. It's nothing but negative!" The woman turned and looked at Birch, who was looking at the roses with his arms folded across his chest. "You seem to speak proudly of this guy," she commented probingly, hoping to learn more.

"I'm proud of all o' muh gym members, but ya do speak the truth. Guys like him make my seemingly impossible goal seem reachable. He was only around for uh short while, but I'm glad that I got tuh meet 'im. I wish I could've spent uh lot more time with 'im He was uh good man, and everyone respected him. In fact, he was even uh bit of an inspiration tuh all o' muh membuhs."

"Oh? How so?"

"Well, he was born only five months intuh his mother's pregnancy. That ain't how it's supposed tuh go, as I'm sure ya know. He was so small at birth that he fit in the palm o' the doctuh's hand. He died uh total of three times while they fought tuh keep 'im alive. They had tuh do uh heart operation on the spot, and since he was so small, they had tuh cut through his back, below his left shoulder blade. That left quite the scar, as you could imagine. Anyway, when he learned about all o' this years later from his parents, he realized that his life was uh blessing, and that he should make the most of his life by helping others. Tuh start, he went through six years of honey sandwiches and liftin' tuh get ripped. Like muhself, he understood that havin' good health is uh sacred gift, and that improving your health is an even greater gift," Birch stated philosophically as he looked past the roses to the reason why he had planted them.

"I agree. My grandmother ended up paralyzed, but she was happy to be alive and always stayed optimistic."

"Hmm. From there, he became uh teacher, and then he powered through boot camp with an injured foot to become one of many great people servin' our wonderful country. So, yes… I do speak proudly of him. Everything I've told you, though, is just the compilation of minor reasons for why he chose tuh work out. There are far greater reasons for why he chose tuh become strong, and they're even more inspirational than his miraculous birth or goal of helpin' others. And that's somethin' I want more people tuh realize: we all have personal or inspirational reasons for working out. Women don't just work out tuh be like men or better than other woman. Men don't work out just tuh impress others or fight. The improvement of our bodies is something far more complex than just pride. Not only that, but havin' improved bodies shouldn't take away from who we are or were. It shouldn't mean that havin' uh strong body and doing uh hobby is different than doin' that same hobby without having evuh worked out."

"Who would have thought that looking at roses that aren't even in full bloom yet could bring about such a deep conversation. Why'd you plant those roses? After all, they seem to be the only thing you've really done around here, so it seems a bit odd."

"Those roses are in memory of muh friend Rose," he answered somberly. "She's no longer in this beautiful world, but she had an everlasting effect on those she knew. So, in her memory, I planted the very flower that she was named after. It was the least I could do fuh her, considering all that she helped me through."

The woman nodded her head. "That's really sweet, Birch. She seems to have meant a lot to you. Was she a girlfriend or something at one point? A wife? I've never even heard of her in anything I've seen online about you."

"That's because I don't talk about her too much tuh anyone but muh buddy Michael. I've only mentioned her once before publicly, and that was yesterday at the fight. Was she my wife? Unfortunately not. I don't date women. She was just uh... really close friend."

"Oh... I'm sorry. I had no idea you were gay. That's also absent from the internet. People can still be unnecessarily judgemental of things, though, so I respect and understand why you wouldn't want that out there."

"As do I, but you mistake what I mean," Birch pointed out with a small laugh. "I don't laugh at ya. It's just that you're the first person tuh ever think that, actually. Of course, it's not uh bad thing or somethin' tuh be ashamed of, but I'm not at all uh homosexual. I don't date women for multiple reasons."

"Like what? We're not *that* bad, are we?"

They were almost at the main road, and the sun was just rising over the horizon. It was not peak sunrise just yet, but the sight created by it was just as mesmerizing. Not only did the sky grow light blue as the horizon faded from orange to yellow, but the rays of golden light cast onto the plants and vegetation of the land, along with the morning dew that clung to everything, made all seem fresh and new.

"Now that's uh beautiful view," Birch commented with a nod of his head. "I should thank ya fuh wakin' me up so early because I wouldn't have been awake tuh see this if it weren't for you. Things like that," he pointed at the view, "are why I love nature and the world. It's why I can take uh deep breath and feel no stress at all. Just the beauty of it all is enough, but it's not just that either. One could spend their *entire* life admiring the intricate details o' pants and animals that make 'em so amazing. That isn't it, though. Nature is so much more than just beauty and aesthetics, and even more than just precious life. It's uhdventure. It's living. There are so many wonderful things tuh explore and do, and it's all thanks tuh everything that this natural world has tuh offer. Not for me, of course, but for regular people… man, is it amazing."

The woman gasped as she turned and looked away from the sunrise and looked at Birch, who stood proudly in his admiration for the view nature was providing him with. "Aww. That breaks my heart, Birch! Being your size must be so rough. I never realized that your size was a handicap." She turned back to the rising sun, which grew more powerful with each second that passed. "This is one of the first sunrises I've seen in ages, to be honest. I never really thought about how much nature provides us with besides just scenic views. I guess you're right. People take the beautiful views of nature for granted. We get so caught up in our daily routines that we forget to *actually* admire the sunrise and sunset unless we're posting about it, and even then, we make it all about us, not nature."

"An unfortunate truth, but as long as one person admires nature, it shall continue to thrive," Birch said with the tone of a wise philosopher as he stared out at the view before him. He shifted the supplies he was carrying on his right shoulder as they started their walk down the main road toward the pickup truck. "Anyway, it has nothin' tuh do with women themselves. I think women are amazing people, but I don't date 'em. O' course, I do 'preciate all that they have tuh offer to this world, and I don't mean that sexually. People are always arguin' over gender equality, but I feel that men and women both have different things tuh offer to the world, and each should be respected fuh that. So, men and women should be equal when it comes to pay and promotions, but people need tuh understand that men and women will always have different things tuh offer that the other gender can't. It's kind o' just how the world works. Just like how people all have different skills and such. Hopefully, that don't make me seem bad. I do respect everyone equally."

"There's no need to be defensive. You're entitled to your own opinion, and I already know that you're an advocate for equality. Well, you've spoken about a few times during interviews and such when people asked."

"Yep. Anyway, the issue with women and me all has tuh do with me. The last reason being the fact that I'm rich, as that tends tuh arouse false love amongst the greedy and selfish ones. It's the last reason on the list, though, because women would have tuh look past all the other reasons why I'm single to want tuh date someone like me. So I know that money would be the only motivation and way that someone could look past everything else."

"That's understandable, considering how much money you have, but you're such a nice guy, though. Unfortunately, gold-diggers do exist, but they're a pretty small part of the population."

"Unfortunately is 'xactly right. Life is about so much *more* than money, or even pride, in fact. It's about livin' life and being there with people and nature. Friends and family are really important too. It's about humbly enjoyin' the precious moments that this beautiful world has tuh offer, and being grateful for everything that we have."

"Then why not enjoy it with someone by your side, Birch?"

"I wish I could," Birch answered bitterly in a way that suggested longing for, but there was a look of acceptance in his eyes, but there seemed to be some other kind of emotion going on behind them. It was something indescribable. "But that brings me tuh the list. I can't have uh romantic life. Love has never worked out with me, nor has it ever even sought me. I can't have sex with anyone. I'm sure I don't have tuh explain why. I'm just physically too large tuh safely perform intercourse."

"Oh... I guess... that makes sense. Hadn't really thought about that, to be honest. That's not what women care about, though, Birch. If somebody truly loved you, they'd look past something like that. Sure, sex is a huge part of most people's relationships, but it isn't everything."

"I assure ya that I know that, but it's not just about havin' sex for fun, though. It's also about havin' uh fam'ly. Most people want one. Not everyone, but most people. I can't make kids, though, so uh woman who wants uh family ain't goin' tuh be with me."

"There's always adoption."

"I know, and I support adoption, considerin' that I was adopted as uh young lad. Not through traditional means, but I know how much findin' uh good family means to an orphan. It can mean everything. It can be what completely shifts their life from uh downward spiral tuh havin' uh good future. I frequently donate tuh orphanages when I have the chance. Those kids aren't mistakes, and the stigma with orphanages is uh growin' disease amongst our society. I feel that they're an overlooked branch of society, and they *need* our help. Uh lot of people don't want adopted kids, however. They want an authentic family, so to speak. The traditional passing of lineage through procreation. I understand that. More than anyone, actually. If I weren't so busy, I would've adopted uh couple of kids muhself."

"I'm sure you could find a woman who shares your values and would be willing to adopt."

"I'm well aware of that, but again, there's uh whole list o' reasons, and every time one of 'em is fixed, there's still another problem."

The woman led the way in silence for a few seconds, but she turned around and looked at Birch with excitement. "Hold on a minute! I just realized something."

"Hmph. What's that?"

"This isn't like back in the day, Birch! You could always take your sperm and your future wife's eggs and have them connect before planting it back into your wife. I don't remember what exactly it's called, but you can have an authentic family filled with your genes!"

"That thought has crossed muh mind uh few times, and it's the perfect solution to muh situation. Except, the problem with that is I'm sterile by birth for some reason. So, that means I have no sperm tuh donate or use. Not entirely sure why I'm sterile as that isn't too common, but I'm glad," Birch said earnestly with a bit of a smile.

The woman scrunched her face together in a puzzling manner as she turned back to lead the way, stepping back a bit so that she was walking by Birch's side. "'Why's that? Wouldn't you want to have kids? You implied before that you want a family."

"Many say that I'm the ideal father figure, but I know that's too kind. I'd love tuh be uh father, though. Not just because the idea seems great, but also because of muh experience with kids. See, at the gym, we have various programs for kids. I teach them all. There's no staff other than Michael and muhself."

The woman was breathless. "You're telling the truth?"

"I'm an honest man if I can say so humbly, ma'am. There is no staff. It's just Michael and me. That makes running the gym harder, but it's the way I like it. The Heaviest Lifters is literally muh life, and it's the path of devotion that I've chosen. That said, I teach all the kids. Some of them are high schoolers getting into fitness or wanting tuh be personal trainers. They can be tricky sometimes, but I try muh best. My favorite, though, are the younger kids. They're adorable, and fuh some reason, they admire me. Tuh them, I'm super cool and just uh regular guy despite muh size. They don't judge, and that's uh nice feeling. Of course, they were all scared at first, but I'm good at calmin' people down. Anyway, I've been working real close with this scrawny boy named Cody. Next year, he'll be a freshman in high school. He's an underdog, and it's takin' uh lot o' work, but I know how much of an impact I've had on his life and still have on his life. It's uh bit o' pressure, but it's mostly uh good feeling. I love it. It's like helpin' people but on uh personal and more meaningful scale. So, in uh way, I've experienced the joy of being uh parent. I know that it's not always like that and that rasing uh kid can be real tough, but still, it's uh tremenduously wonduhful thing tuh experience. So, I'd love tuh be uh father."

"Aw, that's so sweet. I didn't know the gym had programs for kids that young, but I guess all gyms do. I don't get it, then. Why are you glad you can't have kids?"

"Well, I'm gettin' there. I wanted ya tuh understand first that it's nothing tuh do with people or raising uh kid. I'd love tuh be uh father, but I wouldn't wish my genes on anyone. I hate no man or woman, but even if I had uh mortal enemy whom I despised, I'd never wish this horrible life upon them. I've made something of muh life, it's true, but this," Birch gestured up and down himself, "is no way tuh live. Perhaps, if there were others like me, then I wouldn't feel like muh size is uh curse, but I'm all alone in this grand world. Imagine if my genes spread tuh many children of my own descent. They would become the new dominant species of mankind, and uh war between humans and these 'giants' would eventually erupt. It wouldn't be good for either side. It's uh prediction decades into the future, but an inevitable one nonetheless. The food supply would diminish at twice the rate, as well as the oxygen supply. Each breath and meal I have are equal to that of two or three people. Imagine if there were a whole bunch of us. Our beautiful world simply couldn't support such a society."

"That's... well... I *never* looked at it in that way," the woman said depressingly. "That was actually brilliant thinking to even imagine the impact on society if your body type genome spread. You've thought about this a lot, then. It's like finances and the gym, I guess. You think about how adding a new product will affect everything else. I would've never thought that far ahead or anything like that."

"If it's uh dominant trait, that is. If my genes are uh recessive trait, then there's hope, but it doesn't matter because it'll never happen. Even if the 'giants' and the humans got along, my 'people' would always be outsiders, and that ain't the way life is meant tuh be lived. At least not for us humans. Besides, if not many children, what if just one or two of muh kids had the genes and their siblings didn't? That alone would be problematic."

"I can agree with that one," the woman said with a laugh. "Siblings already argue and compare and contrast themselves as it is now."

"Apparently, I came from uh home of many siblings, but that's all the orphanage knew about muh birth. Anyway, the main reason besides that dystopia is that I don't exactly like the idea of artificial pregnancies and such anyhow. The idea is good because it gives people uh chance, but it ain't natural. There are just some rules of nature and science that shouldn't be messed with, and the creation of life is definitely one of them. I disagree with it, but I'm not against it or hate people created from it. If people want tuh have uh kid and that's the only way how, then they're more than welcome tuh do so. I'll respect 'em and their kid. *I* would *never* do it, however, and I fear that it's how I was created."

"You don't know? What do you mean?"

"I know nothing about my origin," Birch replied through a yawn before rubbing his eyes in response to the tears yawns tend to cause. "I don't know where muh name came from or who muh real parents were. Don't think I was born, though, 'cause it just seems like it doesn't line up exactly. I barely know anything 'bout muh body since I hate doctors and medical places, but I do know that I have myostatin-related muscular hypertrophy. At least that explains uh bit."

"Well, isn't that quite the name. What exactly is that? I feel like I've heard of it before. At least the hypertrophy part."

"It's uh rare genetic disorder. There are uh lot of genetic disorders out there, but that one is actually considered uh good one. It's on the internet, somewhere on the list of top ten genetic traits that give ya real-life supah'powers. Basically, people with this condition have reduced body fat and can have up tuh twice the amount o' skeletal muscle, but the exact increase is probably different for everyone. In addition tuh that, people with muh condition also tend tuh have increased muscle strength. Apparently, I happen tuh have the maximum amount and strength of the disorder, which is probably even rarer."

"Well, dang! That *is* a good mutation. Now I understand why it's on the real-life superpower list. It also explains a lot about your appearance and strength. That's actually good news, though."

Birch raised an eyebrow skeptically. "How so?"

"If your condition is the result of a genetic disorder, then there *are* others just like you out there. They might be far and few between since it's a rare trait, but there's hope that you can find them. Then you wouldn't feel so isolated. Maybe make a dating website for people with the condition," the woman recommended both jokingly and earnestly.

"I wish, but that's not necessarily true. My body isn't the typical example o' myostatin-related muscular hypertrophy. The main difference is muh height. While the condition does greatly increase muscle size, it doesn't necessarily affect uh person's height, which is actually based off of bones and growth hormone. People with the disorder are regular people, just more muscular. Not even more muscular, but more like they don't have tuh train and lift at all tuh get the muscles. I'm eight-foot-tall plus two inches. That ain't natural, even with genetic mutations. Nobody's muh height with the muscles and uh healthy body. It's almost unheard of. Usually, people who are really tall are also really skinny. That's why I believe I was created by somebody or some company. Not born. *Created.* Some kind o' unethical experiment. At least if I knew who did it or why, then perhaps I would be satisfied. Although it was probably for a program to weaponize people as cliche as that sounds. Hopefully, it was uh social experiment and not uh military project. I wish I knew."

"True, but who cares if you were created or born? You're still a good person! That doesn't mean there's no hope. A person's humanity is brought about after they're born, not when they're in the womb or passing out of their mother. You of all people *have* to know that."

Birch smiled at the woman, admiring her optimism. "Well, I 'preciate that, and that's uh good attitude tuh have. I assure you that I have more hope than anyone in this world, but... this isn't how life is meant tuh be lived. I've accepted my life, though, and I'm grateful."

"I'm sorry to hear that, but is it really *that* bad?"

"Hmph," Birch sounded in his throat. He nodded his head with a regretful look, although he had not chosen his body. "Allow me tuh paint ya uh pickchuh of what life is like for uh man o' muh size. Think you can handle it? I'd hate tuh dishearten ya. It's worse than just havin' tuh duck under every door of almost every building."

"Go ahead. This is a perspective that most people have never taken into account, and I'd be honored to hear it."

"Well, there's uh whole list. It ain't the worst, but there's uh lot that I miss out on. All the little privileges lost add up to uh whole lot. I can't go out tuh eat at uh restaurant. I can't travel anywhere 'xcept in muh custom-made convertible, which accommodates for muh large size. So that means no buses, trains, or planes. Can't walk anywhere without scarin' people or havin' 'em follow me like the paparazzi and such. Nevuh been on uh ride in muh life at an amusement park. Never been tuh one, actually, and I never will unless it's for uh charity event or tuh speak to people. Barely gone tuh the beach. All my clothes are expensive since I have to get them custom-made. I'm lucky the house and barn are large enough so that I can move around and live. Can't ride uh horse. That's not important, though. Can't properly bowl due to the size of my fingers. Hmm. What else? Can't play hide-and-seek. Haven't been ice skating. Have tuh eat everything with muh hands or large utensils meant fuh serving food. Can't work out using gym equipment or standard pull-up bars. Nevuh gone kayaking or fishing. Oh, and I can't do anything artistic-related except construction. Heck, I can't even hold hands with someone or kiss 'em. I can't do almost everything that uh normal person can. I'm almost not human."

"Almost not human? That's one way to put it, although most people view you as one of the greatest *humans* to ever live. Do you consider yourself something more?"

"Something less," Birch replied earnestly with a cold tone.

The woman decided not to delve any further. She felt that she had already upset Birch and that he had answered more than he had to.

The road was growing narrower and full of potholes as they traveled along the country-like road. They walked side-by-side in silence for a bit, almost at the pickup truck. Birch, as the woman noted, had a steady breathing pattern that seemed to be full of life. She glanced at him frequently, studying his body and face. His body was remarkably strong and pleasing, but his limbs and face did seem tired, as she had begun to notice. Not tired physically, but it was more of an emotional parasite that was draining them of their energy. His gaze was jumping from one tree to the next as he admired their surroundings. She went to speak, but she stopped herself. After a moment, she mustered up the strength to break past the tense air, though Birch himself felt completely fine. "I'm sorry. I didn't mean to pry like that. I never realized how depressing your life was."

Birch was looking off into the trees and listening to a woodpecker as he tried to spot it amongst the foliage by tracking the reverberations created by its beak as if he had echolocation. The majestic bird stopped making noise, and Birch was only able to catch a glimpse of its red-feathered head before it quickly flew off into the forest. "There's nothin' tuh be sorry about," Birch stated, his gaze on the road ahead. "Curiosity is uh common trait. Part of all living things, actually. Even animals are curious, and any dog owner'll tell ya that."

"True, but-"

"I'm not upset at all. I'm an open book for the most part, and trusting. I can't blame ya for your curiosity, either. A man as rare as muhself seems tuh attract uh lot of attention. Everyone thinks exactly as you do. They all think that I've got everything. The unfortunate truth is that I'm not the happiest person despite seeming tuh be. There's uh lot of pain and loneliness inside of me. I'm humble and kind, but it's tuh make up for everything that I've missed out on. I don't take anything in life for granted. It's uh common lesson that many ovuhlook, but probably one of the most important and enlightening ones there is. It's easy tuh see when ya miss out on all of it. Despite that, I still try tuh be respectful and be grateful for what I do have. If I'm goin' tuh have uh boring and lonely life, then I might as well devote it tuh helping others."

The woman nodded her head in agreement. She looked up at Birch, whose gaze was still focused on the road ahead. The eyes of his mind, however, were looking at him from far away and reflecting on everything he had missed out on, and everything that he had made for himself and others. "That's actually really sad. Even though it's kind of your personal problem, it seems like you're carrying this burden for all of us in a strange way. Why *are* you so humble? Everyone says that you're always so helpful and kind and that you never brag, even though you're the strongest man in the world and rich. You're never yelling or threatening or showing off your strength. I just don't get it."

"That's exactly *why* I'm humble. It's because of muh size that my personality has formed. My personality wasn't always the way that it is now. People always wonder why I don't be an Olympian or uh champion of every or any sport. They wonder why I never purposefully go out and try to break the records that have been set."

"Why don't you?"

Birch sighed before he half-looked up at the clear sky ahead. "People think muh size is uh gift, but I think it's an unfair advantage, in all honesty."

"Explain."

"Well, Olympians and athletes train vigorously tuh get in shape and compete. Who am I tuh just waltz in and take everything away from all of them? What right do I have tuh do that? Uh God-given gift? Maybe, but either way, I respect everyone's hard work and sacrifices. That's why I'm humble, and why I mind muh own business and stick tuh muhself. Sure, uh naturally smart person has no problem competing against those who study hard, but I consider that tuh be different than muh situation. *I'm* different," Birch said as he looked at his palms and forearms, noticing the minuscule bruise on his left wrist. "I have no right to hop into their competitions and destroy their dreams. Hopefully, all o' muh reasons make sense."

The woman nodded as she thought about what Birch had said. "That makes a lot of sense, and I actually admire and respect that kind of view. I agree that you're a unique situation, and that physical tests are different than I.Q. ones. Naturally-smart people don't have larger, more complex brains, like how your body is in comparison to regular people. It makes sense. Still… the self-control required to keep yourself from winning everything has to be a lot. It must be so tempting to break those records knowing that you could easily be number one and the champion of the world."

"Not really. Once I established that I shouldn't compete in events and such out o' respect for everyone, thoughts of winning never formed in muh mind again. The intense self-control that you speak of is uh natural part of me, and it has been since I was uh kid."

"But you've broken world records before, haven't you?"

"In public playfulness, yes. I've broken uh lot of records, but that was without using most of muh strength."

"*Why?*"

"I won them because being overly humble is just as bad as being overly prideful. It wasn't peer pressure, but uh lot o' people wanted me to break the few records that I did go an' break afterward. It gives them something tuh look up to, as well as uh better challenge for competitors tuh face. I purposefully threw the competitions so that I broke the records or won by just uh small amount. Don't call me uh fake, but I made it look like I was really struggling and could barely do it." The woman was shocked by the revelation, but her surprise quickly faded when she took into account all that Birch had already said to her. "I broke the records by just enough that uh normal human could beat it one day if they worked hard enough fuh it. That was the fair solution that would please everyone. I want people tuh have the chance tuh continue tuh push themselves and achieve the impossible."

"That's the right thing to do… I guess. Actually, I think you *should* have broken them as best as you could, in all honesty. I know that I agreed with you before, but I'm beginning to think that you should just use your full strength for any competition you enter."

"Hmm." Birch raised an eyebrow and looked at the woman for a moment, adjusting what he was carrying on his right shoulder with a shrug. "Interesting," Birch remarked to himself. "Why have ya changed your mind? I could've sworn you were in total agreeance with me."

"Well, I started thinking about all of the competitions that take place in this world. It's not unfair for you to use your unusual strength to your advantage. Everyone uses what they're given to their advantage, so why shouldn't you be allowed to do the same? It'd actually be inspiring. A man turns genetic disability and physically-outcasted body into blessings as he uses it for the betterment of humanity," the woman proclaimed with a gesture through the air as if she were creating a newspaper title.

Birch chuckled. "That's one way tuh put uh positive spin on it... but muh mind is set. It has been evuh since I was uh child, actually, and I think that it always will be. In uh twisted way, people only want me tuh compete to boost the ego that humanity shares as uh whole, and I don't want tuh be part of that. Anyway, people *do* use everything to their advantage when it comes tuh competitions, but I don't consider muhself physically uh human. Who am I tuh compete with them? And it's not outta pride for thinkin' that I'm not human, but outta consideration for all o' those who are workin' hard, as I said before. Don't mistake muh words, though. I say I'm not uh human uh lot, but in muh heart, I'm just like everyone else."

"Like everyone else? In the heart, you're *better* than everyone else! Everything you've said has been so heartfelt and pure. You're like all of the good humanity has to offer squished into one organic being. They're all words of inspiration, and the best part is that you don't even mean to inspire, but you're just being honest."

The slightest smile appeared on Birch's earnest face, and his eyes seemed to be at peace. "I s'pose so. You're too generous in your praise and compliments. Thank you."

"Oh! Here we are," the woman stated as she pointed to a white pickup truck parked half on the side of the road and half off of it just a few feet away.

The busted-up road was narrow to the point that it was just one lane. Birch had traveled on it once or twice before, although it was a seldom-used road as he recalled. He scanned the surrounding area, checking to make sure that this was not all part of some kind of trap set up by the government or something similar. "Hmph," he sounded in his throat when he noticed four people sitting in the pickup truck bed, supposedly sleeping. "You're not alone?"

"I had mentioned that I was with friends when you and I first spoke. You were still tired then."

"Right." Birch glanced at the surrounding woods again, not spotting anything suspicious. "What were all o' ya doin' out so early in the mornin' anyway?"

"Well, I certainly wouldn't have left it all alone for someone to hotwire and steal. I know this all seems suspicious, but I swear we weren't doing drugs or worshipping Satan. Believe it or not, we decided to unplug from technology and go on a short nature trip. My beliefs aren't so far off from yours, actually. Although, I'm sure you could probably get along with anyone. Anyway, it was a good time until the truck broke down. I don't know what's wrong with it. I mean, if you could fix it, that'd be great!"

"Hmm. It would be, but I'm afraid that mechanics and such have nevuh been muh strong suit. I can do some stuff with carpentry, but that's about it."

"Oh, right. You're hands and fingers are too big to work with the insides of machines. My bad." The woman looked at the passengers in the bed. "One of them was supposed to be keeping watch for my return as well as to flag down any passing cars, but I guess they all fell asleep. We were up late stargazing and having a campfire."

"This road is barely used anymore evuh since they created the other road parallel tuh this one that's wider and faster. Also, I'm pretty sure y'all were trespassing in these woods besides, but it sounds like it was uh good experience," Birch commented as he began to attach the hook and chain to the front of the pickup truck. "It'll be easier tuh pull from the front."

"Oh, is that even possible?"

"I've got it covered. So, how was your trip?"

"It was fun. It felt very refreshing to unplug, and time seemed to slow down. It felt like we were out here for weeks. The problem is that we broke down now on our way to our next destination. We all took off from work, and we're stopping at various spots throughout the state on a bit of a road trip. It was foolish of us to not bring a phone. I thought my friend would since she's always on social media, but even she didn't bring one. Food, drinks, blankets, flashlights, knives... you name it, we brought it. Just not a phone."

"Well, that's how ya truly get the experience, but yeah, ya should've brought one. At least I'm here tuh help. There's uh gas station not too far away, and I think there's an auto shop close by as well."

"Perfect!"

"If they could get out an' walk alongside the truck or b'hind it, that'd make the load uh lot lighter."

"I guess you're right. It's just that we were up all night and the night before that. They're kinda knocked out."

"I bet," Birch muttered to himself. "Honestly makes no difference at this point since it's already uh huge load, but any weight we can take off would be nice."

"Well, it's on wheels, so it's not as bad," the woman stated, still reluctant to wake up her friends.

"Is that what people think? Uh shoppin' cart full o' concrete bricks and dumbells has wheels too. How easy is that tuh pull?"

"Better than pushing it with no wheels."

"Not the point," Birch grumbled as he rolled his eyes. He chuckled a bit internally, however, at the woman's light-heartedness and optimism.

"Oh, and could you give me a lift?" The woman gestured to the front of the vehicle.

Birch cocked his head and then looked back at the woman with an expression of "come again?" on it. "Hold on uh minute. You want tuh sit on the hood of the pickup? What for?"

"Well, you're doing us a great favor, so I was going to sit up here and keep you company. It wouldn't be fair to make you work alone with nothing to keep your mind occupied while you drag this thing down the road."

"That's mighty considerate of ya, but you oughtta head on back and catch up on your sleepin' since you were up all night and then went to get me this morning. After all that walkin', you're probably exhausted."

"Eh, I'm fine," the woman said through a yawn. "I'm going to stay up here."

"Alrighty then," Birch said as he gently picked the woman up and placed her on the hood of the pickup truck. "We'll be good to go in uh minute." Finished with hooking the chain up to the front of the pickup truck, Birch attached the chain to the tight harness and strapped it on so that he was pulling with his whole body and did not have to use his hands to constantly hold the chain. "Here we go," he commented as he started to walk forward, the pickup truck slowly dragging behind him.

The woman swung her legs over the front of the pickup truck, holding onto the edge. "Shouldn't you have done some warmup stretches first?"

"Listen, lady... I'll turn around if you're gonna talk like that," Birch replied jokingly with a laugh. "I should've, but it's no problem. That walkin' got me plenty awake. I just want tuh get ya tuh where you're going because then I can get on with what *I* need tuh do for the day." Birch began to pick up speed, getting into a rhythm. "I'm like an old fashioned train- the ones with the bars on the wheels that start out slow and then slowly get faster."

"I know exactly what you mean. As long as you don't get hurt, I'm fine with it." The woman thought for a moment while Birch pulled the pickup truck along at a steady pace. "Oh, here's a question. You're really tall-"

"Good observation," Birch commented jokingly. "I am tall if you hadn't already noticed."

"Well, I was wondering if you're a world record height or not. I know you see your height as a curse, but it's still cool if you broke a record."

"Not even close."

"There's no way there's somebody taller than you."

"Believe it or not, I'm actually short amongst the giants of human history. There are uh few people who are one or two inches taller than me. In fact, the tallest guy ever was just shy of nine feet tall, so I'm not even close."

"You're making that up!"

"Nope. I'm actually dead serious. My height is not just possible, but it's also not as large as people think. There are at least four or five people recorded at heights taller than me."

"What? That's so crazy!"

"Trust me, I'm shocked just as much as you are. The only problem is that such knowledge ain't common, so most people assume that I'm the tallest man tuh have ever lived. Uh nice title, I s'pose, but I haven't earned it. Not that ya earn it by choice," Birch said with a chuckle. "What about yourself?"

"Oh, I haven't broken any world records, unfortunately."

"Well, I know that, but I meant your life. What's it like?"

"You *know* that? It's not very nice of you to assume that. I could have broken a world record."

"Like what?"

The woman was silent for a moment while she thought before she started laughing. "Okay. Fair point. I haven't done anything crazy or commemorable... *yet*." The woman looked up at the sky for a bit while she kicked her feet back and forth a bit. "My life isn't the best right now, but I guess I can't complain. After spending today with you, I've become a lot more appreciative of what I have."

"Well, mission accomplished."

"Oh, shut up. You weren't trying to inspire anyone."

"True. I wasn't trying tuh inspire, but I did influence uh good change of perspective in someone's life, so that's mission accomplished."

"Even that sounded inspiring. Anyway… I want to switch jobs, but I don't know what to do."

"Hmm. Why do you want tuh switch jobs?"

"Managing the finances for all of these companies and working with such big numbers is very stressful. I mean, imagine all of the financial work you have to do for your gym and then doing that for multiple companies every day. It's a lot of work, and I'm good at what I do, but it's not what I want to do."

"I see. What do ya want tuh do?"

"I don't know, and that's the worse part: knowing that I don't have to be stuck doing what I currently am but not having any passion or the determination to follow something else. There's nothing else to follow, which makes it a lot more difficult."

Birch was quiet for a moment as he tried to think of something to say. "I'm not sure what tuh say. It's uh bit like writer's block, I guess. Hard tuh do something when there's nothing tuh do. I understand why you're frustrated, but it's nothing tuh be ashamed about. Still, you don't have any hobbies or anything that could also be uh career?"

"Nope. All I do is work all day every day."

"That ain't life."

"You're telling me," the woman said depressingly but with a laugh. "I can't even begin to understand workaholics and how they love working all the time. It's so bland."

"I s'pose so. I work all day, but I also love muh job, *and* I'm the boss. What about art an' such? You into that at all?"

"I had been into singing back when I was a kid. I never told anyone, but it's what happens in life."

"Would ya believe me if I told ya I'm actually uh really good opera singer?"

The woman laughed. "You're kidding me, right?"

"Not at all."

"*You?*"

"Yep. I'm telling ya the truth."

"How?"

"I'm not entirely sure, but I s'pose it's got somethin' tuh do with the size o' muh lungs. Not like the long, high-pitched notes, but the deep Italian stuff."

"Why'd you never pursue it?"

Birch's face, which had been hard with the labor he was performing, grew into a solemn realization of failed dreams. "I don't know," he responded in a quiet, regretful voice.

"Was it because of your size?"

"I guess so. It's parudoxical, to be honest."

The woman looked at the moving figure of Birch in front of her, realizing how much emotional burden he truly carried. There seemed to be an even heavier weight upon him than before. His body was at the pinnacle of all beings, yet she could tell that there was a somber expression in the grooves and lines of his muscles and skin. She frowned sympathetically. "I'm really sorry to hear that, Birch. What do you mean?"

"Well, the stage is the worst place for me, since all the attention would be on me. They wouldn't hear my singing, they'd just be looking at me. Yet, at the same time, it's the perfect place for me tuh be since everyone would be ju'gin' me anyway. On the stage, they'd be judging muh talent, not muh size. Then, at the same time, it's all they could focus on. Therefore, it's parudoxical. I s'pose that's why I never pursued bein' an opera star," Birch said gruffly.

"Aw… that's so sad, Birch."

"Hmm. Could you imagine if I went on one of those shows where ya sing anonymously, and it's just about your voice? That'd be somethin' fuh sure. It'd probably be one o' the biggest celebrity reveals on any show in hist'ry. Not that I considuh muhself uh celebrity, but it'd be quite shocking. It's the least of muh worries, though," Birch commented as he picked up speed.

"So, you're trying to tell me to go for it, even if I'm afraid or if it makes absolutely no sense?"

"I don't know. My *greatest* life advice would be-"

Birch was cut off by a loud noise that sounded like a large truck honking, which caused everyone to flinch as the roaring sound echoed throughout the peaceful woods like the roar of a tsunami that destroyed everything in its path. A few birds flew out of the blooming trees, and everyone asleep in the pickup truck bed jolted awake. The loud honking sound was repeated again after a few seconds, and it even sounded more aggressive than before.

Slowing down to a complete stop, Birch glanced over his left shoulder to see a box truck on the road behind the pickup truck with an angry driver yelling through the windshield. Birch turned around to face the woman. "Lis'en, I want ya tuh take care o' your friends since they've been startled awake. Let 'em know what's goin' on. I'll go take care of this guy. Stay back, just in case it's not safe."

"Okay," the woman agreed with a nod of her head. She looked over at the box truck. "Be careful." Birch helped her off of the hood, and she walked over to the pickup truck bed to explain the situation to her friends.

Birch unstrapped the harness around him, letting it fall to the ground. He walked over to the box truck, glancing around the area as he did, and stood a foot away from the driver's door. Birch placed his hands on his knees as he crouched down to be eye-level with the driver's window.

The driver rolled the window down all the way and spat to the side. "The Hell are you supposed to be?" he asked rudely as he squinted his eyes at Birch. "Oh, I know ya, pal. You're that big dude on the internet everyone loves," he said with a noisy scratch at the stubble on his face. "I'm surprised you can fit in that thing. Listen, I don't care if you're famous or not; you can't be goin' seven miles an hour down the road. If you could drive at a reasonable speed, it'd be appreciated."

"I sincerely apologize for the inconvenience, sir, but those folks had uh broken-down pickup truck, and I'm actually pullin' it tuh the nearest auto shop, so I'm afraid it's gonna be uh while."

"Well, *fuck* you, Mr. Nice-Guy! I'm on a schedule here, and I gotta get to where I'm going, *pal*. I get paid to meet a specific deadline, and I get fired for not meeting those times. You can't be clogging up the whole road like this. I admire your helpfulness, but move it to the side or something! That's all I'm asking."

"Sir, I understand why you're upset, but with all due respect, I think you should just turn around and take the other road. It'll be faster that way and-"

"No! I ain't turning nowhere for no one. I need to get where I'm going, and I always take this road as a shortcut. Just move over to the side! It's simple!"

"That would be problematic for me. It'd be uh lot easier tuh just keep goin' straight like I am."

"I don't give a damn what's problematic for you. This is problematic for every other person who'll have tuh take this road and for *me*. I gotta get going where I'm going," the man barked while revving up the motor. "This is a *you*-problem. Just pull over enough so I can get around ya. It's not that big a deal. I'm behind schedule, so just let me use my shortcut like I usually do."

"*Your* shortcut?" Birch's friendly face grew harsher. "Let me explain something tuh ya. Public roads are not uh shortcut for anyone. They are for everyone's use, and when you try and cut through uh public road, you're gonna have tuh deal with traffic and other people. In-"

"Traffic? Other people? This ragtag crew sleeping in the back of the truck there is the only people I've bumped into during my travels along this road. So move it, pal, before I start moving anyway," the driver threatened as he shifted gears and crept an inch closer to the pickup truck.

"Just turn around, please."

"Make me, big *fella*. I don't want to have to go and get the authorities involved with this. Obstruction of the flow of traffic is punishable by law."

"Okay," Birch said aggravatedly. He smirked. "So that's how ya want tuh do things, is it?"

"You bet," the man spat back. "You and your little friends are going to be in a whole lot of trouble by the time I'm done with all of you because the cops are going to hear everything."

"Hmph," Birch sounded angrily in his throat as he stood up straight and began to walk to the back of the box truck. He stopped halfway down at the middle of the vehicle. Squatting down, he gripped the underbelly and bottom edge of the box truck before springing up with powerful force from his legs and a mighty thrust of his arms, flipping the vehicle onto its side. It fell over with an earth-shaking thud, and the woman screamed along with her friends as the man blew the tuck horn and yelled. Birch brushed his palms together as if he were trying to get dust off of them before turning and walking back to the pickup truck.

The woman's friends were shaking in the bed of the vehicle while she cautiously followed Birch to the front of the pickup truck. She hesitated a moment while he put the harness back on before asking, "Birch... *what... happened?*"

"That guy was bein' extremely rude and uncooperative. Plus, his vulgar language was unnecessary. I could tell he was uh troublemaker. Obstruction of the flow of traffic? Well, he's obstructing the flow of charity and kindness. The fine is much more costly for that. I did what I had tuh do, although I wish there were some other way all o' this could've been solved. I try tuh abstain from violent acts and bursts of anger. It's very much unlike muhself tuh behave as such, but we didn't really have uh choice. Now, let's get ya tuh where ya need tuh be," Birch said as he lifted the woman back onto the hood of the pickup truck.

Seemingly energized by his outburst of strength required to flip the truck, Birch pulled the pickup truck even faster than before. The woman adjusted herself on the hood, gripping the front edge of the vehicle. "Birch… I'm okay with what you did if you deem it fair and proper punishment, but won't you get in big trouble for that?"

"Probably, but that won't happen. See, nobody would believe 'im if he told 'em. He didn't know my name, so if he just says that some giant guy he's seen on the internet before flipped his truck, he'll probably get made fun of. I feel bad, but no use in regretting my actions now. Secondly, it'd really just be his word against mine. Anybody he tells would vouch for me even if he did figure out my name, as everyone knows how helpful, humble, and kind I am."

"True, but they don't know how hurt you are, on the inside." Birch did not respond. "Well, anyway, I'm glad you flipped that guy's truck. He was a jerk. According to you, at least. I mean, you told him you were pulling the pickup truck, right? How fast does he expect you to go? I'd like to see him try and pull this."

"Still, we *are* taking up the whole road. Plus, we inconvenienced uh lot of people. Not just him, but also the people waiting for his delivery and the people that will have tuh come and help him. Really, I shouldn't have done that, and normally I wouldn't have, but he really got under muh skin for some reason. I feel bad for him, though. Truck drivers have it really rough," Birch commented earnestly. "They have uh highly sedentary lifestyle of solitude. It's lonely, boring, and ya have tuh deal with people on the road all day. Most people hate commuting tuh vacation or work, so imagine that bein' your life, every day fuh really long hours. Plus, you have uh lot of power with any kind o' truck. That's uh lot of pressure and responsibility they have tuh deal with, 'cause any mistake could cost countless people their lives."

"I've never really thought of it like that before. I feel bad for him now. We shouldn't have flipped his truck."

"His lifestyle is no excuse for his behavior and attitude toward others. At least it shouldn't be. Besides, all shortcuts are risks. If they weren't, then everyone would be taking them."

"True. Thank you, Birch… for everything."

"What do ya mean? It's nothing, don't worry 'bout it."
"I don't just mean pulling us."
"Oh?"
"I mean for your kind words of wisdom as well. I've only spent an hour or so with you, but it feels like I've known you for a long time. You've truly inspired me, and I think I'll remember this day for the rest of my life, so thank you."

Birch half-smiled.

CHAPTER 5

THE PRESENTATION

(Charleston, West Virginia. Later That Same Day: April 13, 2022)

It was approaching 4:00 p.m. as Birch put on an expensive black suit, which was custom-made to accommodate for his enormous size. In fact, it was the only suit he owned. Using a watch extender, he wrapped a golden watch around his large wrist and looked at how much time he had left. It covered up the minuscule bruise he had there.

Birch sat down to eat an entire meatloaf with some string beans and mashed potatoes, which were all drowned in gravy. He ate in silence, thinking about what had happened earlier that morning. After helping the woman with the pickup truck, Birch had asked Michael to take over the gym for the day, as he wanted to rest up before the health presentation he was hosting at the gym tonight. He ate without enthusiasm as he slowly chewed his mashed potatoes, which he managed to get with a large wooden spoon. He stared at the dark meatloaf. *That man could've been hurt when I flipped that truck. He deserved it, didn't he? I don't know. What's with all of these crazy incidents lately? First Old-Spike, then the trees, and then the pickup truck, and finally, the box truck. It all seems tuh be somethin' more than uh coincidence, but I can't place muh finger on it. The Organization can't be behind this, can they? That woman said I changed her life. I have tuh try and be uh better example for everyone if people are goin' tuh look up at me so much.*

Birch left more than half of his food as he got up from the table. He had no appetite. Glancing at his watch again, he quickly washed his hands at the kitchen sink before heading out, anxious to distract himself.

By 5:30 p.m., Birch was back at the gym. He met Michael, who had gotten dressed up in brown cargo pants and a blue and white plaid shirt for the event. The two of them discussed the plans for the evening while they began to prepare for everything.

Occupying the first half of the left wall of the gym was a small stage set up with a projection screen behind it, which would be used for the event. In front of the stage, chairs made up six rows with about eight chairs in each.

Most people in the town had already been to Birch's presentation, so he was not expecting a large crowd. Perhaps, there would be people who had watched the fight, but most of the people who went to the presentations now were either tourists or people from away who had heard of Birch and his gym, and so they came to listen to what he had to say. Many apprentices in the health and fitness field were sent to his presentations to study. People thought that his words alone could change lives and that his plant-shakes were even more miraculous.

Michael walked over and interrupted Birch, who had been intently staring at a laptop, going through the slide show that he would present. Luckily for him, the voice control feature of the device allowed him to actually use it. "Alright, I finished cleaning up the gym. It was a quiet enough day while you were gone. Nothing I couldn't handle, and I even got to work out a bit myself. We should be good to go."

"I wouldn't expect anything less from ya. Were ya able tuh print the new pamphlets for tonight? You had mentioned you wanted tuh change the design and add some stuff."

"Yes. I got them printed just in time, so we're good. It's not much different, but it was about time we had them updated." Michael handed

Birch a stack of pamphlets that would be given to the audience. "What do you think?"

Birch looked at the new pamphlet, which was comprised of a few pages. On the front, it had the gym title with a unique design celebrating the ten year anniversary of the business. The inside of the pamphlet had scientific definitions for all the different types of fruits and vegetables used in the shakes, gardening tips, and recipes for different kinds of shakes that were favorites around the gym. "This is great! Much better than the old ones. The ten year anniversary gives it uh nice look, and the added information inside should be helpful tuh everyone." Birch looked at his watch. "Alright, we got less than half an hour until we get started. Go relax for uh bit and meet back here at ten minutes tuh six. I just have some stuff tuh finish up real quick before we begin."

"I'm going to run out to my car real quick," Michael said with a point to the front door. "I picked up fresh fruits and vegetables on my way over here for the sample shakes tonight, and I'll use the ice from the fridge. That way, we won't have to take from the gym's inventory of food, which will make all of the gym's paperwork a lot easier."

"Always thinkin' ahead. Good call." Birch went to finish setting up a table by the door and placed the pamphlets neatly on it. Over at two rectangular tables, by the bar part of the gym, which served food and drinks, Birch set up an arrangement of deserts, water, and coffee for the audience to enjoy after the event was concluded. He kept an eye on his watch, as it was quickly approaching the scheduled time, and he was growing more anxious. People would be showing up in a few minutes because there were always the people that showed up too early, and the ones that showed up too late.

Birch had just finished setting up all of the refreshments when there was a light knock at the oversized front door. He went over to see who it was, and was relieved at what he saw.

"Hanna, it's you!" Birch exclaimed. "I thought you weren't goin' tuh be able tuh make it. Thank goodness ya came! I already set up all o' the chairs, but there's still work tuh do."

Hanna was a local sixteen-year-old African-American girl who occasionally helped out for volunteer hours. She had agreed to help out at tonight's presentation but was supposed to have been there earlier than when she had just arrived.

"Sorry, Mr. Willow. I'm afraid that having my brother drive me around means I'm always late, but I get my license next month, so I'll finally be able to drive myself around." She had helped out before with some of the charity events and runs, but this was her first time at one of his health presentations. "So, what do you need me to do?"

Birch grabbed the stack of pamphlets from off of the table and handed them to her. "You've made muh life uh lot easier. These are the new pamphlets for tonight's presentation. I just need ya tuh open the front door for tonight's guests and hand 'em one of these. We have enough that every person can get one if they want it. After you've done that, feel free tuh watch the show, and once it's all over, I'd love it if you could help us clean up the chairs."

Hanna quickly skimmed through the new pamphlets as she nodded her head. "I can stay for cleanup. After all, I need all the volunteer hours I can get. How long do you think the show is going to be?"

Birch scratched the back of his bald head. "Hmm. The actual presentation shouldn't take too long, and dependin' on questions from the guests, about an hour is the usual length o' everything. By the time they all leave, and we get cleaned up, I would say about an hour an' fifteen or so."

"That's good. I'm looking forward to tonight. I've heard nothing but good things about your presentations."

"That sounds 'bout right," Birch replied with an artificially egotistic chuckle. "Oh, that reminds me. Do ya have the sheet with you?" He was referring to the community service sheet she needed to have signed as proof of her volunteer actions.

Hanna put the pamphlets down before pulling a pen and a paper from out of her pocket and handing them to him. "Yep. Got it right here for you to sign. I already filled out everything else for you, so you don't have to."

"Well, aren't you prepared?" Birch said jokingly.

"I figured it'd be easier since-"

"Well, you're right," Birch said with a laugh as he grabbed the pen gently between two of his large fingers, tracing a messy signature in the box. "Never been quite able tuh use uh pen for anythin' 'cept signing muh name. If you can even call that uh signature! They'll know it's me, though." He read over the paper. "Hmm. Looks like you're gettin' close tuh those twenty hours ya need," Birch commented as he looked at all of the other volunteer services marked on the paper. "Is the National Honor Society accepting new members soon or whatever? I'm not too sure how all that stuff works."

"Yeah, pretty soon, they're going to be looking over everything. I have the art club, soccer, photography, and I'm almost done with the service hours."

"That's great! I'm proud of ya, kid. Don't evuh forget how far hard work can take ya. Initiative, commitment, and drive are important both at school and in the workplace."

"Thanks, Mr. Willow, but I have to credit you with most of it."

"Me? This is all your hard work, kid."

"It is, but if it weren't for all the events you hosted, I would've never gotten the hours I needed. Besides, you've inspired me to work my ass off to get what I want!"

"Well, thanks, kid," Birch said with a smile. "It makes me proud tuh know that. I'm glad I could help."

"Mr. Willow, why do you host all of these educational events and charities? Most people can't part with money, but you always do so much to give back to everyone and to help everyone as best as you can. All the people I've met in life seem pretty selfish, but you're like the complete opposite. How?"

"You ask how I can be so selfless, but you should be more shocked and confused by how these other people can be so selfish. Bein' kind-hearted should be an instinct and not somethin' inspired or motivated except for reinforcin' your natural kindness. There aren't many good people left, but as long as one gentleman or lady remains, their presence and inspiration will spread. It's not just the right thing tuh do. It's more than just that. It's about equality for those who have suffered or who were born into uh different world than us. Don't they deserve uh chance tuh experience this beautiful world the same way we do? I'm not uh socialist or anything, but the truth is that I don't need all o' this money. I'm uh single man livin' at uh farm. Let the money go tuh those who need it. *I* certainly don't need it. The gym was always about helpin' people, but never money. We don't live in uh supahhero society, but we can all be heroes still. I want tuh help everyone, all while smiling and inspiring. I guess that's what drives me. The important question is: what drives you, Hanna?"

Hanna almost gulped as she stood there speechless, shocked by the pure-heartedness of Birch's words. "Wow, I actually don't know what to say. That was really intense," she remarked with a laugh. "I'm not sure yet, Mr. Willow, but, hopefully, I'll find out along the way."

"Well, you've got plenty o' time tuh figure it out, kid." Birch looked at his golden watch again. "It's ten-of, so people will start filling in soon. Head over to the door and welcome everyone. Think about what I said in the meanwhile. It's important to know your motivations and self. It always is."

Hanna nodded her head, picked up the pamphlets, and headed for the door.

Birch went over to a room to the left of the stage from the crowd's view, which was like a changing room at a movie studio. He turned on the one bright light that hung from the ceiling.

Once Michael announced him, Birch would exit the room and stride onto the stage. For now, he had nothing to do except wait for the announcement. Birch looked at a large mirror that covered the one wall of the room. He adjusted his tie, which was designed to look like the bark of a birch tree, and patted down his suit before sitting down on a wooden bench while he waited. It creaked under his weight.

With nothing else to do, Birch found himself staring into the mirror, the golden light reflecting off of his bald head like sun rays off of stagnant water. He tried to stop what was coming, but it was inevitable, and Birch began a journey of self-discovery and reflection as he looked at the giant in the mirror, who was staring back at him uncertainly. Recapping his life tale to that woman earlier in the day had brought forth some subconscious thoughts that had been creeping around in the background of his large, thick skull. Now his words to Hanna had stirred them even more. *I started out with uh rough life, but it's all worked out... right? Then why can't I shake off this melancholy feeling? It's like something's wrong. As if I'm only half of uh person...* A sense of regret and disappointment grew visible on Birch's face, which seemed to age.

His thoughts growing more powerful, Birch began to whisper to the mirror as if the reflection of him could provide the answers he needed. "What's wrong with me? Why do I feel so sad when I have so much? Money, fame, friends, fam-" Birch stopped short. He had no family except for the animals that still lived on the farm. "No. No family. No, love either." Birch had no person that he held dear to his heart. His love-life had never been right. "I just don't understand..."

Birch licked his lips, which were drying up. He studied his large hands for a bit as he thought back to the very beginning of his life. He looked back into the green eyes in the mirror. "Why did they uhbandon me? If I wasn't created in uh lab... if I was born naturally, why would they give me away? They couldn't have known I would grow and grow into some kind of," Birch froze before sighing, "...what even am I?"

After he ran away from the orphanage he was being raised at, Birch spent a few years of his life wandering from town to town, and so he never knew anyone long enough to love them. Then, when he was adopted and taken in by his farm parents, everything school-related was hard for him. The social aspect of school was awful, and his intelligence was never anything breath-taking. He was just smart enough to make it by. Prior to being adopted and enrolled in school, Birch had received little education. Essential reading and writing skills, as well as math, had been taught to him, but that was it. Had Michael and Rose not befriended Birch and stayed by his side, the whole gym may not have been started.

After high school, Birch and Michael went their separate ways for a while as Birch spent the next few years on the farm doing various jobs while Michael went off to college to become a teacher. It was during that time that Rose passed away, and Birch lost a piece of himself but gained a piece of her voice in his heart and mind.

Michael returned from college and became the state's best teacher of science, and he taught at the school which he and Birch had gone to. Birch, on the other hand, was still just doing farm work and manual labor on the side. He wanted more. He needed more. Taking a loan from a company, combined with the money he already had saved up, Birch started The Heaviest Lifters gym in 2012, and he spent most of his time there for the next few years. He was a big man, over seven feet tall at the time, and continuing to grow. The business took off, however, and Birch was successful. He wanted to help people even more, though. So, he and Michael decided to work on improving the human diet. From there, they would branch off into more prominent aspects of human health. Between their busy lives, the two men started researching, theorizing, and experimenting for a year in an attempt to improve the digestive system of humans to increase the amount of beneficial nutrients that could be absorbed.

Actual scientific progress was not made until 2018. Eventually, the complicated biological and chemical process seemed feasible. Using some animals as test subjects, Michael and Birch tested out their new scientific creation. It worked. Animals that had formally been unable to digest cellulose were now naturally producing cellulase enzymes and digesting cellulose, with extreme health benefits. At least so far, as the results and side effects would take time to appear.

Birch did not wait, however. He viewed his life as lacking value and felt that he should be the first human volunteer for this new era of human health, just in case the experiment did not work with humans as it did with animals. So, Birch experimented on himself with what they had created while Michael was away at a teachers' convention. His chemical and organic composition was changed, and soon, he was able to produce cellulase, which allowed him to digest cellulose. With this new ability, combined with his famous plant-shakes, Birch had developed the ultimate diet. From then on, Birch had more energy than he knew what to do with. He could run faster and work out with seemingly no limit. Each and every cell in his body was now packed with energy and micronutrients from the plant-shakes he drank. His body was also regenerating more quickly than ordinary people, and he had never gotten sick since that day. Even his resistance to the cold had increased, as his body was able to create more heat due to the constant supply of energy and nutrients. The best part, however, was that his brain health skyrocketed, and his intelligence and memory greatly increased.

There was something else that happened, though. Birch's body continued to grow even more massive from its already enormous size, despite his age. In fact, the new amount of energy and nutrients in Birch's body seemed to have boosted his growth. That was never intended, and he and Michael still do not know why that happened, and if it even had anything to do with the cellulose and cellulase experiment. By the year 2018, Birch had stopped growing, but he always feared that he might grow even more, as impossible as that seemed. The two tried their best to discover the strange reason behind Birch's unexplained growth, but it was a dead end. For all they knew, his body had still been producing growth hormones, and it was unrelated to the experiment.

To balance out this worsened body, Birch bettered his personality, which had already gone through a major change after Rose peacefully passed away. Birch thought that if people knew that he was a generous man on the inside, perhaps he could live a normal life. Now, here is where Birch had ended up: rich and loved, but by strangers. He had a lot, but he was also was missing a lot. Birch started to feel sick as he thought about his life, and he turned away from his reflection, which repulsed him. This sick feeling was not just mental, though, and he knew it as he held a hand against his eight-pack of abs, feeling uneasy.

Ever since he had changed his body, his internal organs occasionally felt odd, and it worried him. For the past four years, something had been going on inside of him, ever since the experiment.

Birch could hear people roaming around as they entered the building. He looked at himself in the mirror and gave a half-smile, torn between loving or hating himself. *If I look fine, then maybe I'll feel fine*, Birch thought to himself as he forced a full smile. *They love me. They came here tuh see me. It's not how ya think it is, Birch. Calm down uh bit*, he thought as he closed his eyes and controlled his breathing.

Presenting always made Birch nervous, despite how many times he had hosted events. Practicing could help with a lot, but not with Birch's self-esteem regarding public speaking. He was confident in his body, but it was the judgment of others that he made up in his mind that got him worried. More people were impressed by his masculine physique than scared or disturbed by it, but he could never get himself to believe that. All he could do was wait until his name was called. He knew by now that once he got talking, his nerves would settle down.

The seats began to quickly fill up, and the lights in the gym were all shut off except for a few that were over the small stage. Michael, with professional stage presence, walked onto the stage, used to hosting events. He held a Shake-Show at the gym twice a year, where residents from the town and students from the high school would perform on the stage while the gym served coffee, plant-shakes, and there was an open salad bar. As the humorous host, he was used to being on the stage, and he had even performed himself, being a pianist, singer and songwriter, guitarist, and ladies-charmer. On top of all of that, he was also a teacher who presented to people all the time. To him, the stage was no different than home or school. Michael knew that the more comfortable he was on stage, the better Birch would feel, even if the waiting giant could only hear him.

Michael stopped in front of a microphone at the front and center of the stage. "Folks, thank you so much for coming. It's an honor to host tonight's show, and what a big turnout we have!" Almost every chair was filled except for a few here and there, which was a bigger crowd than usual. Michael recognized several faces from the fighting event. "My name is Michael Kellson, and I have been the co-owner of The Heaviest Lifters gym for *ten* years now."

The crowd broke out into applause, and Michael flashed his white teeth in a charming smile as he waited for them to quiet down. "Thank you, folks. It's been a wonderful ten years, and I can't even believe that it's been that long. For those of you who are unfamiliar with the history of the gym, it was first built back in 2012 by Birch Willow, who is the founder and owner of this gym. He and I have been friends and partners for many years now, and tonight, we would like to share some of our discoveries with you. Here at the gym, we collaborate on diet and nutrition because we all know that just working out isn't enough. I think you'll find what we have to share interesting. Enough of my rambling, because without further ado, nicknamed Charleston Crusher by the town's people, I present to you the legend himself, Birch Willow!" Michael gestured over to his right before grabbing the microphone and placing it at the corner of the right side of the stage before exiting.

Birch came out of the room he was hiding in and walked onto the stage. The wooden boards moaned and creaked under his weight, and each step almost seemed to make the room shake. People in the crowd applauded his announcement, more than usual, but some still gasped or sat there, mouth agape in shock. At least the people who had never seen Birch before. By now, however, he was used to this after the first couple of presentations he had done. It hurt his feelings a bit, but he did not blame them.

Born with a loud and manly voice, Birch had no need to use a microphone in order for everyone to hear him. He waited until everyone stopped clapping. "Thank you for the introduction, Micahel. Everyone, please give uh round o' applause fuh him. Not only is 'e the numbah one science teacher in all o' West Virginia, but he is also the numbah one employee here. He does such uh great job helpin' out here at the gym, and this place wouldn't be possible without 'im."

Everyone applauded. Michael smiled as he passed by the crowd, going behind them to where the projector and laptop were. He would be in charge of changing the slides.

"Thank you. He was right. What uh turnout! Almost uh full crowd! It warms muh heart tuh know that you all made it out here. Thank you all for coming. I'm Birch Willow, uh dietician, nutritionist, personal trainer, motivational speaker, and the owner of this gym. I'm self-taught fuh all o' those, but people say that I'm more than qualified. For those of you who have never seen me before, I'm sure muh appearance is quite shockin' tuh ya. Not only am I really tall, but I also have uh rare genetic disease known as myostatin-related muscular hypertrophy. It causes uh reduction in body fat, double the amount of muscle, as well as increased muscle strength. I just happen tuh have uh really bad case o' it, but I'm not complaining," Birch said jokingly with a slight flex of his arms.

Birch waited for a moment as he let that thought set in. There were a few mild chuckles at his joke. "Now, tonight I wanted tuh share with you an idea that is widely promoted at our gym. That is, the plant-shakes that Michael had been referring to. We serve them along with healthy meals here at our gym bar which is in the area next door." Birch gestured over to the bar to his left which was to the right of the audience. "It's open to the public as uh regular food service, and ya don't need tuh be uh gym member tuh go there. We serve uh variety of different shakes here usin' both fruits and vegetables, and if you look through the pamphlet that was given tuh ya, there are some recipes that tend tuh be favorites among our members. The best part is that the recipes are real adjustable."

The audience members skimmed through their pamphlets, and Birch gave them a moment to do so. "Now, I know uh lot of ya are askin' yourself what exactly are these shakes and why do we claim that they're better fuh ya than most other healthy foods. What's the difference between them and uh regular smoothie or protein shake? Well, when Michael first introduced me tuh 'em, I didn't know what tuh think either. I figured they'd taste pretty bad, tuh be honest. They're actually pretty good, although the first one I had was kinduh too bitter for my liking." Birch chuckled a bit. He liked to keep a light air at the presentations. It made it more comfortable for both him and the audience. "Well, plants are packed with micronutrients, which are crucial for the body. They also have uh lot of macronutrients, and there is uh difference between the two, but basically, they're both important. I'll go into detail later. Plants consist of many essential vitamins and minerals that we, as people, need tuh flourish. Leafy greens act as uh broom through your digestive tract, picking up all o' the waste in the body, and well, it's better than any colon cleanse product without the side effects if you know what I mean," Birch said jokingly with a point of his elbow. The audience subtly laughed at the joke. "Of course, I'm sure you've all heard all o' this from ya doctor or high school biology teacher, so let me talk tuh ya about the things ya probably don't know."

For about the next forty-five minutes or so, Birch went through the slideshow, talking about the exact science behind everything and thoroughly providing evidence and research. He discussed different plants and recipes based on what people were trying to do with their health. He included before and after pictures of satisfied customers and various tricks they could do. There was so much more to the presentation than anyone would have expected. Birch made sure to keep it fun and interesting, so the crowd did not get bored. It was a lot of information to take in.

Birch continued on, going over everything. "The reason people are reluctant to try this, or at least people who know the science about it, is because of a factor called cellulose. This is the term for the material that makes up the cell wall in plant cells. It's the most abundant organic compound on Earth. It makes up your clothes, paper, and many other man-made goods. So if it's that great and all, why isn't everyone eating it then? I'll allow Michael tuh explain the science stuff. I've hogged the stage for long enough," Birch stated with a laugh.

Michael hopped onto the stage and went to the center. Birch stayed in the corner, where he had been the whole time as to not block the projection of the slides. "I'll try not to bore everyone to death, and so I won't get into the atomic science of it all. Cellulose is great, and an amazing source of energy and micronutrients. The problem is that humans can't properly break down cellulose, which is essentially long chains of molecules. Cellulose is tough. Paper is made of cellulose, so think of paper as being vertical layers of horizontal chains. That's why you can rip paper," Michael ripped a piece of paper in half down the middle, "but not pull it apart easily." Holding a piece of paper horizontally, Michael pulled each end in the opposite direction, but the paper stayed whole. "See what I mean? I promise you that I'm actually trying to pull it apart. The chains are too strong, even for our stomach and intestines. A specific enzyme is needed to break apart cellulose, and it's called cellulase. I know, it's really annoying how similar those names are. The enzyme basically cuts the chains into pieces that can be digested. Cellulase is produced in certain omnivores and herbivores, who eat mostly plants, as they need to be able to break down the cellulose. Same thing with certain types of bacteria and fungi. There's a lot more to it, but that's all you really need to know in order to understand how it's connected to plant-shakes. Now, back to Birch." With that said, Michael left the stage and returned to the laptop.

"That sounds real negative, don't it? Y'all are probably asking yourself why you'd want tuh have uh plant-shake if most of it can't be digested or used by your body. Why even tell ya this, besides the fact that I'm honest? Well, we can still use some o' that cellulose, as well as everything else in the plant. Here's what it actually means. Instead of digesting the nutrients outta those dense parts o' cellulose, those indigestible parts serve as gut cleaners and intestinal sweepers. Depending on what ya make, the shake typically ends up working as fifty percent of it goes towards energy and health, with the other fifty percent helping out with digestion. Perfectly balanced, as all diets should be. Minus the hassle of multiple types of meals, as well as the high cost. Plus, it's portable and hydrating."

People in the audience nodded their heads, while others whispered to each other. Some were skeptical, some impressed, and others were simply confused.

"Now, I actually have an excellent theory presentation about the ability to digest cellulase planned for next Thursday. I don't want tuh dabble too much in the subject, as it is uh bit off-topic, but feel free tuh come next Thursday. It is related, and it is incredible, I promise you. Very theoretical stuff. Some of you may have already seen it, as I presented that slideshow just uh few months ago, but I think you'll all find it really interesting."

Birch rambled on for a few more minutes about various aspects of plant-shakes before summarizing it all. "And that about sums it all up, ladies and gents. Tonight's presentation is now concluded, but I do encourage all of you tuh ask any questions that ya might have. If you rather ask your question privately, that's fine as well. Hopefully, you're all astounded by now. Uh restaurant? Uh fighting ring? Uh lounge area? Weight rooms, yoga rooms, uh pool, and uh track? Yes, we do have all of that because we are not just uh gym. We are The Heaviest Lifters!" He pumped his fist into the air. The crowd broke out into applause. The lights in the building were turned back on. "Any questions?"

A woman raised her hand in the audience, and Birch called on her. "Mr. Willow, you talked a lot about the benefits of these plant-shakes but never about any consequences. That concerns me a lot, although I doubt you would ever purposefully withhold information like that from us with ill-intentions. Is there anything we should be worried about?"

"Great question! I'm really glad you asked that, actually. Props to you for looking out for somethin' like that. Michael is the true expert here, so I will hand that question over tuh him, as he actually has some experience that will help you out with that."

Michael joined Birch on stage. "So there are two things to look out for, and neither of them are serious. The first is just a minor thing which involves carrots. I'm sure you all know that too much of anything good is bad. The same thing goes with carrots. They'll help your eyes, but too much beta-carotene will cause orange or gold-like skin. That happens with anything containing carotene, so also be mindful of sweet potatoes and pumpkins, but I personally would never use those in a shake anyway. Again, that's not a major issue, and most people don't experience it, but be mindful of that."

"Understood, thank you," the woman replied. "What's the second thing?"

"So, a major part of health and diet is understanding yourself and your body. That's the most important aspect, and I don't just mean knowing your limits. Allow me to relate it to my personal life. I had been loading my plant-shakes up with spinach, and I actually got kidney stones from that, which are painful, as you can imagine. Now I switched over to bok choy instead to help me. That doesn't necessarily mean that you'll get kidney stones if you have spinach in your plant-shakes or that the person next to you will. Someone here might, or maybe no one will. It really all depends on your personal physiology. The best way would be to check with your doctor first to determine what's best for you or do some online research. Also, Birch is an expert in that, and you could always consult him."

"Thank you."

"Again, it all depends on your body," Birch said to reinforce that the plant-shakes had no adverse consequences. "I've personally never had uh problem with the ones I drink, but I make sure tuh vary muh ingredients. You have to know yourself in order to improve yourself. Another thing tuh look out for is *sugar*. If you're diabetic, havin' multiple fruits in your plant-shakes on a daily basis isn't uh good idea, and I'd recommend goin' with vegetables, as fruits tend tuh have uh lot o' sugar. They're mostly good sugars, but they're sugars nonetheless." Birch looked around at the crowd. "Are there any other questions? After a few seconds, he spotted an arm raised in the crowd. "You, sir," Birch said with a point at the raised arm.

The man hesitated. "A bit off-topic, but while we're all here and you're on stage, could you do the watermelon thing? I've never seen it before, and it's mostly just rumors that I've heard, but if you really can do it, I'd feel honored to witness it right now."

Birch smirked and chuckled. "Is that what y'all want?" Birch asked enthusiastically while raising both hands, palm facing up, to encourage the crowd. The audience all began to talk amongst themselves before cheering for Birch to do it. He had expected this, and being prepared, he pulled out a large smock from inside of his suit and put it on, as well as a pair of gloves. "All right then. Michael, you heard the people."

Micahel, who had been at the bar, ran over with a twenty-pound watermelon to where the laptop had been. "You called it! I guess we won't be using this for the shakes," he commented jokingly. Holding each end of the watermelon with his hands, Michael held the fruit behind his head. Birch tilted his head to each side, cracking his neck. Throwing the fruit forward, Michael released the watermelon with full force using the incredible strength he kept hidden in his toned body, launching it through the air over his head and past the crowd at Birch.

Everyone in the audience was entirely silent as they watched on with star-struck eyes.

As the watermelon got close, Birch formed a T-shape with his body, his arms outstretched to either side, palms facing forward. As soon as the watermelon was close enough, Birch thrust his arms and hands together in a powerful clap that smashed the watermelon into a mess of mostly red liquid with a few chunks of red and green that fell to the floor.

It was quiet for a minute before the audience broke into cheering and applauding.

"He destroyed it in a single clap," someone yelled.

"Such *power*," another exclaimed.

Birch smiled, although his hands were covered in sticky red liquid that could have easily been mistaken for blood. Hanna ran up with a garbage bag for the gloves and the smock, although the liquid mess had mainly fallen straight down. She left the stage and went to go get cleaning supplies for later.

"I'm glad you all found that entertaining," Birch stated. "Any more questions?" A different man raised his hand. "Yes, you, sir?"

"Thank you. I'm part of a marketing team for a small company in advertising. The slideshow and projector screen were crystal-clear. I mean the quality was outstanding, and it competes with television or computer presentations. I was wondering what kind of projector you were using to get such good quality and speed?"

"The projector I'm usin' is from R.O.M.A.B.A. Industries. Their products are amazing, affordable, and the leading innovations in almost everything you could imagine. I would suggest lookin' at their website, and you'll find dozens of different projectors that'll suit your needs."

"Thank you, Mr. Willow," the man replied.

"Are there any more questions?" The crowd settled down, but no one raised their hands. "Before you all go, we are serving refreshments over by the bar. We have some of our most popular plant-shakes that Michael had started whipping up so they'd be fresh if you'd like tuh try 'em. They're cheap tuh make, and if ya want, we'll even make uh custom one, as we bought plenty of fruits and vegetables for tonight. There's also some coffee and dessert if you'd like, but don't tell muh gym members. They'll never let me live it down if they found out I was servin' desserts here."

The audience laughed.

The woman who had asked about side effects raised her hand, and Birch called on her again. "Mr. Willow, you said that Mr. Kellson was blending together some of these plant-shakes for us, and I can see that it's true," she said with a gesture over to the bar, "but I didn't hear a peep from over there. I was wondering what kind of blender you use because it's perfectly quiet. My kids would love it if they could play their video games without hearing me blending stuff all the time."

"I can imagine," Birch said with a laugh. "Again, I actually got that from R.O.M.A.B.A. Industries, which is uh large company over in England for those of ya who don't know that. It's almost uh hundred percent silent, as you pointed out, and it automatically cleans itself, which is the best part. I'd have trouble cleaning it out muhself. We use them here at the gym, and I love 'em. They're uh bit expensive, but they're worth the cost if you're gonna use 'em uh lot." The woman nodded her head, satisfied. Birch scanned the audience. "Well, that concludes our event for the night. Enjoy the refreshments, and have uh lovely evening, everyone." Birch exited the stage as everyone got out of their seats and started mingling around.

A bunch of people went over to Michael and the bar to try some of the plant-shakes. A line formed at the table with the coffee, even though it was night, and an even larger line formed at the dessert table. Hanna started packing up the chairs after she had wiped up the mess on the stage. Flyers for the gym were handed out to everyone, as well. Birch was beginning a new program called Lighter Lifters. It was a program where he would help train people and bulk them up to the body they hoped to have. Time had drastically changed him, and being the selfless person he was, Birch was making the gym less exclusive. It was the right thing to do in all honesty and not just money-wise.

There was an elderly man, about in his late fifties, Birch supposed, who had been sitting in the back row. The man got up and approached Birch, who was walking around. "Excuse me! Mr. Willow, sir, it's a pleasure and honor to meet you." Birch gently shook the man's hand and looked down at him as he had to with all people. "That was a rather lovely presentation tonight, and most certainly informative. I have studied in the field of science as well, and so when I heard of your special plant-shakes, well, I knew I just had to stop by," the man said enthusiastically. "You completely exceeded my expectations!"

Birch smiled and nodded his head. He had run into encounters such as this before. He was careful to make sure no one got his research or even thought about stealing it, but that came at the cost of distrusting strangers, and especially those with backgrounds in science or the government. "Well, thank you, Mr.-?"

"Sir-"

"Mr. Sir?"

The old man shook his head joyfully and laughed. "Not at all. It's Thomas. Sir Thomas, as I'm called. My apologies."

"Ah, no need for that," Birch said with a forgiving wave of his hand. "Between the good manners, the title of Sir Thomas, and the slight British accent, I take it you're an Englishman or were one?"

"Indeed, I am. Although I'm afraid I didn't fly all the way over here just for you, Mr. Willow. I have a couple of other stops across the country while I spend the year here. Charleston just happens to be where I'm spending my first few weeks. Thankfully, it happened to line up so that I could attend your presentation."

"Well, I'm glad you could make it over here tonight. I try my best tuh put on uh good show."

"And a good show it was indeed. Biology isn't my exact specialty, so I found all of it quite interesting, and I especially found your discussion about cellulose and cellulase rather intriguing. That's something that you certainly don't get at your local smoothie shop. These plant-shakes... they're what you use?"

Birch was suspicious since Sir Thomas was a scientist, as far as he knew, but it was not the first time he had encountered a person like this. People believed that if they drank the plant-shakes like he did, then they would then become like him, but that was far from the truth. The plant-shakes were not miracles in a bottle. "Yep, I drink at least three uh day. They changed muh life."

"Well, as you can clearly see, time is starting to catch up with me, and I hope to perhaps restore some of the damage that it has done to my body. Get a little bit of pep in my step, if you know what I mean. Do you think these plant-shakes can help me out with that?"

"Sir, you look fine, and I do believe so. Or perhaps, I should say I *know* so. They have helped me greatly, and anyone of any age can benefit from them. All of the nutrients you absorb will boost brain productivity, slow its decay, improve digestion, and help your skin look better. Also, as I mentioned, the shakes will pack you with tons of energy tuh help keep you going throughout the day. They'll also help you go tuh the bathroom more easily, which some people of your age begin tuh have trouble with. Feel free to check out our new program in the flyers being handed out. It's called the Lighter Lifters. If you come, I'll make sure not tuh overwork you, and I have plenty o' tips for maintaining health as well as body strength. After uh certain age, maintaining muscle or building new muscle becomes uh bit of uh different game."

"Well, thank you very much, Mr. Willow. You're a good man, and our society is lacking that, so I really admire you. Most would say I'm too old to be starting again, but I say to Hell with them! I've still got plenty of time left, and a whole other part of life to live. Perhaps I'll swing by tomorrow if you're open and available to work with me."

Birch handed a paper and a flyer to Sir Thomas. "We'd love tuh have you join. Here's uh schedule of the days and hours that we are open. The track outside is open twenty-four-seven tuh the public as well if you'd like tuh use that. We keep it lit all through the night, so use it anytime you'd like." Sir Thomas thanked Birch and started to walk away. "And make sure tuh bring your friends!" Birch called after him. "We love all the new members we can get, and not just for the money!"

"Don't worry, I will!" Sir Thomas shouted back to Birch as he exited the building. Then to himself, he muttered, "Oh, I will, Mr. Willow. Kronos will be more than happy to learn about all of this." He smirked before disappearing into the night.

CHAPTER 6
THE SECRET BREAKTHROUGH
(Charleston, West Virginia. The Same Day: April 13, 2022)

His reconnaissance mission finished, Sir Thomas quickly left the gym, making sure that no one followed him. Everyone was still inside, enjoying the refreshments, but they would be coming outside soon, so Sir Thomas picked up his pace as it began to drizzle slightly, opening up a fancy umbrella to cover himself. His path lit by dim street lights, he walked across the road and over a block and then turned down another street. There, in the pitch darkness of an alleyway between two large buildings, Sir Thomas stopped short, pulling out a pistol in his left hand.

In the alleyway darkness, slightly illuminated by yellow light from a streetlight at the end of the pathway, Sir Thomas saw the sinister silhouette of a man in a lab coat with messy hair. Though the man's features were shadowed in the dark night, Sir Thomas could tell it was Kronos. The two men had flown to West Virginia, as teleportation was too risky for living beings right now. However, they had teleported Kronos' custom-made car to a specific location to pick up. Kronos had stayed behind with the unique vehicle in the alleyway to do research online while Sir Thomas was gathering vital information on Birch.

Kronos was out of the car, for some reason, and seemed aggressive, which concerned Sir Thomas. He slowly walked forward as he watched Kronos repeatedly smash something against the one wall of the alleyway near a dumpster. Whatever it was that Kronos had in his hand cried out in vicious pain, but its whines for help were quiet compared to the contempt in Kronos' voice.

"You filthy creature," Kronos hissed. "How vile! You are nothing but a groveling creature that begs others for help. I am **King Kronos**, and I stand at the pinnacle of all humans who stand above all other lifeforms. How dare you touch the vehicle I created by hand, which is the envy of all others!" He smashed the animal violently against the wall one final time with a violent thrust. With that, Kronos loosened his grip on the animal, which fell to the ground with a bashed-in head that was a mixture of cracked bones, torn skin, and blood.

Sir Thomas squinted through the darkness and saw that the animal had been a cat. "Well, isn't that unpleasant," Sir Thomas remarked, hiding his terror and disapproval inside as he put his pistol away. "This situation has gone all to pot. I might chunder, in fact."

"Spare me of your fancy British talk, Thomas."

"Perhaps if you were ever social during our time in England, you would understand me better. It's not fancy talk at all. Then again, you never listen to anyone other than yourself anyway. That aside, I do believe that's commonly called animal abuse, Kronos. Or rather, animal cruelty, considering what I just witnessed. It's punishable by law, in fact. I wonder what that cat must have done to deserve such merciless treatment. Then again, just the fact that it exists was probably enough to provoke your aggressive nature."

"Do not mistake power for aggression, Thomas," Kronos retorted firmly. "Either way, that was not the case. The cat's futile existence had nothing to do with the punishment it brought upon itself. That insignificant creature decided that it was all right to jump onto the hood of the car I built by hand. *The* car which embodies every idea of science fiction and the future into an actual existing vehicle."

"Ah, my apologies. Cats are to be beaten to death for jumping on the hood of a parked car in a dark alleyway. How could I have forgotten such a standard rule of society?"

"Tone down your sarcasm, old man. That's not why I killed the cat, although that is a grave offense in itself. Its claws could never even put a micro-scratch into the masterpiece I created. Nor does my hatred for cats have anything to do with it, as I look down on all forms of life equally. When I got out of the car to tell it to scram, it jumped at me, so I caught it and punished it as it deserved. No animal could ever hurt a being such as myself, but even the attempt is pitiful and insulting."

"Hmm. You and I shall discuss this some other time when it is more convenient to do so. I thought we had a long talk about how you *are* a human and should stop viewing yourself as something much greater, but I suppose you tuned out everything I said. It wouldn't be the first time you did that. We'll have to talk again about it and the respect that animals deserve, but I'm afraid that we have more important matters to go over. I learned a lot today."

"So the mission was a success then. Excellent. That brings me great joy," Kronos said creepily with a twisted grin.

Sir Thomas rolled his eyes. "I don't doubt that it does, Kronos." He reached into his expensive suit and pulled out a white handkerchief that had gold embroidery around the edges. "You've gotten cat blood on your hand. You best wipe it off before you get in the car," he commanded as he threw the handkerchief to Kronos. "Oh, and wipe off that creepy grin while you're at it." Sir Thomas looked at the innocent cat, which lay dead in the alleyway, and a sick feeling overcame him. Yet, there was nothing he could do.

Kronos had a despicable expression on his face. He wiped off the cat blood from his hand, using the drizzling rain to his advantage. "It *is* a great insult to have such filth stained on my royal flesh, so thank you for doing the honorable thing and helping me cleanse myself, Thomas." Kronos reached into the brown satchel that he always wore and pulled out the D.O.O.M. Shooter, which he used to swiftly eradicate the bloody handkerchief. "No evidence as always," he hissed with a cruel smirk. "Those who threaten beings far superior than themselves will learn the most solid theory of science ever established: survival of the fittest." Kronos looked to each end of the alleyway and then hopped into the car, joining Sir Thomas before driving away.

They drove in silence for a brief moment, Sir Thomas shaking his head. "Disregarding what just happened, let's get straight to business. The sooner we complete this whole 'mission' of yours, the sooner I can finally relax in comfort and luxury. Every day, my stress increases exponentially, and I'm surprised that it hasn't killed me yet. It's been a long and tiring journey raising you, so it's about time that I finally get what I want. My whole life has been about you. Now it's time for my life to be about me."

"Ha! And you call *me* the selfish one? Spare me of your tiresome lecturing, Thomas. Every day you lecture me over and over again. You never stop."

"You never listen."

"Correct. Oh, and this isn't just *my* mission. I don't know how many times I must tell you that it's for the sake of everyone in this world."

"You can keep saying it, but I don't believe such rubbish."

"You don't believe, or you don't understand?"

"*No one* understands."

"I understand. I always do."

"Then explain it to me, Kronos. What is your goal?"

An honest frown formed on Kronos' face, although Sir Thomas did not notice. The ends of his lips were dropping as if heavy, and his sour expression was the embodiment of concern about an inevitable fate. Even his eyes were not glowing with malicious joy as usual. They actually appeared sad and tired. The vein in his forehead was not visible. His lab coat was not shadily shifting around, but it seemed to be nothing more than an article of clothing, for once. The ego, the aggression, the grand delusions, the sarcasm, and the power were all gone, leaving

Kronos as an emotionless being with just truthful knowledge and logic. "Thomas, you're my guardian, aren't you?"

Sir Thomas had not looked over at Kronos, so he did not realize that the man sitting in the car with him was far different from the one he knew. "Unfortunately, yes. I try to be, anyway. Although, it doesn't make a difference when it comes to you since you practically do everything yourself and never listen."

"It was strictly a yes-or-no question, Thomas. There's no need for the whole explanation." Kronos sighed.

Glancing over at Kronos, Sir Thomas saw the man there, and he began to realize that it was not the usual Kronos who would have argued back with him or been sarcastic. "My apologies. The situ-"

"Incorrect. The answer is that you are my guardian, and you have been for a long time now. The position is of no importance, but rather I'm talking about the standards of the relationship. As back-and-forth as our insults are, I know you love me, and I know that you know me better than anyone, although most of my evil-genius-intellect is beyond your comprehension."

"That's true, but what does that have to do with anything?"

"My point is that you know that I'm a man who resists change, although I am seeking it on my behalf and for the future. Ironic, like all things in life are. You also know that I'm loyal to my past-self. I always shall be. The truth is that I'm actually unsure for once, as we've established that already. I'm not totally confident and egotistic, as I always have been. Losing my memories is the only thing that could ever defeat me. My schemes are always hundreds of steps ahead, and I always win. Yet, I didn't foresee losing my memories, and losing my memories means that I don't understand all the steps in the plans I had set into place. Now, I'm stuck trying to figure out what my past-self was trying to do. Even I, the most intelligent being in all of the universe, can't understand what was going on in that mastermind's head."

Sir Thomas scrunched his face in confusion, the wrinkles on his forehead pressing together. *Why now? You're repeating yourself. What are you trying to tell me? You're never serious. You believe that geniuses are the only ones who have the privilege to act stupid.* He took a deep breath. "I see… and you think that this mission will help you figure it out?"

Kronos slowed down before parking on the side of the street, which was dark, as the streetlight there had died and never been replaced. He turned to face Sir Thomas. "It doesn't matter whether this mission was for me to finish or for my past-self to complete. I'm not worried about figuring out what I was trying to do. I know what I must *do*, as I've figured at least that much out. What I'm concerned about is what I was trying to *prevent*. My past-self was doing something vital to the whole survival of the world, and I actually mean that. It's a threat so great that the only one who can oppose it is me, which is why I had to lose my memories- to disappear from the enemy's radar."

Sir Thomas gulped as he looked at Kronos' face. It was not vile as it usually was, but it actually looked aged. His teeth seemed flatter than their usual sharpness, his lips were uncurled from their regular sinister curl, and even his amber-yellow eyes were dim. There was fear in them. Sir Thomas had never seen them like that before. There was no ego, sarcasm, or joking in the intelligent voice speaking to him. Every word Kronos said was something that he believed full-heartedly and undoubtedly had evidence for. Sir Thomas pressed his hands against his legs to stop them from trembling as his heart began to quicken its pace. Getting through to Kronos had always been his goal, but he realized now that perhaps someone or something far more terrifying had been buried the entire time. "Kronos, this is terribly serious, isn't it?"

"I fear something beyond all of us, is coming," Kronos replied gravely with a solemn expression overtaking him, draining him of all emotion. "I am selfish, self-centered, overly prideful, greedy, and a plethora of other negative traits, but the way my past-self was hunting for power is different than any of that. It was out of desperation… as if there was limited time left. A man slowly growing in power, such as myself, would not behave in that way. The videos I saw of myself, the papers I read, and the blueprints don't add up to *me*. It's like I was trying to prepare for something. It may not seem like I can ever be satisfied, but I essentially have my dream life. I sit around in a world of my own creation with unlimited money, intelligence, no government bothering me, servants who heed my commands, and the power to basically do whatever I want. I even have you, old man."

Sir Thomas grew internally weary, and there was a sadness that rose within him, visible in his eyes and mouth, as he looked at Kronos. "I don-"

"Yet, there was something about everything I saw that throws me off. The blueprints for all of those nonsensical hero-like weapons and armors. Why would I make those? I don't think it was just for fun or an impulsive idea from my insane imagination. It's for a major battle that's coming. And the profiles of those people don't make sense either. Why would I care about these scientific rivals? *Rivals*? The truth is that their scientific discoveries are impressive, but they're nothing in comparison to everything I've created at R.O.M.A.B.A. Industries. I mean, having their research would greatly boost my power, but I already am the most powerful man in the world." Kronos turned and looked through the windshield at the night sky, which was covered with wispy grey clouds, the moon's light partially visible. "At least, that's what I had thought."

Every muscle in Sir Thomas' body was clenched tight, and his heart twisted as if it might stop. He never understood Kronos, but what he now witnessed was obvious. He hesitated a moment, held back by fear, but he needed answers. "I think I finally understand, but I'm terrified to accept what I believe to be true." Sir Thomas grew silent for a short moment, but he let his fears turn into words. He knew the truth now. "The only reason you would crave such power from people you consider much weaker than yourself is if something more powerful than you is coming."

"Correct," Kronos replied gravely, as if for the last time. "I've figured out that my past-self determined that a threat was coming that no one on Earth would be prepared for. Not even our work in atomic manipulation would be enough, and so that's why I was doing all that research regarding these other people who have made scientific breakthroughs. The whole concept of a world of survival of the smartest and most powerful people... that anarchy world that my past-self spoke of was a cover-up. The video logs were a code that only I would be able to interpret."

Sir Thomas gasped. "But that would mean-"

"Correct. I, too, fear such unimaginable intelligence. My past-self knew he was going to lose his memories, and that's why he made those video logs. Not for the future, but for me." Kronos looked away from the fading light of the moon, which was now covered entirely by the evening clouds, and turned back to face Sir Thomas, who appeared to be on the verge of death from utter dread of the terrifying future that Kronos was predicting.

"Kronos, what exactly is coming?"

"I have no idea, old friend. I have no idea."

"Your past-self didn't tell you?"

"He didn't know either. Otherwise, he would've told me."

"Bollocks! To Hell with it all! We'll just have to prepare for anything and everything."

"Correct," Kronos replied as he turned his view back to the dark sky. "That's precisely what we're doing out here on this insane adventure of illogical sense and seemingly fictional ideas." He closed his eyes for a prolonged moment before slowly opening them back up. "Yet, preparing for anything and everything is not easy. Especially when even the ability to manipulate atoms on an individual scale isn't powerful enough. That's why I must have their research, Thomas. I need it in order to save us all, or at least most of us."

"No!"

"Hmm?"

"I think that you're looking at this all wrong, Kronos."

"Really? That'd be impossible."

"I'm not sure what's coming, but you're not going to have to take it on alone. Create an alliance with these other scientists, and we can fend off the threat together."

"**Then they'll all die!** Even working together, they'd be too weak. I don't want their deaths to happen when they don't have to. In order to save them, I'm going to steal their research and take away their ability to even think of partaking in the upcoming battle. **It has to be *me* with all of their powers.** I fear the battle will be one-on-one, and it has to be me. Only I alone can fight this incoming threat. **Mr. Monatomic** versus the unknown embodiment of all power."

Sir Thomas' face and heart grew even rougher as he turned and faced Kronos. His blood ran cold, and his skin grew paler. He struggled to hold back tears. "Don't tell me-"

Kronos had a single tear trying to escape his right eye, but he blinked and crushed it into atoms that dispersed. He let out a long, slow exhale of acceptance. "Correct. I don't need to tell you that-"

"It's a suicide mission," Sir Thomas said slowly in utter shock. He looked at Kronos, who was focused on something beyond the night sky. As shocked as he was, Sir Thomas was more affected by the sudden wave of guilt that came over him, every negative thing he had said about Kronos stabbing him over and over again. *You've been carrying around this secret burden for all this time? I'm so sorry, Kronos. I never realized that. Yet, as your sworn guardian and caretaker... as your father, I must accompany you. Except, you'd never allow that.* He looked at Kronos, knowing that the evil genius had already made up his mind. "You're truly going to go through with this mad scheme, even if it means your death?"

"I assure you that the idea of dying for the world is a noble cause that sickens me a bit, but I do love the attention it'll bring to my name. Of course, I doubt anyone would even know. At least not for a long, long time. The battle will take place behind the scenes of society. You should honestly be proud. I've always been making the world a better place with my inventions, but I suppose this will be the ultimate and final gift of my astounding intelligence. It will be a nuclear explosion of complete prosperity, freedom, and safety, once we split my intelligence like a uranium atom. The teleportation split my brain, and now the intelligent cells are bouncing off of each other and splitting in a chain reaction that will cause the explosion I speak of to occur relatively soon. The disease was to trick the enemy because it gave me an excuse to go after the rival scientists without seeming suspicious."

"It can't be true."

Kronos did not respond. He continued to stare into the black abyss above him as the rain came down even harder. Thunder softly sounded in the far distance. It appeared as if he might squeeze out a tear or two, but Kronos did not shed any tears. His mind was made up, and he understood it all logically. There was no reason to cry. In fact, his acceptance was so solid that he seemed to have already peacefully died in the car. "I know it took a lot of arguing and negativity to convince you to tag along with me on this journey, Thomas, but I wanted you to be able to spend time with me before I died. I wanted to spend my final days with you. I thought it'd be a fun little adventure before I disappear forever, and along the way, you'd be able to learn some things that might help you out when I'm not around." Kronos waited a moment, which felt like an eternity for the two men pondering in silence before speaking. "**My death is inevitable, father. For the world to be saved, I must die.**"

Sir Thomas, a good-hearted and loyal caretaker until the very end, dropped dead in the car seat upon hearing that his son would have to die in order for the world to survive. Though he had instantly died of heartbreak, tears were still streaming down his face, containing the last particles of his life essence as he moved on from the physical world. His heart, already weary, had been unable to handle the shock.

Kronos looked over at the lifeless body of his caretaker in the car and cried out.

❋ ❋ ❋

Worried about what was taking Kronos so long, Sir Thomas got out of the car. He looked over at Kronos, who was still standing ominously in the alleyway. "I'm a patient man, but how long does it take to wipe a few drops of cat blood off of your hand? You'll catch a terrible cold staying out in this drizzling rain for too long, and then I'll have to take care of your miserable self."

"I'm afraid I got lost in theoretical thought, old man," Kronos replied, his back still turned to Sir Thomas so his caretaker would be unable to see his eyes, which were on the verge of tears. "I have a lot on my mind, given recent circumstances. The harshness of reality is able to occupy the simplest of minds, and it is certainly more than capable of taking unwanted refuge in the greatest minds as well, if not more likely to do so. Thanks for your concern, though."

"Oh, well, aren't you in a charitable mood. You actually thanked me for once in your life. Suit yourself then. I'll be in the car with the heat blasting when you're ready. I want to get to bed soon, so hurry up. Sitting at that presentation for so long has my legs and rear feeling rather sore, and I'd like to relax with a cup of calming tea."

"Roger that, Thomas," Kronos replied, straining to keep his voice normal and not choked-up. He stared at the damp ground by his feet as Sir Thomas got into the car. He tightened his grip on the fancy handkerchief, his mind going over the conversation he had just played out in his head, living every moment of it as if it had been entirely real. *I'm terribly sorry, Thomas, but I can't tell you any of that. As much as I hate to seem like the world's biggest jerk, I have to keep up the act. I have to use my sickness as an excuse for this mission, even though you and I both know that I'm actually cured. Otherwise, you'll either die or try and make a team to fight off the threat. You'll try to save me, as good of a man as you are, but my death is inevitable. My death... is necessary. You think that I hate these scientific rivals of mine, but I actually admire them. I wish to form an alliance with them more than anything. I'd finally have friends. Yet, I can't befriend them. I must keep them away from the path I walk... even if that means having to be their enemy. The same goes for you. I know that you wouldn't be able to handle the truth, but even if you did, you'd only get in the way. Only I know the truth, and it must stay that way. They can't know that I'm one step ahead.* Kronos hopped into the car after destroying the blood-stained handkerchief with the D.O.O.M Shooter. He pulled out of the alleyway and drove off without saying a word.

"Bloody Hell. I'm almost terrified by the silence of this eerie night. You're awfully quiet," Sir Thomas commented, raising an eyebrow as he glanced over at Kronos. "It's rather unusual for you not to be bragging, scheming, or insulting someone or something. No snarky remarks for me or sarcastic comments? Is something the matter? You know you can't keep secrets from your caretaker."

The back muscles in Kronos tightened up, and he clenched the leather steering wheel. *That's true. Most people can't keep secrets from you, but I can. I'll have to continue acting like the version of me that you know, and it's awful, but it is what must be done in order to preserve the world we know. I'm sorry, Thomas, about everything, and hopefully, I can properly apologize to you if there's ever a chance. You'll understand one day when I'm gone. Ironic how you'll outlive me, old man. Then again, all things in life are ironic. Most often, the irony of this world is cruel. All things are paradoxical.* Kronos relaxed his tight muscles so he would not give away that something was wrong. He sighed, acting frustrated by the question. "Other than you interrupting my valuable thoughts, nothing is bothering me. I'm just doing some internal scheming, as usual. There's no need to worry yourself over me, Thomas. Nothing of this corruptive and pitiful planet could ever cause even the slightest distraction in my mind or heart. I'm more than capable of maintaining a perfect mindset."

"Is that so?" Sir Thomas glanced over at Kronos again, and keen eyes like sharp daggers of suspicion and skepticism tried to pierce through Kronos, but his ego-embedded fibers were impenetrable. "I trust you, so I'll leave it alone." Kronos sensed the word-trap and made sure to not react. "Anyway, you should have gone with me. The presentation was the opposite of a damp squib. It was brilliant! Of course, the honest truth is that I would've preferred to have gone to the fighting tournament, but we just missed it. Even this old Brit enjoys a good fight or two. What a bloody shame."

"Correct. I, too, would have enjoyed witnessing the power of that giant as well as the individuals trying to desperately survive his brutal attacks. Other than that, however, I'm entirely fine with having missed that presentation. Overly nice guys like Birch Willow make me feel sick, and I don't mean with guilt. I hate those generous bastards with their overwhelming kindness and careless disposal of money."

"A lot better than overwhelming ego and aggression," Sir Thomas grumbled.

"Incorrect. Besides, I bet that giant is hiding some kind of monster in him. Disregarding your twisted views, what did you learn?"

"*I'm* the one with the twisted views?" Sir Thomas laughed. "Now that's ironic humor. Anyway, I personally enjoyed it. In fact, I think everyone did. The information was thoroughly researched, and it was all interesting to learn about. The different perspective on fruits, vegetables, and their uses was mind-opening. Mr. Willow did a good job of keeping the crowd entertained. I'll show you a video later of him smashing a watermelon with a single clap. That was absolutely remarkable to witness in person. Oh, I did find something intriguing out about h-"

"What? What is it?" Kronos asked excitedly, almost drooling at the thought of a new scientific breakthrough. The truth, however, was that he could not care less. He was trying to keep up his act, as well as distract himself from the conversation he had imagined.

"Well, if you didn't impulsively interrupt me like that, I'd be able to explain," Sir Thomas replied with scorn. "Pfft. I could've sworn that I raised you better than that, but then again, you can't tame an egocentric maniac."

"There's no need to tame a perfect being. *That's* your issue."

Sir Thomas rolled his eyes and sighed. "Perhaps you saw this online somewhere during your research, but I found out that Mr. Willow has myostatin-related muscle hypertrophy."

"Correct. I picked up on it right away. An astounding condition, to say the least. You know that I stay away from genetic research, but I know that the chances of a man getting tall height genes and a rare genetic mutation such as Birch's would be extremely low. It's quite possible that he also has hypertrophy of the pituitary gland, but that would result in health problems that he does not have. The chances of muscle and height genes lining up so perfectly are not entirely impossible, but very close to it. The exact math would be-"

"There is no need for the mathematical equations behind the calculated probability of the genes lining up, Kronos. You're just trying to show off. It is highly unlikely, though, and I agree with that. *However*, are you suggesting he gave the mutation to himself?"

"Correct. That's precisely what I'm implying."

"That's almost malarkey, in all honesty."

"Incorrect. He'd be a true genius to do such a thing, or just to even come up with such a concept. Realistically, a man his height would never be anything other than lanky. No offense to really tall people. It's just a historical fact that muscle development for people of such tall heights is not easy. Yet, if you applied the myostatin-related muscular hypertrophy to a person of that height, and then add in his discovery regarding the plant-shakes, you'd have one remarkable being. You'd actually have a real-life superhuman and the strongest human in the world. That's why he messed around with his genes. He's not just tall and muscular. He's a *big* guy, including his organs and skin and everything, not just his skeletal muscle."

"A plausible theory, as always, but I don't think Mr. Willow gave the mutation to himself. I'm pretty sure he was born with the condition. Genetic manipulation in adults is still almost impossible as of right now. Well, it's really complicated and expensive, to say the least. Not to mention all of the ethical issues. Besides, I don't think he's actually smart enough to pull that off. He is, indeed, an educated man, but he's not the brain behind the operations, as far as I know. He co-owns the gym with a man named Michael Kellson."

Kronos thought for a moment. "Michael Kellson? I think I remember seeing his name mentioned in one of the articles I saw while researching. He's considered the number one teacher of science in this state. His forte is biology, which would make sense given what we're proposing. I hadn't paid much attention to the information regarding him, but now it all makes sense. Did you meet him as well?"

"I did not directly speak to him, but I saw him at the performance when he introduced Mr. Willow and later on when he discussed some of the science regarding the plant-shakes. He seemed like a genuine guy, and he was completely composed on stage. It's clear to me why he would be considered such a superior teacher."

"He's a regular human?"

"As far as I know, but there's no telling, considering the fact that we don't know what their discovery is. Presumably, it has nothing to do with manipulating the growth or size of the human body. I wasn't able to gather enough intel to figure out who's running everything, but they're probably working together. They're literally the perfect example of the brains and the brawn working together."

"Speaking of the breakthrough… did you manage to get any hints to what it might be?"

"Mr. Willow talked about the plant-shakes, just as the file you had typed up stated. He went over the benefits of drinking the shakes, and everything to do with that was actually normal research. He mentioned cellulose and cellulase, however, and that made me a bit suspicious. He has a presentation about those two things in a few days. I've come up with a few theories on how Mr. Willow has used these shakes to grow to such an immense size, but I don't have enough information to prove any of them. He wasn't at all The Ruthless Root, as you call him. In fact, he was a very nice guy."

Kronos nodded his head. "It's a shame that we'll have to kill him."

"*Kill* him?" Sir Thomas asked in shock, almost coughing the words up, although he was used to Kronos' ideas by now. "Why must you be so swift to inflict pain for answers? You are so violent by nature, and you always have been. That man was very kind and selfless. He even invited us back to the gym tomorrow. Well, he invited me and said to bring a guest, and not just for more money."

Kronos rolled his eyes before breaking out the one thing his body could never erase from his brain: his sarcasm. "*Oh, he did? Well,* I suppose that was *extremely* kind of him." Kronos slammed on the brakes as a vehicle with rafts on the roof sped by.

"Bloody Hell! Easy with the brake slamming!"

Kronos looked around in shock. "Oh, so it's my fault that they sped across the intersection?"

"Most likely. It usually is, given how reckless of a driver you are. Anyway, it was nice of him to do that. It's also exactly why we are going back there tomorrow to talk to the man."

"What?" Kronos yelled as he sharply turned a corner. "I don't want to go talk to this guy. Let's either steal his research or force it from him. We don't have time to waste!"

"Funny that you say that, seeing as you pulled me out of my relaxing life to be here with you on this quest for a cure that you don't actually need."

"We don't know that, Thomas, but I do know that it'd be easier just to shoot up his gym and get the research."

"Oh, and shall we fight the police afterward when they show up? Then the F.B.I.? The American government?" Sir Thomas shook his head in frustration. "Kronos, you have to learn to be sympathetic and caring. I know that you've had a troubled past and present, but you can't always pick the violent way to do things. Sure, it might be easier, but it doesn't guarantee complete success or additional future success. Think about it logically. If you kill Mr. Willow, you might not get all of his research, or even any of it. Then where would your permanent cure be? He's a charitable person. He'd rather hear your charity case than fight you. He is a very genuine guy, and I think he would be more than happy to help us. Talking to him will get us a lot further than any other method. It'll be best for all of us. I can only imagine what damage he could do to us with a body like that."

Kronos clenched his teeth and tightened his body before sighing angrily. "Fine! Fine! We'll do it *your* way, Thomas. But if it doesn't work right away, we're doing it my way. I brought the D.O.O.M. Shooter for a reason." Kronos whipped the gun out of his satchel just in case Sir Thomas needed proof. He started aiming it around the car, ready to fire, driving with one hand.

"Blimey! Get that thing out of here!" Sir Thomas started yelling before forcing Kronos to put the gun back into the bag. "I don't care if you're ambidextrous! Driving with one hand is reckless. Are you bloody mad? That's a highly dangerous weapon, Kronos. It's not a toy!"

Kronos reluctantly shoved the D.O.O.M. Shooter back into his satchel. "Seeing as I'm the evil genius who built it and created all the ideas for it, I already know that."

Sir Thomas nodded his head. "Ah, yes. How could I forget that you built an atomic weapon behind my back?"

"Whatever," Kronos said in frustration, ignoring the comment that was meant to shame him. "It'll be useful to us."

"Perhaps. I can't argue against that point. Anyway, there was something else I wanted to tell you, but I can't quite remember what it was. It was something that I knew would make you happy." Sir Thomas thought for a moment, trying to remember what it was. "Ah! I remember now. Mr. Willow was using one of the high-quality projectors we created. *And,* he uses our blender at the restaurant in his gym. He has three of them, and you know how expensive they are."

"He does? You've earned him some respect from me now. But that means he'll know our company. If it's not against us, that might work to our advantage." Kronos swerved into their parking spot at the hotel they were staying at. "What exactly is your plan?"

Sir Thomas handed Kronos the schedule that had been given to him at the gym. "It's rather simple, actually. We'll go first thing tomorrow morning before the gym gets busy. If I can even call the place a gym. It's a brilliant building, and a company worth a fortune. It's much more than just a gym, and Mr. Willow is much more than just a man. We'll talk to him then. Now, let's get to bed. I could use a good night's rest."

CHAPTER 7
MEETING THE COMPETITION
(Charleston, West Virginia. The Next Day: April 14, 2022)

Morning came after a night that seemed to have dragged along slowly for the two men. Kronos had spent the majority of the night outside on the balcony of their hotel room, thinking over every variable and possibility of the upcoming days and weeks. Beyond that amount of time, he knew that he would be gone, and nothing would matter except for everything else that had already been planned out by him. Sir Thomas, on the other hand, was a bit restless as he tried to figure out what was going on with Kronos and what this whole quest of theirs was actually about. Either way, neither of them had definite answers, and staying awake had served them no good.

Exactly at opening time, Kronos and Sir Thomas were already at the gym, having managed to get a few hours of sleep. Sir Thomas was running on two cups of hot tea, and Kronos was being fueled by a variety of sugars he had digested. They had parked their unique car one block away from the gym to make sure no one would see it in the case that they had to escape. Sir Thomas was hoping for everything to go well, but he could tell that Kronos was already in a foul mood.

Birch had just flipped the open sign in the front left window of the building when the two men walked in. "Sir Thomas! So glad ya made it!" Birch smiled and shook his hand. "You even brought uh friend!"

"Good morning, Mr. Willow! I figured I'd make as much use of the gym as I can while I'm here for the time being. It may end up being the only chance I have to experience what it's like to work out at such an establishment as yours, so I can't afford to be sleeping all day while the sun is already up and the birds are already flying. Anyway, I'd like to introduce you to my son, Dr. Kronos Nephus."

"Oh, wow. Pleasure tuh meet ya," Birch said to Kronos as he shook his hand. "You've got uh mighty firm grip there," Birch remarked in surprise, as he had never really felt the other person's hand in a handshake due to the size difference. "I have tuh say that you're the first person tuh ever enter this gym with uh lab coat on. That explains the doctuh part."

Kronos half-smiled at Birch to humor Sir Thomas, though his eyes grew more wrathful with each word that left Birch's mouth. *He has such a despicable dialect! His speech makes me sick...* Kronos had to bite his tongue to prevent himself from spitting on the floor in disgust.

"Well, I'm wearing an expensive business suit as usual, so I suppose we're both out of style here," Sir Thomas commented jokingly in an attempt to calm Kronos down.

"Please, do come in," Birch said as he stepped aside and gestured to the enormous interior of the gym. "An' don't worry 'bout it at all. Uh few people who come straight from work are usually dressed up too. You're probably the earliest customers I've ever had, though. Then again, I open early, so I can't complain. As uh guy who lives on uh farm, I've been up for quite uh while now." Birch was hospitable, and he loved meeting new people. Socializing with people at the gym made up for all of the friends he had missed out on while growing up. At least here, he was not judged, and people actually got to know him. Besides that, exchanging advice, life stories, and experiences with others always fascinated him, and he loved doing it.

"I'm afraid that when you get to my age, waking up early becomes an everyday thing," Sir Thomas said while stretching his back. "Not that I much enjoy it, but the body has its own way of doing things."

"Indeed it does, Sir Thomas. Are ya both here tuh start working out today, get uh tour o' the whole place, sign up, or somethin' else?"

"Not entirely sure yet." Sir Thomas switched to a more serious tone while still remaining friendly. "We actually have to discuss some important matters with you, Mr. Willow. Is there anywhere we can sit down?"

Birch, although a bit suspicious and confused, just went along with it. *I guess they want tuh talk about their health and workout plan. It's probably easier fuh him tuh sit down. He seems pretty healthy, though, but it might just be uh preference.* Birch nodded his head. "Of course, just follow me." Then he looked over at the restaurant part of the gym and yelled, "Michael! Can you take over fuh me? I have some new clients tuh take care of. If anyone comes in, you know the drill."

Michael answered that he could and went about doing business in the gym. Birch turned his attention back to Kronos and Sir Thomas after leading them away from the entrance and toward the right side of the gym from a front view. "Back when I was first draftin' up the blueprints fuh the gym, I had the guys add uh small lobby over here. Figured people could rest or wait for someone else. Whatevuh they have tuh do. Couldn't hurt tuh have it. Anyway, what seems tuh be the matter? How can I help you two gentlemen?"

Sir Thomas and Kronos sat in two white leather chairs with Birch in a chair across from them, hunched over with his elbows on his knees. Between Birch and the two men was a wooden table, which was five feet by two feet, with magazines about health and working out on it. The setup kind of reminded Kronos of the dentist's office, which he hated.

"I suppose we'll start this off with this," Sir Thomas said as he handed Birch a business card for R.O.M.A.B.A. Industries. "We're from England, and this is the company we own that deals with scientific experiments and the newest innovations in all fields of technology, as well as a bit of artwork on the side, although that's not important." Birch flipped the card over, reading both sides. "We're actually considered the number one company in the world right now, but heed that no attention. The company's name is pronounced Row-Mah-Buh, by the way. You pronounced it as Rom-uh-bah at the presentation yesterday regarding the blenders and the projector."

"My bad," Birch replied with a chuckle. "If I had known the owner himself was attending muh presentation, I would've prepared better. Your blenders are perfect. I love 'em, although they're nothing compared tuh some o' the other stuff I've seen on your website. You have uh ton o' mind-blowin' stuff."

Sir Thomas nodded his head. "Thank you for your kind words regarding our company. You'd be surprised by how difficult it is to create self-cleaning blenders that are nearly silent."

"I see. However, there is uh problem."

"Hmm? Do tell, Mr. Willow."

"I've seen the people who own R.O.M.A.B.A. Industries on the news and such, and they ain't the two of ya. So who exactly are ya? I mean, perhaps the company was just bought by you two rich Englishmen, but I haven't heard about anything like that. Plus, the amount o' money tuh buy that company is far beyond that of any person at this point."

Kronos tensed every muscle in his body, aggravated by the doubt Birch had. He struggled to hold in an exhale of contemptive frustration.

"Ah, well, that's a brilliant point, Mr. Willow! You see, we're the *true* owners of R.O.M.A.B.A. Industries. The faces on the media are simply faces for the company. Sometimes, when people have a company bringing in as much money as ours, they prefer not to be associated. That's the case with us. Of course, we're proud of everything that our company has accomplished and continues to, but for our own personal safety, Kronos and I prefer to act behind the scenes. It isn't cowardice but more so a clever move to keep ourselves safe in public. I suppose we have no proof of that, but I urge that you take our word for it. On my honor and that of all my ancestors, I swear that I'm telling you the truth. May God strike me down if I lie. We do pay the two people you see online and on the telly a good deal of money for the risk they take."

Birch nodded his head and smiled proudly. "I have tuh say that I'm very impressed. I believe you. In fact, I don't blame ya at all. Your company rakes in somewhere in the quadrillions each year as far as I've heard, so I prob'bly wouldn't want tuh be associated either. Especially with all the court cases and everything. That aside, what do ya want from me? I'll tell you right now that I'll never sell this place."

"You can relax about that, Mr. Willow. I assure you that Kronos and I have no intention of buying The Heaviest Lifters. This is an absolutely astonishing business you have here, but I can tell that you're a man who would never sell out. It's one of the things I respect the most about you."

"Well, you're right about that. Thank you."

"The unfortunate reason that we're here is because we've had a remarkable breakthrough in one of our latest research projects in the field of atomic science, but there have been some side effects, as I'll put it."

Birch placed the business card down on the table. "Side effects? Well, that's the inevitability of new scientific research. What seems tuh be the problem?" Birch internally sighed, frustration and caution building up inside of him, slowly making him more irritable. *So much fuh maintaining uh low profile. This sounds like shady stuff, and I don't want tuh be involved. I've heard rumors about R.O.M.A.B.A. Industries. Buyin' uh blender from 'em was one thing, but uh scientific breakthrough with side effects is another.* Birch kept a straight face, however, and he was interested in learning about the discovery.

"I'm afraid it's a terribly long and boring story, but allow me to explain as best and as swiftly as I can." Sir Thomas started by talking about the properties of atoms and molecules. He spoke quickly and as best as he could, for he knew that he did not have too much time before Kronos' patience ran out. Besides that, he wanted to justify everything before Birch's suspicion came out in violence or aggression. He knew that he was in between two potentially dangerous people, and he was trying his best to avoid conflict by appeasing both of them.

Birch put his large hand up in a gesture to stop. "I know all about that kind o' stuff. The stereotype that us gym guys are meatheads isn't true. At least not fuh me, since I studied science back in high school with Michael. I know uh thing or two 'bout atoms since he keeps me updated on all o' the science stuff goin' on in the world. What you're talkin' about is basic science, but I assume it's essential tuh the research you were doing."

"Very well then, Mr. Willow. My apologies. I assure you that I had assumed you to be educated based on your presentation last night, but I wanted to refresh you in preparation for the revelation of the new science. I'm glad that you're intelligent, as what I'm about to tell you would utterly shock and go over the heads of most people, as they wouldn't be able to scientifically back up such claims and theories. They probably wouldn't believe us, but what I speak is, indeed, true, and I ask that you bear with us while I explain." Sir Thomas took a bit of a pause and a deep breath before dropping the seemingly-fictional idea on Birch. "R.O.M.A.B.A. Industries is an acronym-based name that stands for the rearrangement of matter and biological assets. This is due to the foresight that we would create the ability to manipulate atoms on an individual scale, which we successfully have. With that concept in mind, we have used this to further manipulate and exploit the properties of atoms, along with waves and frequencies, to create teleportation."

Birch's face, when he was not smiling or laughing, was gruff and emotionless. Many had even suggested that he become a professional poker player. So, it was easy for him to hide his disbelief, but it required a lot of his willpower to hold in a laugh. *Teleportation? Granted, Michael and I have our own secrets and discoveries, but somethin' like that? I don't know. Now, this seems more like uh prank than uh shady deal. But I'll go along with it. It ain't uh prank. I've seen the things that they sell from their store, and I've read the articles. The manipulation of atoms on uh single scale? This is above muh intelligence level, and I admit that. What do I have tuh do with any of this?* Birch scratched the back of his bald head. "Hmph. Teleportation? Like actual teleportation from one place tuh the next in an instant?"

Sir Thomas nodded his head seriously.

"Well, that's an absolutely remarkable accomplishment!" Birch commented as he shifted in his seat, leaning in loser to the two men across from him. "Most people wouldn't believe it, but I'll have tuh trust ya fuh now until you explain the science. That would prob'bly be the most significant discovery in all o' history, actually." He thought for a moment. "Hmm. I'm assumin' that the side effects are why uh breakthrough o' this magnitude hasn't been released yet."

Sir Thomas would have to lie, which he hated doing, as they had not planned on releasing anything to the public. At least not for a few years for a multitude of reasons. Kronos, getting tenser and more cautious of Birch, had the D.O.O.M. Shooter ready in the brown leather satchel that he always wore on his left side. There was a sensor built into the top that would open if he moved his left arm or elbow above it in a certain manner, giving him quick access to the weapon. If this man turned on them for their technology and science, he wanted to be prepared. He knew that a simple fist ready to be sprung would do nothing against the giant before him.

"Precisely the case, Mr. Willow. I assure you that we had no intention of keeping such a discovery to ourselves. Until we work out the kinks and side effects, we can't release the teleportation or patent it, as we don't wish for anyone to suffer the consequences of untested science. Otherwise, we would have started to change the world by now. You see, the problem has to do with the brain cells, as we have focused mainly on the teleportation of living organisms. That is far more important than the teleportation of non-living things."

"Uhgreed."

"Before I get into any of that, however, let me explain how the teleportation works. It's an extremely complicated process, but I'll simplify it as best as I can." Sir Thomas went into explaining the process of the current, the vibration of particles, wave frequencies, and everything else that went into making the whole idea actually real and functional. Through science, he brought to life what would have seemed fictional, as many people had done over and over again throughout the unsteady course of history. Sir Thomas paused for a moment, catching his breath. He was still talking relatively fast to keep Kronos calm. "Are you following me so far, Mr. Willow? Have I lost you yet? I understand that this is all rather complicated, but I'm afraid that it has to be."

Birch quickly thought over everything Sir Thomas had said, trying to confirm the possibility of it using what he knew and what seemed possible. "It's all beyond muh intelligence level, but I understand ya so far. Everything you've stated is mostly theoretical, but it seems feasible, in uh way, although uh bit of uh fantasy as well. How did ya even think of somethin' so idealistic and complex?"

"He does most of the thinking," Sir Thomas replied with a point of his thumb at Kronos. "It was his brilliant idea, but he's also the guy who formed R.O.M.A.B.A. Industries and made almost all of its inventions, so no surprise there."

Birch nodded his head and smirked as he looked at Kronos, trying to figure him out. "I see. *Very* impressive. You're an extremely intelligent man then, Dr. Nephus. You have muh utmost respect. I could nevuh think o' somethin' like this, so good for you. Any single one o' your inventions by itself would make your intelligence terrifying, so tuh have uh whole company of 'em really shows me how smart ya are, and I am truly impressed." Birch turned back to Sir Thomas. "Anyway, there are side effects as of now?"

"Unfortunately so," Sir Thomas answered. "Like all pioneers of science, we've run into some unforeseen issues that must be fixed. I assure you that they were the most elusive variables, and part of that is due to how experimental all of this is."

"That's understandable."

"We encountered a problem when we first tested out this method of teleportation on a human subject. The animals we had tested prior to our human subject hadn't been able to show signs of the side effect, which is a major reason why it went undetected. The brain cells, when teleported, lose any information that was contained in them that branched across multiple cells. Specific pieces of information on individual atoms and cells did remain, however, along with frequently used day-to-day functioning. These functions included semi-writing and the ability to make noise to a certain extent of understanding. Actual words were neither spoken nor written, but the marks and sounds were close enough to resemble a small remembrance of such things, which is better than nothing."

"Makes sense tuh me," Birch replied. "The animals didn't show any signs since they can't talk, and that's really the major way of noticin' memory loss. It's kinda like uh puzzle, I s'pose. When the whole thing is taken apart, each individual piece keeps uh part of its detail tuh the picture, but the images made by groups of the pieces and the overall puzzle image is lost. Only puttin' it back together doesn't create the original image. Interesting. I've heard about theories on atomic and cellular memory. Losing one's memories and skills are uh terrible side effect, but it's better than havin' everything lost. Plus, anything that's genetic should still be there. At least the small pieces retained give ya uh possible understandin' of the problem."

"Right you are, Mr. Willow. Using that, we immediately began working on theoretical ways to keep the information stored. Kronos found a way to fix this problem rather swiftly, although I wish we could have avoided it in the first place."

Anxiety and worry soon replaced the suspicion within Birch. With each second that passed, he realized more and more how much danger he was in, considering how smart the two men across from him were. "You two are on uh whole different level tuh have fixed it so fast. That's great. How'd ya manage tuh fix it, though? The brain is uh delicate matter tuh be dealin' with."

"It is indeed, which was certainly an obstacle in our path, but we overcame it. We had the brain cells kept together in a liquidus-gaseous state and then teleported separately. This experimental state allowed everything to phase through matter and teleport while still keeping the information from breaking apart. At the same time, we were able to ensure that no damage occurs to the cells, although there might be long term effects besides the problems we've already encountered. Then, the cells were injected back into the skull, where they solidified back into a functioning brain. This kept all of the stored information together, and none of it was lost."

Birch scratched the back of his neck. "Kept in uh liquidus-gaseous state, you say? Now that's impressive, although hard tuh believe. You've lost muh faith and belief, as far as muh brain goes, but muh heart is still with ya on everything. Not too sure how that would work, but I s'pose that makes sense given the situation, and it sounds possible. I'm guessing that fixed the problem but created another one in its place?"

Sir Thomas nodded his head. He glanced over at Kronos and noticed that he was rapidly tapping his foot up and down silently now. His patience was running thin and what happened when all of it was inevitably depleted was something that Sir Thomas hoped he would not have to see today, or ever. "I'm afraid you're correct, Mr. Willow. Our cheerful celebrations were, unfortunately, put to an end when the new side effects revealed themselves after weeks of concealment. This solution to one question led to a new and even worse problem."

"Worse than memory loss?"

"Far worse, Mr. Willow. I know that is unbelievable, but I assure you that memory loss, although a horrible condition, is not equivalent to death or the process of it." Birch's face grew stiffer, and he subtly nodded his head. "Since the brain cells were being injected separately into the body after it was rebuilt, we came across an autoimmune disease of the sort. After repeated teleportation and injections, well, the body began mistaking the cells for some form of bacteria or pathogen entering the skull. The immune system started attacking the brain cells somehow, and we have several theories on how it managed to do so."

"Sorry tuh interrupt, Sir Thomas, but that don't seem right. I'm no biologist or doctuh, but I know that the brain operates the body. How could the immune system attack the brain without the brain powerin' it tuh do so?"

"Don't worry about such a paradoxical situation as that," Kronos said coldly. "That's a minor detail with only theoretical explanations, and explaining all of them would waste a lot of our precious time. Until further research is done, we don't have an exact answer to the cause of such an immune response. The only way to get an answer would be to have several people contract the disease and allow us to run tests on them, but the disease is fast, and without an absolute cure or way to slow it down, it'd be highly likely that they'd all die. I assume you of all people would hate for that to happen."

Birch was caught off guard by the power and lack of humanity in Kronos' voice. "U-uh... yeah. Of course. I don't think anybody would want tuh lose people tuh the disease, even if it meant gettin' an answer or research. Includin' you, Dr. Nephus. After all, scientists aren't exempt from ethics. I understand the stress you're both under, as well as how important time is in regard tuh diseases, and especially when those diseases are new. While you may seem cruel, I think you're just uh logical kind o' man who states the facts."

"Correct," Kronos replied sharply, his eyes unreadable. "It's precisely the attitude we need regarding the situation. It's imperative that we remain calm and power-through all of this. We'll have to skip the 'how' of how the immune system operates despite the lack of brain cells, as frustrating as that is for you. Thomas can explain the rest. It gets worse, but I'm sure you can handle it."

The atmosphere had grown tenser, and Sir Thomas began to worry about a fight breaking out between the two men. Kronos had not been subtle about his dislike for Birch, although he had not been contemptive either. It was as if Kronos was intentionally trying to irritate Birch without directly saying anything that would justify an angry response from the giant. On the other hand, Birch was doing his best to stay calm and be understanding, acting as if Kronos' attitude was justified, given the severity of their conversation.

Sir Thomas straightened his tie and subtly gulped. "Unfortunately, we had a test subject die due to this disease, as we were unaware of its presence within the subject, as there are no symptoms right away. Part of what makes it so dangerous is the fact that it is a silent kind of disease until the final stage. Either way, Kronos here has suffered from it as well, and that's how we know what the final stage looks like."

"*What?*" Although Birch did not entirely understand Kronos, his shock replaced his dislike with sympathy and curiosity. "How is he alive? I thought it was fatal? It's not just somethin' you can cure."

"Incorrect," Kronos stated as he cracked his neck. "There *is* a way to cure this disease. Actually, I suppose the cure could be given ahead of time to stop it, but that would be an extreme risk. While a cure is a cure, the one we used is not preferred."

"Why's that?"

"The only way to cure this autoimmune disease is to destroy the immune system. A rather simple cure, and one that can be done quite easily with the right resources. The problem, however, is that you have to destroy the immune system to a total state of uselessness, leaving the subject entirely vulnerable during the long time of recovery that it takes for the immune system to be restored. If not kept in quarantined confinement, the subject would most likely contract something and die. At the same time, it depletes all of their energy and weakens their body, as well as damages the mind. Recovery from that is long, and a person may never be the same again."

"That's an awful situation. You're lucky tuh have access tuh the best resources in the world. I'm assumin' that's how ya survived and recovered? It's not that easy tuh destroy the immune system, though. Do you use uh virus or some kind o' chemical reaction?"

"Neither of those are unintelligent guesses, but the method of the destruction is of no importance right now," Kronos replied coldly. "The point of meeting with you is to never have to use that method again unless absolutely necessary."

"He's actually right about that," Sir Thomas said. "I'm afraid that the cure was a one-time thing, and to destroy your immune system again is risky and more difficult. Had Kronos not had a large supply of medicines and chemicals to help quicken his recovery, he would have been in bad shape for quite a while. Of course, the destruction of the immune system affects everyone differently. The disease is difficult to catch, and destroying the immune system takes a while. He," Sir Thomas gestured to Kronos with his thumb again, "had already lost a good amount of his recent memories by the time I was able to stabilize his body, and it was only due to the grace of God that he happened to be with one of the brightest minds in the world at a place with everything modern science has to offer. If it had been anyone else or any other place, death would have reigned supreme over him. The cure is being tossed aside because to make this project global, we need to prevent this disease from ever happening in the first place."

Birch breathed in deeply through his nostrils, his face still neutral, although it was more hostile than friendly. *These people are tellin' the truth. Everything seems scientifically accurate, so far, and what would they even have tuh gain from lyin' tuh me? They don't need money. Can I trust them? Why have they come tuh me about this? Is it because some people considuh me uh health expert? I'm certainly no doctuh.* Birch nodded his head in understanding, crossing his arms across his broad chest.

Sir Thomas grew worried. "Are you still with us, Mr. Willow? I understand that it's a lot of science to take in, and I sincerely apologize for dumping all of this on you."

"It's certainly uh lot, but I understand. Destroying the immune system is uh poor substitute for uh cure, and we don't want that. I'm assuming there's no way tuh make the brain cells immune tuh the body's immune system. Besides that, upgrading the brain is not only theoretical but would also be extremely complex and almost impossible. The only thing that comes tuh mind is putting uh selectively permeable membrane around the brain that doesn't allow white blood cells tuh pass through, but that could pose several risks."

"I applaud that statement," Kronos commented earnestly. "We had already thought of that, but to even think of that idea is genius. Most people would have never even thought of that, and if they did, they would not have taken into account all of the resulting problems. You're far smarter than you seem, but I already knew that. A selectively permeable membrane is a good idea, but it can't be done for several reasons, as you just said."

"Yeah, 'cept it don't matter anyway 'cause I know you didn't come here for muh ideas on how tuh fix the situation. I ain't bright enough tuh catch yer eye like that. So, that being said, I don't understand why you're coming tuh me 'bout this at all. I assume you two think that I can help somehow?"

"That's exactly why we're here, Mr. Willow," Sir Thomas replied. "It's no coincidence that Charleston was our first stop. You're a famous health expert, after all. A nutritionist, a dietician, a researcher, and so on and so forth, in fact. However, we also know what else you are, and *that's* why we've traveled here seeking your help. There are *others* like us."

"*Others*? What do ya mean by that?"

"I'm afraid we're not quite sure about them ourselves. They might be scientists, or they might just be geniuses, but either way, they are people who have discovered remarkable breakthroughs but are being held back by side effects and the consequences of self-experimentation. Either that or they're just hiding and maintaining a low profile as of now for various reasons. We know only of theories to explain their breakthroughs and abilities, but as far as who they are and why they have done what they have, we are yet to know. Except for one person, that is. You're one of these unique individuals, Mr. Willow."

Birch felt his chest and shoulder muscles tense up, although he tried to keep a skeptical look on his face to keep his secret. He wanted to lower his massive chest, but it was clenched tight. *Not good. This is* not good at all. They know I have uh secret. Hell, they might know what it is. How? That's impossible! There's no way I'll be able tuh convince them otherwise. They're too smart for that. People who know your secrets can cause ya big trouble, and I don't want any of that. What do I do? What should I say?* Birch raised an eyebrow. Despite knowing that it would fail, he planned on trying to convince them that he was not who they thought he was. His ginormous body and past feats made it rather difficult, however. "Others like us? I'm one of 'em? Self-experimentation and abilities? I'm not sure I follow what you're saying. What do you mean?"

Kronos let out an aggressive exhale of impatience and frustration, his eyes closed for a brief moment longer than a regular blink. "I would urge you to-"

"What I'm referring to are people like us who have discovered something remarkable," Sir Thomas quickly interjected. "The speculations include an immortal man, a magnet-master, a time-bender, and others. We have a whole list, in fact, but that's not the point I'm trying to make. It's obvious that you've received some kind of scientific help yourself, either through your own research or Mr. Kellson's work. No man could be your size and live a healthy lifestyle. The amount of energy you require would be hard to gain through a regular diet, but you have even more than you need, which is incredible. Even with your genetic mutation, the strength you possess is beyond believable. People at your height often die young, but you're healthier than any normal human being. It's not just your muscles, but your entire body seems to be double the size of a man who is already far larger than the average human being. Many consider you a superhuman, in fact. Your research may help us, and we can help you, as we know you're probably in need of help. You said yourself that side effects are inevitable regarding new science. *Please*, Mr. Willow, we need your help. Whatever you've done to make you into this superhuman, we hope that it might be a major piece of the cure to this teleportation-disease. You could fix the one problem that is holding back the *entire* future. From what I've observed, your goal is to help all of humanity, is it not? Here's your biggest chance to do so!"

It was a lot to take in, and even Sir Thomas had surprised himself by his speech. However, he had acted instinctively, cutting Kronos off and trying to prevent a conflict.

Birch sighed, unsure of what to believe anymore. Given his own life, between his body and the research he had used on himself, Birch found himself believing in a lot more than a normal person would, but he still had his doubts. *An immortal man? A magnet-master? Are those as fictional as I think? I basically am uh superhuman, so it's not that hard tuh believe. These two seem smart enough tuh make teleportation, and if you can manipulate atoms, it probably wouldn't be that hard tuh do. They're not wrong about me either, which is scary. I have received scientific help. What Michael and I discovered is remarkable. But I know what I have tuh do. I'm not selfish, but this is best. Perhaps, I can save them from continuing down their path of scientific destruction. Their inventions will inevitably impact the world negatively, even if they have good intentions. I have tuh stop teleportation and the manipulation of atoms from growin' anymore than it already has.* Birch went with his gut instinct, which, despite his charitable reputation, was to not help them but rather help himself and make sure that he was safe. "I know that I seem like some kind of uh superhuman figure, but I'm just uh man. And how do I know that this isn't some sort o' plan tuh come after me or con me of muh business? It sounds reasonable and all, but I don't entirely believe everything about it. I'm sorry."

"Is that so, *liar?*" Kronos had already planned out last night how to handle this exact situation should it occur, and he knew that it would.

Birch looked over at Kronos with a distasteful look in his eyes, although they were not entirely hostile. "*Excuse* me?"

Kronos let out a fake sigh and shook his head as an evil chuckle escaped his throat. His foot had stopped tapping. "Oh, it's nothing, Birch. I didn't want to have to do this, or at least the old man didn't," Kronos gestured to Sir Thomas, "but you leave me no choice!"

Kronos instantly swiped his left elbow over the stachel at his side in a pattern, and the top and front side opened up instantaneously. With incredible speed, he whipped out the D.O.O.M. Shooter with his left hand and aimed it at a large training dummy across the gym, behind Birch to his left. The dial already set on maximum power, Kronos held down the trigger which caused a flash of light as the yellow beam of electricity, about the size of a cardboard paper towel roll, shot out of the gun and across the gym. He let go of the trigger after a few seconds, and the electrical current burst inward-out. The training dummy fell backward, the head of the figure wholly gone, drifting around in a bunch of atomic pieces. A few of the molecules clustered back together, forming small clumps of whatever material the dummy had been made out of, but for the most part, the head had been completely destroyed.

A malicious grin of sharp teeth formed on Kronos' face as his amber-yellow eyes seemed to glow like the electric current of the gun. *And that was just with a weak shot in comparison to the full experimental potential of the D.O.O.M. Shooter. Hopefully, I won't have to shoot too much stronger than that, though. I'll enjoy it too much, and when you really enjoy something, you don't want to stop.* He licked his lips with a snake-like tongue.

Birch jumped up out of his chair, sending it flying back a bit. He tensed up and began to clench his fists, but he tried to remain cautious and calm, knowing that even he would be killed if hit by the gun's beam. "Woah! I didn't need that kind of proof. Who's gonna' pay for that! What even was that?" That training dummy was one piece of a business that he had worked hard to build up from nothing. To have strangers come in and disintegrate it into thin air, that made Birch extremely angry... and he was seldom angry.

"Isn't it obvious, Birch?" Kronos teased maliciously. "You should have been listening to everything we said. I can manipulate any and all atoms. You doubted us, so I gave you physical evidence since your mind was unable to grasp the unbelievable. Unfortunately, many must see in order to believe."

"So, destroyin' muh life's work is your way of makin' evidence for seemingly fictional claims?" Birch raised his left leg up and stomped forward a step, snapping the table in half as he stepped toward Kronos, the magazines and wood a mess on the ground under Birch's giant foot. "I assure ya that I was listenin' tuh everything."

Sir Thomas quickly stood up and put his arms between the two men, who both seemed to be far more than human. He reached into his suit pocket and handed Birch a thick wad of cash. "This is more than enough money to buy two training mannequins to replace the one he just destroyed. That's the D.O.O.M. Shooter. It sends out an electrical current that tears apart the bonds of the atoms of the object that it's shot at. The current it's based on is part of how the teleportation process works."

"Hmph." Birch was still tense. He looked around the gym, glad to see that the few people who had walked in had been too busy to notice what had happened.

"I sincerely apologize for his rude behavior, Mr. Willow. That was entirely inappropriate of him to do. He isn't accustomed to leaving the house."

Kronos rolled his eyes at the comment and shot air out of his mouth between closed lips. "Pfft." He snickered internally. "It's a castle, actually."

"*Now*... put that away," Sir Thomas commanded Kronos, glancing back and forth between the two powerful beings. After a mischievous grin and a glint of death in his demonic eyes, Kronos reluctantly put the D.O.O.M. Shooter back into the open satchel. He left the satchel open so the weapon could be taken back out in an instant if necessary.

"Why not close the bag?" Birch asked in a demanding way as he looked down at Kronos.

"Kronos, close the bag," Sir Thomas commanded.

Planning on refusing to do so, Kronos listened and closed the satchel, seeing the situation he found himself in now more challenging, and therefore, more entertaining to him as a sharpshooter.

Looking down at Kronos, Birch could see the satchel without taking his eyes off of Kronos. He noted that, despite it being closed, Kronos was still ready to draw and shoot. "Hmph."

"Thank you." Sir Thomas turned his attention back to Birch. "As I mentioned earlier, his brain isn't entirely stable after such an illness." That was not true, but it made a good excuse, which he hoped Birch would believe. "Now, back to the business at hand. I assume you believe us now. I don't lie, Mr. Willow. We're not the only ones, and we know that you're one of us. Your participation in the creation of a cure could benefit all of humanity in drastic ways, and I mean that."

Sir Thomas sat back down, and Birch did as well after a long moment of hesitation, as he tried to think of what would be the best course of action. He kept glancing over at Kronos, whose villainous face was unreadable as always, although he seemed to be up to something utterly terrible inside his large skull. *I trust you, Sir Thomas, but I don't understand Kronos. Is he actin' like this out o' desperation because he's afraid of dying from this disease, or is this who he truly is? Is he tryin' tuh make uh cure fuh everyone so badly that he's willin' tuh do anything? I can't figure 'im out.* Birch's veins were bulging out of his body, and his large muscles were flexed to the point that the tightly compacted fibers seemed to be on the brink of tearing through his skin. Yet, he was barely even flexing. His whole body alternated between tense and relaxed, and he was ready to attack at any minute. He was not going to let anyone destroy his gym. It was all that he had.

The three of them sat in awkward silence as the tense atmosphere hung heavy around them. Birch finally relaxed his body a bit before he let out a long sigh that contained the thoughts of a hard decision made. He felt bad for them, even though Kronos had chosen to use unnecessary violence. "Listen, fellas, I'm real sorry. The truth is that I believe ya, as crazy as it all seems. I understand the situation that you're in, and I do feel bad, but I don't think I can help you guys. Even if I wanted to, I can't. That's the honest truth of the situation, and even though it's not muh fault, I do feel bad."

Sir Thomas' heart almost stopped, as his breath got caught in his throat. *Oh, bloody Hell. Don't say you can't help us! Not after I convinced Kronos to come here and talk to you. Not when we're so close to going back home and forgetting about all of this. Please, Mr. Willow! This isn't just for the future sake of humanity. This is for my sake as well, and his.* Sir Thomas tried to control the internal wave of panic and bitterness that had filled his body. "I'm afraid I don't understand your reasoning for that, Mr. Willow. Why don't you think you can help us?"

"I feel bad, so allow me tuh explain. You both deserve that, and it'll make sense once I explain it to ya. You're both very smart, but you're desperate, so you've overlooked somethin' that changes everything. Just look at me. Muh research has greatly improved muh health. As uh result of what I did, I've experienced uh tremendous increase in overall health, speed, energy, muscle recovery, blood circulation, mental energy, sleep benefits, strength, regeneration, and various other improvements. The list goes on and on. That's actually the opposite o' what ya need. In theory, the healthier you become, the closer you'll get tuh dying. Sure, muh research will help your brain uh bit, but that won't actually do anything. In fact, it'll improve everything else about your health at the same time, which is the worse possible situation for ya. Uh healthier body means that you'll have uh stronger immune system, and then your brain cells will only be attacked harder and destroyed faster. My research won't cure your disease, but it'll actually make it worse by greatly improvin' your immune system. That also makes your destroy-the-immune-system-cure far weaker."

A bitter expression was on Sir Thomas' face, which faced the floor, but he attempted a half-smile in admiration of Birch's honesty. "I see. What you say is the unfortunate truth, not just regarding the science, but also how foolish we have been in our desperation. Even if we were able to supercharge the brain cells, it wouldn't be enough."

"Besides, not all of us are hidin' fuh selfish reasons."

Sir Thomas looked up at Birch with shock and concern.

"That's what you said, right? That some of these scientists have experienced problems too? You said that I've had muh own side effects that I've had tuh deal with, and you were right about that. Fatal ones too, and I don't want anyone else gettin' hurt 'cause of the information I know. In uh sense, I'm the guardian of the knowledge I've discovered, as it is beneficial but comes at uh cost. In the end, it will destroy ya. Should I fail in muh duty tuh protect others from such information, I would feel both responsible and guilty. I'd regret this day fuh the rest of my life. My goal is tuh help everyone, but not if it means they might get hurt in the process. Especially when the risk isn't necessary and when there are other ways. I hope ya understand."

Sir Thomas could hear the honest and shameful tone that underlined Birch's voice, and his half-smile drooped to a frown in bitter sympathy. He looked at Birch, the pinnacle of human strength and the healthiest person alive, and felt pity. It seemed impossible to do so, yet it was happening. *Astonishing! I suppose that Kronos was right about these people. He tracked them down perfectly. Who would have thought that such people existed in secret among our society? Not even in secret, in your case, Mr. Willow. This quest has just begun, but it has undoubtedly turned out to be something. I never expected to encounter a man like him. Everyone looks up to you, but no one actually knows what you're going through. What you've already gone through. That has been said about many others, but it's a different case for you. I'm considered a gentleman of good-heart, but you far exceed me, Mr. Willow. Bravo.* Sir Thomas locked eyes with Birch, both of them understanding what lay in their hearts. He nodded his head. "My deepest sympathy, Mr. Willow. I'm terribly sorry to know that."

"As am I, Sir Thomas... but our field of work will always come at uh cost, and that cost is our lives. It takes away from us, physically, mentally, socially, and emotionally. I've devoted muh life to helping others, and you should do the same. I can't help muhself at this point, and I'll prob'bly start countin' down muh days soon enough, whether it be weeks from now or uh few years. There's no turnin' back from what I've done tuh muh body. Not all science has an on-and-off switch. I was tryin' tuh create somethin' better fuh everyone, but no good deed goes unpunished, as they say. Ironic, I suppose. Again… we're the pioneers of science," Birch stated as he shook his head in regret. *Poor guys. They're just like me. But I can't help 'em or muhself. Nobody can. We're all beyond regular people and help now.* He sighed bitterly. "I'm sorry, guys. Truly, I am, but I can't help ya. From the bottom of muh heart, I urge you both tuh leave the path you're on and take another one. I know that abandoning teleportation is the last thing you'd want tuh do, but it'll be the most beneficial tuh everyone. The atom wasn't meant tuh be manipulated by humans, and if ya continue tuh do so, it'll only get worse and worse. The problems you've encountered are just the smallest obstacles on the beginning of uh long path with seemingly no end tuh it."

Sir Thomas sighed in disappointment, but he nodded his head in agreement. He understood Birch and believed him. The problem was whether or not Kronos would. Sir Thomas stood up and shook hands with Birch. "Despite how gutted I am, I have to say that those are some of the finest words I've ever heard, Mr. Willow. You aren't called a motivational speaker and inspiration for nothing. This outcome is rather disappointing, but I thank you for your time. I understand and respect your choice. I'm sorry to have troubled you with all of this, but you were one of our only chances of finding an answer. I'm afraid we can't abandon this quest just yet, but we'll keep your advice at the front of our minds. I expect you'll understand and respect that we wish for this to be kept a secret between us, as we shall keep yours."

"Of course, Sir Thomas. From one sick scientist to another, you have muh word," Birch said with a salute half-jokingly, although the bitter truth was embedded in each word as well. "Best o' luck tuh both of ya. If you want tuh continue down the path of the unknown as many feel they must, I won't stop ya, but take care of yourselves out there. Not everyone you meet will be as hospitable and understanding as me. Some of 'em will be dangerous menaces who will undoubtedly do everything they can tuh stay hidden or destroy those who learn about them."

Kronos twitched, and he felt sick to his heart. *For a while, you actually had me feeling earnest and admiring you, but abandon teleportation and the power to manipulate atoms! You would dare to cheat the future generations, The Ruthless Root? That's a disgrace to everyone who has ever tried to do what we have done. How sickening! To every scientist, pioneer, and-* He shook his head, unable to understand.

"I wish we could help you, but I don't think that there's anything we can do," Sir Thomas stated regretfully. "It's truly a shame to think of your demise, as this is a brilliant business you have here. Although, I can't conceive a man such as yourself giving up hope so soon. Have faith that you will find a way to cure your own side effects, Mr. Willow. Keep on helping people, because your work *is* appreciated." Sir Thomas turned to Kronos, who had a mixed expression of shock and rage across his face. His eyes were covered by the shade of his forehead as his face looked at the ground. He was exuding an aura of dread and power that only grew stronger with each second that passed. His teeth were clenched, and his body was twitching as his veins pulsed along his rough flesh. "Let's go, Kronos," Sir Thomas said firmly. "There's nothing more for us here."

After a final nod of his head toward the two men, Birch started walking back to the main gym area, which was in the opposite direction of the entrance of the building. He saw a few people coming into the gym, as it was now later in the morning, and he waved at them. Turning away from the members, he headed for the bathroom and then to see how Michael was doing.

Sir Thomas was halfway to the gym entrance when he realized that Kronos was not right behind him. He sighed, assuming that Kronos was just slowly moping behind him. "I'm sorry. I know you're disappointed, and I am too, but stop dragging your feet, Kronos. Let's get going," he commanded as he stopped and turned around to face Kronos. Sir Thomas' breath got caught in his chest again, and his heart twitched when he saw that Kronos was still sitting in his chair, brooding in a dangerous aura of desire for vengeance. *Oh, bollocks... What is he going to do? This isn't good at all,* Sir Thomas thought to himself as he started to walk toward Kronos. He instantly stopped.

Kronos stood up from his chair in a smooth motion with a body like steel, not using his arms to help him, but merely getting up with the strength of his legs. A ruthless expression of determination had taken over his entire face. He snickered psychotic laughter with pride and power as he spread his legs apart in a fighting stance with the knees slightly bent. His voice grew twisted and deeper, filled with absolute power and domination. "Well, if you won't give us your research freely, we'll just have to take it! Every peasant must offer what is theirs to **King Kronos**!" Faster than humanly possible, Kronos whipped out the D.O.O.M. Shooter and began to use it freely, shooting down anything in sight, from workout equipment to random pieces of the building.

"*Stop* this madness," Sir Thomas cried out as he watched the grand gym get destroyed internally, one small piece at a time. He had no idea what to do, his eyes bulging with shock. His cry of fear and desperation was not heard over the sounds of metal and plastic scattering in deformed chunks as if the place were under mortar fire. Debris was beginning to litter the place like a street after the hurricane waters that had flooded it dried up and left everything behind. "Bloody Hell!"

Bored of merely shooting random objects, Kronos held down the trigger of the gun, which increased the electrical current's power with each second that passed as he swept the beam left and right across the gym, atomically deconstructing everything in the gun's path. People who had at first looked at Kronos when he yelled were now running out of the gym in a frantic panic. Michael crouched behind what was left of the bar and began calling the local law enforcement.

Birch came out of the private bathroom, which was in his office, whistling happily to himself, glad that he had taken care of the stressful conversation. But upon seeing the destructive commotion, his giant heart sank like a rock in water to the dark depths he had been struggling to stay above for so long. In that single moment, everything terrible that had happened to him flashed in his mind, though he did not know why. It was a subconscious reaction, brought about by how unfair all of it seemed to him. All of the horrible memories stacked on top of each other, crowned with what he now saw happening to his gym. The moment he had been struggling against... the snap inside him that would ultimately take over his monstrous body... had finally happened, as he had always feared it would. The inevitable beastliness that had been creeping around inside of Birch, held back by his pure-heartedness and love of life, had grown too strong for him to handle. He thought that the two men had left. He thought that he had dealt with the situation properly. Yet, here was the opposite of that. Everything Birch had ever cared about was being destroyed. Everything that he had worked hard to create to help others was being destroyed. The only thing he had was on its way to being gone forever.

Overwhelmed by the negativity building up inside of him, Birch roared louder than a territorial polar bear, almost shaking the whole building as all of the hot air inside his body, heated even more so by his uncontrollable anger, rushed out of his giant lungs. His hands instantly clenched into fists that could easily punch through bricks. He stopped and quickly scanned the scene to see what was going on, but he already knew the cause of the chaos. It could only be one thing. His green eyes, which many had compared to the very essence of life, locked focus with Kronos' demonic eyes of amber-yellow.

Kronos shot Birch a malicious smile of death, his sharp teeth glinting in the yellow light created by the D.O.O.M. Shooter. "*I warned you,*" his condemning expression seemed to say.

Quickly squatting down and picking up a whole weight lifting machine, Birch launched it at Kronos with a heaving throw that sent it flying across the room as if it weighed nothing. It flipped and spun in a circle as it cut through the air at Kronos.

Kronos, the modern-day sharpshooter of the world, flicked his wrists and hands in a frenzy of lines in front of him, the electrical current following the paths he marked out and slicing the machine into an artificial hailstorm of small pieces, which went scattering across the floor. Birch was shocked by what he just witnessed, and Kronos used this to his advantage. He aimed the gun and shot its destructive beam above Birch at the ceiling and traced a jagged-lined circle. The ends of the line connected, and the large chunk of the ceiling, with a rough circumference of thirty-two feet, fell straight down. Birch caught the massive piece of ceiling material with his arms at right angles, his knees bending a bit. *Why didn't he jus' shoot me and kill me? That evil genius is up tuh something.* Birch cracked his neck in a threatening manner before thrusting the large piece of material away from himself in Kronos' direction. It thudded as it slammed against the ground and broke into several parts.

Kronos smirked. "Not bad," he muttered to himself. "That was rather impressive, although a feeble weight and effort for a man of your strength. That might work in the final battle, but I can't allow you to attend despite your potential. Therefore, I will weaken you to the point of immobility, for now, The Ruthless Root."

His sorrow and desire for revenge rising with each passing second, Birch seemed to grow stronger and more muscular as his humanity started to slip away. His pulsing veins were more visible, his compacted muscle fibers were close to tearing through his healthy skin, and he was beginning to sweat, each breath sounding like a roar of thunder. His giant heart's powerful pumps could almost be heard out loud as testosterone and adrenaline flowed throughout his massive body. With each flex of the large muscles across his body, the air around him almost flew back. Birch tore his black muscle-tee in half, throwing the pieces to either side of him after letting loose another earth-shaking roar. His scars glistened in the light as his eight pack of abs tensed to a hardness of steel. His eyes were still the green embodiment of life, but they now represented the dangerous and opposite side of life: death.

"So, this is how ya repay muh kindness? Then so be it," Birch spat out angrily. He took a threatening step forward, the ground cracking underneath his foot as he exerted strong force from it. "It is only in the natural and desperate defense of other precious life that one shall be taken, should no other option be at my disposal. You leave me no other option, Dr. Nephus." Birch tensed up, ready to actually kill Kronos, seeing him as a terroristic threat to both himself, the gym, and the local people. He had never killed a person before, and the idea of just hurting someone had always made him sick, but he felt different. He understood his duty to everyone relying on him. "Rose... forgive me," Birch whispered through clenched teeth to himself.

Quickly grabbing a small medicine ball with one hand, Birch pitched it at Kronos as lethally as he could, almost breaking the sound barrier with his throw, but Kronos jumped up and kicked the medicine ball back at him with both legs. *Impossible! Uh dropkick? To kick that ball at that speed would have shattered all of the bones in his legs! How is he still standing?* Birch backhanded the flying ball that came back at him as if it were a fly, and it went soaring away from him toward the ruins of the bar. The defensive hit against the ball left a small patch of red on his hand with a slight stinging sensation, but Birch ignored it. He had smacked the speeding ball away from him with such force that it smashed through what was left of the wooden bar, almost taking out Michael, who was just getting off of the phone. He quickly escaped the gym, hesitant to leave Birch behind.

Birch instantly threw another small medicine ball at Kronos, aiming for his heinous face this time. That was merely a distraction, however, as he knew that a ranged attack against Kronos was pointless. He charged forward at cheetah speed with rhino strength while Kronos was ducking to evade the medicine ball. Birch was still concerned about the experimental weapon in Kronos' hand, but a head-on attack seemed to be his best option. He pulled back his right arm at full power and tensed every fiber in it as he swung forward with every massive muscle in his body backing the punch. His deadly punch expelled all air with a loud snap-crack sound. At the last second, he saw that Kronos had velcroed his lab coat shut and spread his arms wide, allowing himself to be hit directly by the full force of the devastating blow.

The punch sent Kronos flying fifteen feet across the gym into the wall behind him at an insane speed. A crater with three rings formed upon his collision with the wall, crack marks spreading outward from the center of impact.

Birch looked over at Kronos, who was slumped against the base of the wall. "You must have uh death-wish tuh have opened yourself up tuh muh punch like that. If you thought relaxin' your entire body would save ya from the damage, you're not entirely as smart as I had thought. See, I'm uh different case than regular punches or impacts that would have been mitigated by that martial arts technique. I'm the Charleston Crusher. I'm-" Birch grew speechless as he noticed that his right hand was slightly bleeding at the knuckles. *Impossible. That scientist must have some tricks up his sleeves. My skin and knuckles are tough enough tuh punch through uh brick wall without bleeding, so why am I injured from punchin' him?*

Psychotic laughter comprised of harsh cords of utter villainy and condemning ego echoed threateningly across the partially destroyed gym. Birch stepped back in shocked panic as Kronos stood up from the floor, brushing the grey dust off his black cargo pants. The aura of pride and power exuding from him was overwhelmingly intimidating. "**Incorrect.** Curiosity and a death-wish are two drastically different things, though the two can sometimes cross paths." He cracked his neck and spine, his evil eyes and monstrous mouth more twisted and sharp than barbed wire as he clenched his left hand into a fist. "Although, I did actually feel some damage from that. You're one of the only beings in this world powerful enough to hurt me. You should quit the humble act and be proud for once," Kronos said with a menacing smile that exuded an intense wave of power, "as that is **indeed** the **greatest** accomplishment any person can ever achieve."

Birch's eyes grew hollower than his current heart of sorrow and revenge. He clenched his fists even harder and tensed the muscles in his feet, ready to move in an instant. There was utter fear in his lifeless eyes, brought about by the unforeseen and uncomprehensible. While he had held back just a bit, he had expected that punch to knockout Kronos. In fact, he had expected to kill Kronos with that, his mind clouded by anger and adrenaline. "I don't understand!" Birch noticed that Kronos' lab coat was now parted down the middle once again. He thought back to when he punched Kronos in the chest, and the lab coat had been closed. "Oh, I see. Relyin' on your fancy gadgets, are ya? That's why it's velcro instead o' buttons. Makes it easier tuh close up on short notice."

Kronos laughed out of pity for Birch. "You're strength is inversely proportional to your intelligence. Don't make me laugh at you any more than I already have. It *is* bulletproof, cut resistant, and shock-absorbant to a degree, but it was never designed to withstand the devastating blows of a superhuman such as yourself. It's only a prototype, and the real one is for someone else. Any person wearing this would have died from that punch, or at least been paralyzed. Not to mention, my skull still made quite the forceful impact against that wall."

"Then how the are you still standing? At the very least, all o' your ribs should be cracked, and all o' your internal organs should be inflamed or expellin' whatevuh was in 'em!"

All emotion drained from Kronos as he looked up at Birch coldly, an ominous aura of power seeming to spread out everywhere from his body. Now there was just pure ego, which he had rightfully earned. His gaze was enough to paralyze even the most strong-willed people. "Well, I find the answer to that question rather obvious. Still, your ignorance is justified. I'm still standing because I am **King Kronos**, and I stand at the pinnacle of all humans, which stand above all other lifeforms. My genius is just one of countless abilities. You're not the only one with a rare genetic mutation that gives them real-life powers."

"There's no way-"

"**Incorrect** yet again, The Ruthless Root. My bones are more than eight times denser than the bones of regular humans, thanks to a beneficial mutation in my LRP5 gene. They're essentially steel."

"You expec' me tuh believe that?"

Kronos laughed maniacally. "Cast aside your foolish doubt. I have no reason to lie to a being so much weaker than myself. My bones are practically indestructible, although that does come with a few downsides. That dropkick was the first time I've jumped in years, as it is a difficult task considering my body's weight. My bones aren't the only part of me that put me above everyone else. My skin is often compared to the skin of a shark, which is comprised of dermal denticles. To rub my skin is enough to make a person bleed, and my skin is hard to damage even with blades. Those who punch my bare skin only hurt themselves. In your case, however, it must've been the roughness of the lab coat material, which is meant to serve as a microscopic thorn-like defense against attacks. It couldn't have been my skin or steel-like bones, as my clothes were in the way. Having a large brain is the key to becoming the ultimate being, but a vessel strong enough to protect it from any threat is just as vital." Kronos coughed up a small amount of blood, which was only enough to fill two teaspoons. His blood was so unnaturally dark that it was almost black. He smirked as he wiped it away with the backside of his left hand. "You're the first being to ever make me bleed. So, you have slight potential, but I'm afraid you're not good enough to survive what is coming. If you can't even hold you're own against me, then you'll surely die."

"You're completely insane!" Birch exclaimed with a sharp point at Kronos, his voice thundering throughout the entire building. "I don't even know what you're talkin' about, but half of what you say is delusional. Are you sayin' ya let me hit you so you could finally feel pain? That's sickening," Birch spat out. "You're too powerful for your own good."

"Incorrect. I'm not a masochist or something. I let you hit me as a scientific field test to measure your strength. That data is critical to my analysis and predictions of events that are beyond your comprehension. So far, you've proven to be quite a remarkable specimen, although you haven't done anything too impressive yet. Then again, I haven't taken out the Atomic Gauntlet against you."

"You're not goin' tuh be takin' anything out against me. It's time tuh end this, Dr. Nephus. I have no choice, but tuh crush ya!" With that stated, Birch charged at Kronos once more, giving it everything he had, his feet cracking the ground below him with each powerful step.

As fast as Birch was, however, Kronos' incomprehensible mind and reflexes were faster. He knew that the fight between them could drag on forever, should he allow it. However, that was not what he wanted. He began to fire a beam from the D.O.O.M. Shooter.

Time stopped entirely for Kronos as his quick mind entered its own world of thoughts, all being passed around his skull in a single second. *I could kill you right here and now, Birch, but that's not what I came here to do. The more I theorize, the more I realize how much I don't know about the upcoming threat. My plans have gone awry, and you'll have to be prepared for what's coming. However, your inhumane strength and potential are held back by your meekness and humanity. I have to destroy those chains, unfortunately, so you'll be able to survive the future. I have my reasons for why everything is happening the way that it is. By destroying your gym and injuring you, the impending threat won't be interested in you, and you won't be able to get involved either way. Then, if I fail, you'll need to be strong enough to stop whatever kills me. That's why I'm only slightly injuring you. Honestly, I was deeply touched by a lot of what you said today, and I secretly admire you. Trust me. You'll understand one day, or perhaps not, but I always will.* Kronos frowned bitterly.

Kronos held down the trigger and clipped Birch's right shoulder, atomically destroying a majority of it. That was the problem that everyone overlooked due to their hopefulness and exaggerations. Birch was only human, and he shared the same weaknesses as them. His skin was the same as anyone else's, and so were his atoms. Large amounts of blood spurted out from the unnatural wound. As the giant stumbled backward, clutching his shoulder, which was in unimaginable pain on an atomic level, with his left hand, he slipped on a fragment of debris and fell backward. His bald head smashed into a metal weight, and the back of his head began to bleed as he fell unconscious.

Kronos looked at the large body that lay on the floor, his head lowered in bitterness. *I'm sorry, Birch. You're a good guy... for the most part. You'll thank me later, if I'm right about everything, and most of the time, I am entirely correct. Even if you never find out the truth, I'm fine with you hating me for what has happened. It's a far more desirable situation than the countless others that plague my vast mind.* Kronos turned around and sprinted toward the entrance of the gym. Not having time to open the front doors, he shot a gaping hole through the wall by quickly tracing a circle and then expanding it ring by ring. He jumped through the opening and onto the street, which was abandoned. He could hear sirens in the distance, and they were approaching fast.

Turning around and holding down long and firmly on the trigger, Kronos fired the D.O.O.M. Shooter, directing the increasingly more powerful electrical current back and forth across the building several times in non-straight lines. He sprinted away as the gym collapsed in on itself and crumbled to the ground. Running like an eccentric madman, Kronos sprinted over to where the car was hidden, using the gun to destroy any cameras and traffic lights he saw. Without stopping, he quickly hopped into the vehicle.

Sir Thomas, having warmed up the engine already, sped out of there. He had made a swift exit as soon as Kronos had begun his attack, as he knew there was nothing he could do except ensure their quick escape.

Sirens were heard throughout the town as the two men sped back to their hotel. Kronos continued to use the D.O.O.M. Shooter to vaporize every camera he saw. They slowed down as they approached the hotel, and they pulled in without raising any suspicion. Their meeting with the first rival scientist was over.

CHAPTER 8

ANALYSIS AND NEW RIVAL SCIENTIST
(Charleston, West Virginia. The Same Day: April 14, 2022)

Kronos and Sir Thomas walked calmly up to their hotel room on the second floor. They locked the door firmly behind them. The room they had paid for was a master suite with a view of the Kanawha River. It featured two bedrooms, an open concept living room with a kitchen, and a walkout balcony. They had more money than they needed, and it showed, as this hotel room was not only expensive but also unnecessary for the two of them. They were just staying for a maximum of three days to meet with Birch and gather their intel. However, Kronos always insisted that they get the best option since they were the best.

Sir Thomas walked into the kitchen and leaned against the refrigerator, trembling with disbelief. He tried to remain calm as he felt taming one's temper was most appropriate, although how he was feeling was clearly visible. He had more steam coming out of his ears than one of his fancy English tea kettles.

Going over to the sink in the kitchen, Kronos spat into the drain and washed away bloody spit. "How utterly displeasing," he muttered to himself. "That unnecessary risk was illogical. I'll be fine, though." Kronos used a paper towel to wipe his mouth, and then he stuffed it into a small trashcan underneath the sink. He pushed the trashcan back into the small space and then closed the cabinet, leaning his side against the counter as he turned his attention to Sir Thomas.

It was silent except for the subtle humming of the refrigerator and the ticking of an analog clock on the wall above the sink. The two men stood there staring at each other for a while, unsure of what the other was thinking, though they both knew the other was thinking a lot.

"Pfft." Kronos slowly exhaled through his nostrils. *Unfortunately, I can't tell you the truth, Thomas. Yell and lecture at me all you want, but I'm doing the right thing. I won't ask for your forgiveness. I already know that you'll forgive me once you find out the truth. Not that it matters since I'll be long dead by then.* Kronos almost laughed a bit at himself and the situation, finding it all to be a cruel joke being played on them by some powerful threat. "You're so flustered and angry that you don't even know what to say," Kronos snickered. "I suppose I'll break the silence then and start since you could probably stand there all day thinking horrible thoughts about me. Not that there's much to say about anything. That was quite the ordeal, though, was it not?"

"Are you kidding me right now, Kronos? I don't even know what part to begin with, but that meeting certainly went all to pot. I didn't stick around to see what happened after you started yelling like a wanker, but I'm well aware of what went down: disruption of the public peace, shooting, illegal use of experimental firearms, destroying personal property, aggravated assault, murder charges, and terroristic actions! The endangerment of innocent lives! The list of horrible deeds goes on and on, but you'll just ignore all of my remarks and the evidence because you always just turn everything around so that it praises you or blames someone else. This is unbelievable and immature behavior for a man such as yourself, Kronos! This is the last straw. I've completely had it with you. I thought you killing the prisoners you had gotten sick was immoral and unforgivable, but this completely surpasses those heinous deeds in all aspects."

"Is that so? You mean to tell me that the destruction of personal property is worse than killing test subjects? Intriguing."

"You're so selfish that you're not even thinking about this whole quest of yours anymore, since you've clearly treated it so recklessly. That just proves how arrogant you are behind all of that breath-taking intellect. This mission that we're on was supposed to go undiscovered by anyone except for the other scientists when we confronted them."

"And so far, it hasn't been discovered by anyone."

"Bloody Hell! That's what *you would* say right now. We may not have been seen or recorded, but our plans will undoubtedly be discovered, and either Mr. Willow or the government will begin cracking down on us, which is the very last thing that either of us wanted. I especially didn't want this to turn into some affair with anyone other than the other scientists or us."

"Incorrect. How exactly are people going to relate today's events to you or I? Hmm? You and I exist as ghosts both in the digital world, as well as in society, thanks to my immeasurable genius and methods of staying unknown."

"Our business card could be somewhere amongst that mess, which would jeopardize *everything* we've created. Plus, it probably has our fingerprints on it. The chairs could have pieces of lint from our clothes stuck to them!"

"Correct. You're absolutely right," Kronos said sarcastically with a meaningless wave of his hand. "I should've realized that a small business card in a building that has products from our company could lead directly to us and jeopardize *everything* that we've created. How stuuuupid of me!"

"It doesn't matter if he had products from our company in that gym or not. Our business card could still be a lead, especially since the authorities aren't going to know when he got the blenders. They might think those were delivered today with the business card right before the attack happened. You believe that you're invincible and untouchable, but that's not true, Kronos. Don't you realize that you've put everything at risk with what you did? I mean *everything*. Not just our lives. The company that we started from nothing, our quadrillions of dollars, our castle, or rather *our home*, Kronos! You had to know there might be consequences that even you couldn't handle if things went horrible. Didn't any of those things cross your mind at all when you thought about attacking Mr. Willow and his business?"

"Not at all," Kronos stated without care.

"Of course you didn't! I-"

"It's not because I'm emotionless, Thomas," Kronos retorted. "You might think that, but it's not the truth. None of those things being lost upset me because I never feared them being taken away or destroyed in the first place. I barely fear theoretically possible consequences, let alone fictional consequences. I am confident in myself, and I know for a fact that the business card will not be used as a lead. A step ahead as always, I destroyed it during the fight. Many believe I can predict the future day-for-day or even for years at a time, so why would you even doubt me after all these years?"

"That's not entirely true, but I know by now that there's no point in arguing with you. Many people? The only person who believes you have psychic foresight is *you*, Kronos. I'm relieved to know that you destroyed the card during your... tantrum, as I'll word it, but I'm still completely gutted by your behavior."

Kronos rolled his eyes. "A tantrum? And you're the one calling me immature? That wasn't a tantrum, Thomas. What occurred was merely an act of revenge in retaliation to Birch's refusal to help us with our efforts to find a permanent cure and obtain research that could help expand our empire of scientific knowledge. The man refused to help us or disclose what his breakthrough was. He clearly took no sympathy for my poor dying body, which is the exact opposite of what you had predicted."

Sir Thomas crossed his arms across his chest, tapping his right index finger rapidly against his left arm. He sighed, shaking his head in disappointment. "His refusal to help was the opposite, but his reaction actually makes even more sense than what I had predicted. You're so self-centered that you fail to hear anything that anyone says, and as a scientist, you should be ashamed that you don't observe all variables."

"Oh, spare me, please. You always talk in these riddles about the personalities of people and such. What are you trying to say? The truth is undeniable: he refused to help us."

"You were so busy brooding in frustrated defeat that you ignored everything he said after he denied to help you and countered your cure with the scientific facts that his research would make the disease worse. Bollocks. You frustrate me! Were you not listening? He couldn't help us because he's dying!" Sir Thomas yelled with an angry swing of his hand. "He wanted to help us but knew that there was nothing he could do, but that's not the worst part. The poor fellow is dying of some unknown ailment, and then you went and destroyed everything that he worked hard to make."

"I suppose I did him a favor then. Now he won't have to worry about writing a will or anything." Kronos glared over at Sir Thomas and flipped a grey strand of hair away from his forehead. "Don't tell me that you're actually pitying that man. Your heart is too good for your own good, old man. First off, there can be no sympathy when he made the decision to delve into the world of experimental science."

"Are you serious right now? That is so bloody ironic that-"

Kronos raised his hand in a gesture to stop. "Birch said that he had experienced side effects of his own, which doesn't automatically imply death. As a scientist, you should be ashamed that you assumed something. Even if what he was referring to did imply death, we have no evidence of his statement being true, so it could merely be a fabricated excuse to protect himself and his research."

Sir Thomas sighed again as he shook his head in frustration. "You are, indeed, the smartest human in the world, Kronos. I don't doubt that for a second. Yet, this right here," he made a circle in the air with his finger, "is what you lack. Understanding Mr. Willow is something you failed to do at that meeting, and part of me was afraid that would happen. As always, I had hoped for the best, but of course, I received the worst. It's always that way, and it always shall be. You've memorized the periodic table in its entirety, you can speak and read several languages, and you can list almost every chemical and atom in the air of a room with a single inhale, but when it comes to people... you simply can't understand them. He was telling the truth about his research. He is sick, and I could tell how gutted he was over the fact that he could help neither himself nor us. You've studied body language, from voice tone to eye movement, in an attempt to read people, but you can't understand people or emotion just from observing those variables. I know that you can predict people's actions based on patterns, past data, and hundreds of theoretical possibilities, but you can't understand them, which is critical when dealing with people. *Especially* when you want something from someone. A major part of understanding others has to do with observing with your own heart and emotions instead of your eyes and ears."

"Correct. That's true, Thomas. I don't quite get people, and I most likely never will. Having exceeded every intellectual limit to be beyond humanity, I have, unfortunately, separated myself from humans to the point of failing to understand their insignificant actions and meanings. I suppose emotions are something I lack in so that I may thrive and function in a proper and logical way. However, let's suppose what you say is true. It's quite possible that he's experienced unfortunate side effects as a result of self-experimentation, but that leaves a single question of vital importance then."

"And what might that be?"

"How is Birch dying, and why?"

"That was more like two questions," Sir Thomas grumbled. "I'm unsure of how or why he's dying, but I have some ideas and science that could, theoretically, explain exactly what is going on with his body and why it's happening. Without knowing what exactly his experiment was, our range of possibilities is too broad. As far as I know, Mr. Willow gets his superhuman status through the use of his plant-shakes in combination with his already humongous body. He never claimed that, but a major part of it has to be connected to those drinks somehow."

"Correct. I agree with you on that part. By connecting the experiment to his consumption of these plant-shakes, we can at least narrow our range of possibilities down to something more feasible. Based on my knowledge and research, however, they seem to be regular smoothies in all honesty. I don't even like smoothies."

"According to him, they're far superior to smoothies, but they *are* just regular drinks nonetheless. It's combining them with his research that makes them so valuable. During his presentation, Mr. Willow brought up cellulose and cellulase, which you're more than familiar with. He also mentioned that he had a presentation about theories and research regarding those topics planned for this Thursday, which is rather odd. Except that's canceled now, thanks to you. Those two terms aren't mentioned too much in the world of diet and exercise, but they're used more commonly in the field of biology, which also happens to be the field that Mr. Kellson studied. The fact that he brings so much attention to them makes me suspicious that he hopes humanity will one day be able to do something with them that we are currently unable to do. He had mentioned the fact that humans cannot digest cellulose and hinted that it would be beneficial if we could. That said, my theory is that his body somehow produces cellulase and so he is able to fully digest and absorb the nutrients of what he eats."

Kronos began to pace back and forth. "I see what you're thinking, and it would explain his unusual interest in those topics. Humans naturally producing cellulase to break down cellulose? Now, that would be an absolutely remarkable achievement, in all honesty. That does make sense, considering his impressive health stats, as the extra benefits resulting from the digestion of cellulose would be tremendous. Yet, it doesn't quite add up."

"How so?"

"It's true that such a process would be beneficial to the body, but simply absorbing extra nutrients from plants isn't enough to make a person that large and powerful."

"That's exactly what I had initially thought, but I've figured that part out. His size actually has nothing to do with it, and really, his body type is a coincidence in this whole debacle. That's what we had been discussing before, and although a small chance, it may just be that a unique man like himself happened to also make a unique breakthrough. The process isn't supposed to be some kind of superhuman pill or drug that makes you taller, larger, or stronger. Mr. Willow was born with myostatin-related muscular hypertrophy, which made him ginormous when combined with his extreme genes for height. His discovery of the ability of humans to naturally produce cellulase and digest cellulose is a coincidence, and it was most likely Mr. Kellson who discovered it, as far as we know. If *I* had discovered or created this ability, I wouldn't be his size. I'd be the same old man I am, but with twice the energy and a much stronger and healthier body. I might see a slight restoration of youth, but it wouldn't be anything too shocking. That's along with all of the benefits he had listed during the meeting. Understand?"

"Of course, I understand all of that, but astronomical coincidences such as that are almost paradoxical in the realm of science. They aren't since they are backed by logic and solid facts, but I'm skeptical of the idea that a person could have been born with extreme height genes, a *rare* genetic mutation in skeletal muscle, and then discover the ability to digest cellulose as well. The mathematical probability of those three occurrences aligning like that is slimmer than a line the width of a single atom. What are the chances, then? Not to mention that it happened to be during our lifetime and during the time that all of the other people on that list made their breakthroughs. Don't you think that there's something much larger at play here?"

Sir Thomas laughed. "Well, I'm gobsmacked by what I think you're implying, Kronos. Although, I doubt you would mean something as illogical as that, or at least it's illogical in your mind. Yet, I suppose we all have a change of mind and heart eventually. Are you saying that you believe God's power is at play here?"

"I assure you that such coincidences on a scale as large as this are shocking, but they aren't mind-blowing to the point of converting to a religion due to the fact that there is an actual probability of this happening. However, something isn't right, and I know that for a fact."

"I thought that perhaps your damned soul might have begun a journey of salvation. Then what did you mean? Are you just being skeptical and paranoid, or do you *actually* believe that there's some master puppeteer manipulating science and people?"

Kronos shook his head. "Just forget it," he mumbled, realizing that he was hinting too much at the truth. Of course, he knew Sir Thomas would not think much of what he had said. "You think there are side effects for this production of cellulase? As far as I know, it could only be beneficial. Then again, I haven't thought that much about it, and I honestly don't care that much."

"Of course, there are side effects."

"How bad could it be? Cows and mushrooms do it all the time. Digesting plant material is nothing harmful."

"Mr. Willow isn't a cow or a mushroom, though. Anything you force or manipulate the human body to do that it naturally can't do is typically harmful. *Especially* in the whole realm of self-experimentation in regard to untested and undertested theories." Sir Thomas walked through the kitchen and sat down on a couch in the living room, Kronos sitting in a chair across from him. "You're living evidence of that, considering your new disease and possibly dying body."

"Well, you got me there. Even I have no retort for that. Let's get to theorizing about those side-effects then. I enjoy scientific discussions like that. You said you had some ideas?"

"Indeed. The first major problem would be his heart. Any person of his height or size usually dies young. The heart is unable to keep up with how much blood his body needs and the long span that it must pump blood across. The heart is the engine and motor of the body, but it's a standard one that is basically the same for everyone, even though we're different vehicles. Sure, some are not as healthy as others and some are stronger, but they're mostly all the same. Mr. Willow requires an engine and motor far stronger than that standard, however. Yet, he does a lot more than any other person of his size. His heart, as it has been witnessed, is probably in top condition. Otherwise, he would have been dead long before now. I don't know whether this is due to his ability to digest cellulose or if it is something else that he does. He does have extra energy from the extra nutrients, but he could have a special mechanical heart for all we know, or a biologically-engineered one."

"Correct. Most people who are diagnosed with gigantism or similar conditions usually die of heart failure or something similar. The heart is a muscle, but it's not skeletal muscle, so his genetic mutation has no effect on it. Do you think he's just lucky?"

"His luck would have run out by now, even if his heart was in top condition. So, I've decided to assume that his heart is powerful and not the problem."

"Again, this is all theoretical, but I think you're correct regarding his heart. It seems to be just as strong as the rest of him."

"Since that's crossed off the list, I started thinking about what else it could have been. Certainly, it can't be anything to do with his brain or lungs. That's when the idea hit me. I suspect that he suffers from abnormalities within the digestive system. This idea occurred to me during his presentation based on some of the things he said. Not to mention that a new form of digestion would undoubtedly affect the digestion system itself. I also did some additional research last night to make sure these ideas were accurate."

"*Well?* What did you find?"

"I found two things regarding how his experiment was meant to work, as well as how it might have gone wrong. The first theory is that perhaps Mr. Willow has bacteria in his stomach that produce cellulase, rather than his body actually making it."

"Bacteria? That's just like cows and some herbivores. That would make sense, but that poses a lot of risks if you think about it."

"That's precisely what concerns me. The additional bacteria would increase the internal temperature of his stomach cavity, which could be life-threatening. Spicy foods do the same thing, but only briefly and on a much smaller scale. This would be a permanent increase, and it would most likely grow exponentially. The resulting symptoms would be mistaken for a fever, making the problem hard to detect. If his body couldn't handle the new temperature brought about by the additional bacteria, he would surely die. His internal organs wouldn't be able to function properly. Of course, it would all depend on his body's ability to maintain homeostasis, but to cool his internal temperature would be no easy task, and he'd probably be unable to live a regular life. He'd also be entirely unable to work out that way that he does, as that would raise his increased body temperature even higher." Sir Thomas looked up at Kronos, whose face had grown stern as he fidgeted with his fingers. "Are you all right?"

"Hmm." Kronos remained in thought.

"Are you pitying Mr. Willow now? It's only a theory, and as far as I know, he isn't suffering from this, or he's coping with it somehow."

"Incorrect. It's not that." Kronos took a deep breath. "I'm a scientist and afraid of nothing, but the idea of death from the inside-out such as that case horrifies me," Kronos admitted gravely. "I'm not squeamish when it comes to anatomy, but the body rotting on the inside and decaying both internally and externally disturbs me. We're humans, after all. We aren't meant to die like that. Just heating up internally to the point of death is unthinkable and unbearable. The pain would be different from natural death, though I could never describe it or even imagine how it would feel. I suppose once you're ranked among the most powerful beings, you're the only one strong enough to defeat you. Having your own stomach burn your insides is horrible. Having your own blood cells engulf your brain cells is horrible."

Sir Thomas slowly nodded his head as he looked at Kronos. *Shame on me. I never stopped to ask you how you've been feeling after your experience with the disease. We've been so caught up in this quest, and you've seemed so fine that I failed as a caretaker to check-up on you. You don't necessarily remember what happened, but just hearing about it probably makes your insides clench and your head throb. This whole time, I've been insulting you and assuming all of your goals to be selfish, but, perhaps, you truly are afraid of getting sick again. Are you afraid of dying? Have you been living in constant fear that your own body might suddenly begin to destroy itself? If I ask you, you'll just change the topic or ignore me. Such is how it's always been. Still, I feel awful now.* Sir Thomas sighed. "Such is the consequence of science, sometimes. I don't blame you for being disturbed. No one would ever care to die because their own body destroyed them from the inside-out."

"Yet, that isn't the case for Birch. He wouldn't have lasted this long, and that's a fact. So, what are your other theories?"

"Besides his stomach cavity temperature being raised, the new bacteria could be fighting with his healthy gut bacteria and killing them. They're taking up more room in his stomach, and upsetting the balance. The microbiome is a very delicate thing, and it affects us a lot more than most people even know. Of course, he might be trying to manage it as best as he can, but there'll come a time where he won't really be able to do anything."

"Theoretically, it might not even be the other bacteria in his gut."

"What do you mean? An immune system response?"

"That's exactly what I'm suggesting, but it would all depend on how he was and is getting the bacteria into his gut. It's quite possible that the immune system keeps trying to destroy them, and he has to keep adding more. This would be physically taxing, and he might even constantly feel sick."

"That's certainly a microscopic war that I wouldn't want going on inside of me."

"But everything we've theorized so far is only possible if he has cellulase-producing bacteria in his stomach. The other way would be for him to either have an additional organ, gland, or something else in him producing the cellulase enzyme."

"Indeed. Between the throat, gallbladder, saliva glands, and the many other possible areas of manipulation in the body there are several ways that he could have his body producing cellulase. However, the problem isn't with how the cellulase is being produced, so it doesn't really matter."

"Hmm. You believe the digestion of cellulose is the cause of the side effects?"

"Mr. Willow said that the cellulose that doesn't get digested acts as a broom which then 'sweeps' the colon. If he were able to produce cellulase and break down the cellulose that he eats, then there's no broom. He, theoretically, has no broom to help clean his colon. The intestines mainly rely on this. They can't push waste out if there is basically no waste. Essentially, he probably can't even go to the bathroom without a colon cleanse or some other kind of medication. If not, he'd be sitting on the toilet for an hour, slowly pushing a few specks of waste out. At the very least, he'd have unhealthy fecal matter or possibly no stool at all. It depends if he can fully digest cellulose or just a majority of it, and I have no clue as to how much he can break down."

"Oh, crap! No pun intended." Kronos smirked, laughing internally. "That was a *shitty* joke. What a *waste* of my intelligence. I see exactly what you mean. He's digesting a majority of what he eats, and his diet primarily consists of plants, ones that are blended into a liquid, in fact. Yet, he is not a vegetarian. The meat he eats would help create waste, but it would be the smelly mushy kind often excreated by carnivores, and it wouldn't be enough."

"The question is essentially a matter of the adaptation of intestinal strength. Are his colon 'muscles' stronger because they aren't relying on the cellulose-broom, or is it more of a symbiotic relationship between the organs and the waste?"

"Intestinal strength has been proven to increase due to kegel exercises in cases of people trying to overcome the reoccurring problem of constipation or improve bowel movement. The strength actually has nothing to do with it, though. See, the problem is the lack of waste. It's easier to clean a room full of large objects than to search the walls to eradicate a few specks of dust. Understand?"

"I do. Still, those small specks are problematic."

"Correct, but it's not like they are permanent. Eventually, the small specks will add up to something his intestines are able to push out. In fact, he might not have to go to the bathroom for days or weeks at a time. That's actually beneficial, although waste hanging out in the colon is never good. Still, unhealthy or small amounts of stool aren't necessarily lethal. Unless you think that-"

"Indeed I do," Sir Thomas replied gravely. "I think that based on these assumptions, it's highly possible that Mr. Willow has colon cancer. Had it in the past, has it now, or will have it. Any of those three. If not cancer, then he probably suffers from an unusually high rate of digestive ailments. The stomach flu, for example. It is even possible that he needs to get his stomach pumped every now and then or that his system has gone septic before or even often."

After Sir Thomas finished speaking, it was silent for a moment as the two men thought over everything they had just discussed.

"I'd rather have my insides heat up until the point of death," Kronos muttered. "I suppose this could all be possible. Birch did say that he had encountered side effects of his own. Yet, that is considered a preventable cancer, or at least one that's easy to detect and eradicate, for the most part. Perhaps, what he did to his body is advancing the cancer at a destructive rate. Considering the energy his body gets due to his digestion of cellulose, the cancer cells must be thriving. At the same time, he has increased cellular regeneration and duplication, so that cancer must be feasting."

"It doesn't matter if they take it out. It'll just grow back."

"The problems don't end there."

"I beg your pardon? What else could there be?"

"There is one other thing that you perhaps didn't think of that has just occurred to me now. With the ability to digest cellulose, that means Birch has more energy than anyone. He could work out all day if he really wanted to. That explains his speed and strength. However, this is why he has to live such an active lifestyle. If he weren't so active, he would be obese beyond belief, which would result in death. The number of extra calories from those normally nondigestible parts of the plant would be so many added on to the already high-calorie diet that many follow. Besides the digestive tract problems, if this were released to the public, there would be a widespread obesity epidemic unlike any ever seen before. Everyone would become immobile and useless. Perhaps a lot would die too and-"

"Nope! I know what you're thinking, Kronos! Let's fatten everyone up so we can take over the world. Not going to happen!" Sir Thomas having been Kronos' caretaker for years knew what he was thinking.

"Well, clearly I wasn't the only one thinking about it." Kronos raised his eyebrows and smirked at Sir Thomas. "You're actually the one who brought it up, so I have nothing to do with it. Good idea, though. I'll have to take it into consideration."

Sir Thomas laughed a bit as he stood up from his chair. "Not a chance. We already have enough to take care of." He thought for a moment. "Really, it'd actually be useful to those who suffer from hunger. Third-world countries and such. It would basically double the amount of food and nutrition a person could get from plants. That could do a lot more than you would think. In fact, you could actually digest wood, shirts, paper, grass, and anything cellulose-based. We could end world hunger and slow down the decimation of food resources." Kronos thought that idea over before swiftly rejecting it. Sir Thomas ignored Kronos' disgust at the noble idea. He walked over to the balcony and looked around outside. The river was flowing beautifully. Closing the sliding glass door behind him, Sir Thomas sat back down on the couch. "No coppers outside yet."

"Cops? Ha! You think they could ever find us? You think that anyone could ever find me? I want you to understand something, Thomas. It's not my fault that I'm an evil genius. It's almost as if it is genetically coded into me."

"Whatever you say," Thomas replied, rolling his eyes.

"Anyway, hopefully, Mr. Willow isn't dead. Then when he comes to find us, we can get him and the Immortalizer at the same time." Kronos reached his arms out in front of him as if capturing them there and bringing them toward him. "We'll catch two scientists with the same trap. It's foolproof."

Sir Thomas let out a sigh, believing that was a bad idea. "I understand that you live by your philosophy that multitaskers run the world and everything, but soon you will destroy yourself in such haste. Fighting a man who is supposedly immortal and a man who is considered a superhuman at the same time seems like a suicidal plan and absolute rubbish. Anyone would agree. It'd be more than just a bloody skirmish. We can't just kill them with the D.O.O.M. Shooter. Otherwise, we don't get the research to its fullest. Capturing them instead, though? That's just as wrong."

"It almost sounds like you don't want to do any of this and that you would rather just be home relaxing in your castle back in England with a classic novel and a warm cup of tea," Kronos replied jokingly, knowing that was exactly what Sir Thomas wanted.

"You know *what*, for *sooooome* reason... I *do* want that. *Very* selfish of me isn't it?" Sir Thomas replied sarcastically.

Kronos shook his head. "All this digestive talk has made me lose my appetite. So much for breakfast."

"Unfortunately, I lost my appetite when you vaporized the training dummy and then destroyed the whole Goddamn gym!"

Kronos laughed. "You're going to have a stroke! Calm down. I suppose stuff like that could cause someone to lose their appetite, but I'm actually in the mood for a victory meal now. Thank you for curing my lack of hunger by reminding me of what I've achieved so early in the day."

"My God, you're bloody annoying," Sir Thomas replied as he rolled his eyes, secretly enjoying Kronos' humor.

"Don't call me your God. I'm not even a prophet." Kronos grabbed a snack from a cabinet next to the fridge before walking back over and sitting on the couch next to Sir Thomas. He put on the flatscreen television that was mounted on the wall across from them.

The news was automatically the first channel that played when the television was turned on. A lovely, dirty-blonde-haired woman with elf-like ears was on the screen. Although a reporter who was supposed to focus on the news she was reporting, the young woman talked and acted as if she was the center of attention rather than the story itself.

"This is Natalie Anderson from American News 50, reporting live from Charleston, West Virginia, where a tragic accident has just occurred about half an hour ago. Reports say that The Heaviest Lifters gym was attacked in what is believed to be a terrorist attack. The only victim was the town hero and gym owner, Birch Willow, where witnesses have reported that he was shot in the right shoulder by the main attacker. His wounds have been reported as nonfatal. Mr. Willow, called Charleston Crusher by the locals here, has been taken to the hospital for treatment of his injuries, and we will continue to report on his condition. There were no other casualties, as everyone else was able to escape safely. Here are what some of the witnesses have to say."

The scene was chaotic, still filled with police, firefighters, and local residents who could not help but come out and see what was going on. Despite all of the commotion, the footage was sorrowfully quiet as Natalie walked over to Michael Kellson and began questioning him. He answered as best as he could, although he was still shaken up from what happened.

"We still aren't entirely sure what happened. The last thing I remember was that Birch was helping out some clients and so I went and started taking care of some stuff in the office room of the gym. After that, I came out and was chatting with one of our regular customers. I didn't see who it was, but a man started yelling something at Birch, who was in the restroom. The man then began to shoot up the place, and I didn't see any explosives, but a lot of stuff did explode. You can tell that just by looking at the ruins of the building. I immediately called the authorities and got out of there. We still don't have a lot of information until the forensics and police figure out what exactly happened."

Natalie agreed with what he had to say. "Thank you, Mr. Kellson, and our prayers for Mr. Willow. We were told he was injured badly, correct? And do you have any idea as to why anyone would target your gym?"

Michael answered what he thought correct, but he truly had no idea about Kronos or Sir Thomas. "Birch was shot in the shoulder with whatever weapon they were using. From what I saw, the back of his head was cracked open too. He is currently in the hospital being treated for his injuries. In fact, the police and firefighters actually had to pull him out from under the rubble of the gym as you can see here," Michael gestured to the crumpled piles of the gym. "Birch was unconscious when they retrieved his body, but he is alive. Given the weight and amount of rubble that fell on him, it's likely that he might have some broken or fractured bones as well. However, it's nothing fatal, as far as I know, and that includes the head injury. As far as the attack, perhaps money? I have no idea why anyone would attack our business. We are a kind and charitable place. Perhaps it was meant to serve as a public statement, but I really don't know. Birch is considered a celebrity, so it opens him up to a lot of attention and possible threats. Given the recent fighting event we just hosted, it's even possible that this was an act of revenge from one of the losing contestants, but I'm not trying to point fingers at anyone. Until the criminal suspects are apprehended and questioned, we still don't know the reasoning behind the attack, and whether or not we should expect Charleston to fall victim to any other attacks soon."

Natalie thanked Michael for his time and answers before walking over to one of the police officers. She asked the woman the same questions, and the officer gave almost the same answers. Everyone was entirely clueless as to what happened, or what kind of weapon had been used to create such havoc.

"Well, folks, there you have it. Is it a terrorist attack, or is there something else at play here? Tune in later to find out more, and of course, our thoughts are all with Mr. Willow as he recovers. As always, this is Natalie Anderson reporting live. Back to you, Justin."

The news footage went back over to the main center with the other news hosts sitting around the newsroom. Anchorman Justin Ingain began to introduce a new story, his deep voice earnest. "Thank you very much, Natalie. Quite the story, and more on that later as we get new information. Our best wishes to everyone there as they attempt to figure out what happened. I've always admired Mr. Willow. Coming up next: a speedster spotted running through Minnesota. Is it an online hoax, or do superheroes exist? More on that after the break."

The news cut out as the television cut into a commercial break about colon cleanse. The room became silent as Kronos muted the television, although the fridge still hummed, and the clock continued to tick.

Sir Thomas reluctantly looked over at Kronos, who was smirking with mischievous and greedy intentions behind the wicked smile. "No, Kronos," he stated firmly. "Don't even think about it! We're already in a mess that we can't handle without violence. We don't need to start trouble with this person too."

Kronos shook with feverish excitement, and he laughed with the joy of hope in defeat that came about when the odds suddenly seemed to completely turn around. "Thomas, didn't you just hear that? A speedster was *just* seen in Minnesota! That has to be The Chronological Changer! It has to be! I went there searching for them, but it was a dead end. I think. I don't entirely remember, but I couldn't find them. Maybe. Yet here they are, once again in action. It couldn't be more perfect for us. We're already in America. We might as well pay them a visit while we're here."

Sir Thomas frowned, and he grew sourer in disbelief. *Damn telly! You're one of my only friends, so why are you encouraging him? This is why I prefer to read!* Sir Thomas let out a frustrated exhale through his nostrils as he turned and looked at Kronos with judgment in his eyes. "And do what, Kronos? Create another enemy? When you showed me the files for the scientific rivals, I didn't think you meant the rival part literally. I thought it was just a code, but after your last two visits to these people, I don't believe that anymore. You set a trap for The Immortalizer, and I don't even need to explain what happened with Mr. Willow."

Kronos was laughing gleefully to himself, too happy over the mention of a real-life speedster to even be annoyed. "You're getting all emotional and frustrated, Thomas. Given your past heart problems and age, I'd suggest you take a deep breath and relax for a minute. You need to think about this logically, which means understanding and realizing that the pros greatly outweigh the cons in this situation. It's true that I 'failed' the last two missions, but this one is going to be different." Sir Thomas gave Kronos a look of utter disbelief. "Listen, if you hadn't convinced me to sit and talk with Birch, this all wouldn't have happened."

"You would dare blame me?"

"However, I have taken your lectures on connecting with humans on an emotional level into consideration. Given our situation, I believe, logically speaking, that it would make sense to do what you suggested. We are going to befriend The Chronological Changer and have them help take down The Ruthless Root and The Immortalizer."

"*You? Befriend* someone?" Sir Thomas laughed in an exaggerated manner. "Blimey, you've gone absolutely mad to be speaking such unbelievable rubbish. I'm terribly angry right now, but that actually made me laugh. "Oh, and I suppose that we should film all of this while we're at it? We'll have everyone take a gander at it once it's all pieced together: a real-life speedster and a teleporting man versus an immortal man and a superhuman. This dodgy project of yours is getting too out of hand in all honesty. It should end. Actually, all of this tosh shouldn't have even started to begin with, but I suppose this was bound to happen one day or another. Perhaps not with us, but people like these rival scientists are sure to attract one another, just as they attracted you." Sir Thomas was quiet for a moment, knowing he was going to regret tagging along. "I'll help you, though. I don't wish to see you get harmed trying to tackle all three of these guys at once. Hopefully, I might be able to settle the entire matter between everyone using my persuasive personality and charming manners." He glanced over at the analog clock in the kitchen. "It'll probably take us a while to get there. Pack your things, as we're leaving tonight. After this person, however, we're done, and I mean that. I'm retired after that!"

The two men turned their attention back to the television. The news was back on, and Justin was introducing the new story. "Welcome back everyone, I'm your anchorman Justin Ingain, and as always, this is American News 50. Around the country, covering the states, we're here with the most important updates. Well, in Granite Falls, Minnesota, there have been reports of a real-life speedster who saved the lives of many in an apartment building fire just today. Witnesses say the vigilante left without talking to anyone or even being seen. Reporter Rebecca Wright is on the case."

The footage went over to Rebecca. "Thank you, Justin. I'm here live in Granite Falls just half an hour after the victims were saved. As you can see, the firemen and first responders are still here helping out at the scene. The fire itself was fast spreading and was finally just put out. No one knows how it was started, and there will be further investigation into the cause of it. There are suspicions that a smoker's cigarette was at play here, although it has not been confirmed. Now, as for the speedster part, here are what some of the locals have to say."

Rebecca began interviewing a woman who had been saved from the fire. The woman's face was sunken in, and it was apparent that she had been scared and crying. "Well, I was trapped with my daughter when suddenly a person came into the building. They had some kind of crazy costume on, and it seemed like time had slowed down. They weren't moving at super speeds, but they were moving faster than any person I've ever seen. They even left a visible particle trail behind them, as if they were moving at super speed. It looked like green lightning. A piece of the ceiling came down, and they caught it before throwing it off of themselves. So, they were really strong too, even though they looked really skinny. They picked me up, and I was out of the building before I could even blink twice."

"They? So, you're saying that you couldn't tell whether they were male or female?"

The woman shook her head. "No, I couldn't tell the gender. They were moving too fast, and I was confused besides. The smoke made it hard to see. After saving me, they went back to save my daughter. I don't know if they're watching this, but my daughter and I thank them very much. I don't think she would have made it." The woman started weeping at the thought of her daughter being trapped in that fire.

Rebecca thanked the woman, who was clearly not listening anymore, and then went to one of the firefighters. He had been talking to the other firemen but immediately turned his attention to her once she approached. "Excuse me, sir, I'm with American News 50. Can you tell us anything about what happened here?"

"Yes, ma'am, I can. Is this all being streamed?"

"Yep. We're live right now."

"Roger that. Well, 'bout forty-five minutes ago, we got a call over at the station about a fire that was happening right over here in this building." He gestured over to the apartment building that still had some smoke coming out of it. "We quickly headed over to respond to the call and take care of the situation. For about the first five or so minutes, it was just us firemen. We had started putting the fire out but hadn't yet gotten to saving any civilians. Part of our team had just entered the building. All people on the bottom floors were cleared out immediately, and we set up a perimeter. We were sending up the ladders and sending in men and women to rescue the trapped civilians when this 'speedster' figure showed up." He made air quotation marks with his hands when he spat out the word speedster.

"Speedster? You say it as if you don't believe it or like it."

"That's because I don't. It's true that a masked vigilante did save a lot of people who hadn't yet been rescued, but as far as the rumors about incredible speed and time slowing down, they're just the result of inhaling fumes from the fire. Nothing more than that. Besides that, a lot of people in traumatizing or dangerous situations often idealize and dramatize their rescuers. Of course, there's nothing wrong with that at all, and it's not necessarily a bad thing, but it is partially to blame for the rumors that are going around. I certainly didn't see anyone moving at superspeed or even cheetah speed at the most."

"I see. So there was a hero, just not a superhero. No green lightning trail?" Rebecca was no longer shaking with excitement. Her face now had a severe expression to it. She had really been hoping there was a speedster.

"Not that I know of or saw. We have to thank this person for their assistance in rescuing civilians, as they did put their life on the line and helped others, but *we* have it covered. It's our job, and they should stay out of the way. We're the closest things to real-life heroes. Their costume is just some person roleplaying. It's dangerous and an irresponsible thing to do, both for their safety and everyone else's."

Rebecca reluctantly thanked the man, and he went back over to a firetruck. "Well, there you have it, folks. Is it the result of toxic fumes, traumatic exaggeration, or was there really a speedster here? Stay tuned as we find out more."

The television went to another commercial break.

After muting the television, Kronos and Sir Thomas sat on the couch in silence for a minute, absorbing all that they had just heard and seen.

After a minute, Sir Thomas broke the silence as he went over to the kitchen for a snack, his appetite back. "They said this person had a green lightning trail, what do you think of that?" He started eating a plum, which was one of his favorite foods to eat.

"It's very intriguing." Kronos turned off the television and strolled over to the kitchen, his hands in the pockets of his lab coat. "It's not from speed… I can tell you that much. Now in my research and this journey, I have seen some crazy things, but that is too crazy. They'd have to be moving faster than the eye could track it, or around that fast. Real-life speedsters don't exist. It's a nice idea, but too unrealistic."

Sir Thomas abruptly closed the refrigerator door and looked at Kronos, accidentally spitting out pieces of plum in disbelief as he almost choked on laughter. "Too unrealistic! Are you kidding me? I'm absolutely gobsmacked. You teleport around with a gun that disintegrates stuff for God's sake! How could you even say that? Mr. Willow is over eight feet tall and has super strength. You claim that there is an immortal man, and there is a file for a magic man you call The Dark Depressor. A terrible name by the way." Sir Thomas shook his head in disbelief. "To me, it seems like a person who runs fast would fit in perfectly with this whole journey. I can't believe you just said that."

Kronos sat down at a table in the kitchen area. He chuckled at the comments. "I suppose you have a fair point, Thomas, but I'm not entirely sure that speed that fast could be achieved via the human body. Secondly, The Dark Depressor is a brilliant name, by the way. I had to find something that wasn't already taken and copyrighted, now didn't I? Not that I'm publishing anything about these people, but just out of respect for fellow creators and original works. That's an extremely difficult thing to do. The Chronological Changer's speed-powers are probably just some time-warping illusion that they create. That's precisely why I named them that. They aren't actually super-fast, as far as I know. We'll just have to find out for ourselves."

"I'll give you credit for that one. The comic book industry is full of aces who have taken a lot of good names for speedsters. If we do find this person though, I call dibs on getting their research. I don't move as quickly in my old age." Kronos smirked, knowing that Sir Thomas did secretly want to be involved in this, even if it was just a little bit. "Don't use what I just said against me, though. I still disprove of all of this, for the most part. Anyway, what about The Ruthless Root? Why did you make that name? Mr. Willow is the complete opposite of ruthless. He's actually a very nice guy."

"Except for when he threw a weight machine and a medicine ball at me. You barely saw what I saw, since you were so busy hiding outside in the car, soiling your fancy British britches or whatever you wear. He was screaming like a savage caveman. He had perfect scars across his chest, and his eyes were even more vicious than mine. Plus, he punched me. He smashed pieces of the ceiling and everything. If only you had heard him roar. Also, he drinks plant-shakes and is named after two types of trees, so it seemed to match the theme. I prefer all of my nicknames to be alliterative." Kronos thought for a minute. "Hell, I saw a clip of a video of him fighting a bear, breaking a neck on one and the jaw on another. That's what I call ruthless, as well as efficient."

"I'm not sure if I entirely believe that or not. You're an exaggerator and delusional. Since you aren't clever enough to come up with good enough names, I call naming everyone on the rumor list! Magnet Master or such." There was a lighthearted and joking tone in Sir Thomas' voice. It was almost as if everything they were doing was part of some kind of video game or something. Perhaps he even thought it all to be one horrible nightmare that was coming to an end as the sun began to rise in the real world.

"Sure, okay. Once I'm dead, you have full permission and rights to name them. Until then, I am the official namer, and it stays that way. Magnet Master? Really? I kind of like M.O.M. Master of Metal!" The two of them laughed at the ridiculous idea. "As far as this speedster goes, we won't know anything for sure until tomorrow. Now get some rest, Thomas. It's been an eventful morning, so we should relax for a bit. We have a long drive ahead of us."

The plan was to start driving before night and be there before morning.

Sir Thomas had a glass of water before going to his bedroom to read a book he had packed with him for the trip.

Kronos found himself walking out onto the balcony, looking around at the world outside. *You're a good caretaker, Thomas. Perhaps the best. You shouldn't be here. I truly wish that this could all go down a different way. Don't be sad. I've accepted it all. But if my sickness and memory loss wasn't intentional, then what exactly have I gotten myself into? Is it possible that I developed Schizophrenia? My own immune system had been eating my brain, and now I'm going against others who are just like me. Super smart scientists, yet we're stupid and self-destructive. I admit it, and I'm not ashamed to do so. Just regretful about it, and that's different. We're greedy and have kept our research to ourselves. I'm sure those are only a few of our terrible traits, but I know we have plenty of good in us as well. Still.. we were impatient and experimented on ourselves.* "And in the end," Kronos mumbled to himself, "we've all just ended up sickly…"

CHAPTER 9
RECOVERY AND REVENGE
(Charleston, West Virginia. The Same Day: April 14, 2022)

Birch Willow woke up to the beeping sound of a heart and vital signs monitor. It had a somewhat relaxing rhythm to it, but the rhythm swiftly changed into the soundtrack of a horror movie, pulsing faster and louder as Birch fully gained consciousness, realizing he was in a strange place. His head throbbed with massive pain, and he felt dizzy. He squinted his eyes shut and tried to drown the stinging sensation out. His head stopped ringing, and Birch reluctantly opened his eyes. Now that his head was not a mess, Birch was able to see that he was in a hospital. He felt as if he would faint and fall unconscious from anxiety and shock, but his body was still on high alert from the battle at the gym, and so, instead, he was instantly filled with panic and an instinct to bulldoze out of the building.

Slowly, the memories of what happened came back to him like flashbacks, and Birch flinched and twitched with each horrible memory. He turned his head to the right and looked at his right shoulder, which was wrapped in thick layers of bandages and medical tape. All Birch remembered was being shot, but after that, everything was just nonexistent in his memory except for brief glimpses of blurry images that he must have seen while half unconscious.

Flexing his massive arms and legs, Birch felt them weighed down by something he could not move, just as he had felt during the sleep paralysis he often had. However, he could tell this was different. Strapped down to a large bed, he noticed that metal cuffs held down his body, located at both of his wrists and ankles. These metal cuffs were not ordinary, and he knew that. Standard ones would not have fit around his body, and even if they had, he could easily break them.

The fact that he could not break the strange cuffs made Birch even angrier, and his giant heart began to beat louder than an ancient drum. He let out a powerful roar that physically shook the windows of the room, and he was almost foaming at the mouth. His eyes had utter fear in them, backed by complete defiance. He squirmed and moved like a wild animal strapped down.

Upon hearing the inhumane roar, an African-American man in a lab coat, who seemed to be in his early forties, rushed into the room through a door to Birch's right. "Mr. Willow! Please calm down!"

The Ruthless Root instantly stopped moving when he heard the voice. He turned his head toward the figure, and as soon as he saw who it was, his whole body grew tenser, and every fiber of muscle in his body became backed by anger beyond comprehension. He now understood what was going on. "You," Birch yelled out in a deep voice that threatened life. "Let me free right now, before I get even more pissed off!"

"Or what?"

"I'm never angry, but you know what'll happen if I'm enraged. Normally, the idea of havin' blood drawn makes my arms completely numb and weak. I can barely move them. Medical buildings make me feel weak like that too, but I'm not goin' tuh stay here for another minute. I'll break these cuffs off, and then I'll snap your neck and twist your head all the way around, Abraham. I'm strong enough tuh even rip it all the way off I wanted to. Your head could be attached tuh nothing except you're slimy spine like uh fish skeleton."

"Break free of those cuffs? A very tempting thought for you, I assume, but there's a problem with that. The Organization was in contact with a figure a while back. There were reports of a man who could control metal with his mind and body. He's not a part of us, so I assure you that it caught our interest right away. I met with him a while back and made a deal for some of his technological inventions, and I assure you that they are indeed remarkable. Some are calling him the California Crusader since he's doing vigilante work in the state. The point is, he made those cuffs using strong metals and powerful magnetic forces. We took into account your size and strength during the drafts for those cuffs, and we even made them stronger than your predicted strength. So, try as you might, Mr. Willow, but you won't break those cuffs."

Birch laughed heartily.

The echoing sounds of Birch's loud laughter worried Abraham a bit despite his firm belief in the calculations that had been made. "What's so funny, Mr. Willow?"

Birch continued to laugh, the sounds almost contemptive. "Well," he grew more serious as he stared at Abraham with pure rebellion in his eyes, "I just find it funny that you think The Organization can predict uh person's strength. That's impossible, even for you guys. You can use all the technology, equations, data, and whatever you want, but you will *never* be able tuh predict uh person's strength!"

"Say what you will, Mr. Willow, but I trust the California Crusader and the mathematicians on our team. We all know you hold back, so we weren't able to calculate and plan for your true strength, but we planned for you to be a lot stronger than your past feats have shown. I simply can't take your word over the statements of The Organization."

"Of course, you won't, but I understand that actions speak more powerfully than words!" With that declared, Birch flexed his large muscles so strongly that his skin almost tore open. His veins bulged. His body became as hard as his bones. He pressed his arms up against the cuffs. The tough metal, held down by magnetism, resisted at first, but Birch's strength grew with each passing second, and the cuffs only grew weaker with each second as they were moved further away from the magnets. Then, with an impressive burst of power, Birch sent both of the metal cuffs flying off of his arms across the room, destroying the magnetic power. Sitting upright, he used his arms and legs to quickly break the cuffs around his ankles. He jumped off of the bed, and when he landed, the whole room physically shook. Standing tall and proud, he turned and looked down at Abraham, his face stern and defiant. "You seem unafraid, Abraham. Do you have snipers outside? Think they're faster than me?"

"Not at all, Mr. Willow. It's just us. I'm certainly impressed by your feat of strength, but I expected nothing less. I'm not afraid because I'm not your enemy. We had nothing to do with what happened today."

Towering in front of Abraham menacingly, the massive figure of Birch seemed ready to kill in an instant. "You really expect me tuh believe that?"

"We healed you, didn't we?"

Birch looked at his right shoulder, which was wrapped up. He turned his angry gaze back down at the man below him as if he were nothing more than an ant to be stepped on. "Hmph. You've got me there. What did you do?"

"Curious, aren't we?"

"Answer the question."

"For someone who is constantly praised as being helpful, humble, and kind, you're certainly impatient and rude. I know that you secretly have an unstoppable angry side, but there's no need for me to experience it. Anyway, the surgery was experimental, but you should be rather appreciative of what we did. You're a man of nature, so I'm sure you'll hate what we did, but it was the best option."

"*What* did you do?" Birch asked again, more aggressively this time. He clenched his giant hands into lethal fists.

"Allow me to give you the whole medical report then, Mr. Willow. It's approaching noontime. After we rescued you from the rubble and debris you were buried under after the gym attack, we brought you here. I had a group of agents quickly set up this room for you. You've suffered a mild head concussion, which isn't bad, considering the fact that the whole back of your head was smashed. There was some split skin and bleeding, but there was no need for stitches. Your skull is entirely intact, which is good news. You were knocked out from that, plus the rubble crushed you, but no broken or fractured bones from that even. You're fortunate to be alive, considering how much fell on you, but I guess you're more indestructible than everyone thought. You recovered relatively quickly once I.V. filters were set up, and we patched the back of your head up, but then we kept you knocked out to perform the surgery on your shoulder."

"What exactly even happened tuh muh shoulder? It was ripped apart atomically?"

"Part of it was. You were missing several layers of skin and muscle from your right shoulder and upper arm. Specifically, your deltoid was the most impacted. You lost a lot of blood from that injury, and it was hard to stop the bleeding and repair some of the damage to your veins and arteries. However, I do have some good news for you. You'll be able to leave before tonight if that's what you want. Given your extreme anxiety and dislike of medical facilities, I assume you want to leave as soon as you can."

"So this was all uh setup, wasn't it? I already declined your offer politely. I just want tuh live uh peaceful life. That's all I've evuh wanted. I'll send you the science and research, but I still have tuh work out the side effects. I'm telling you the truth! You think you can just come here and destroy everything that I've created? I'll kill all of you! You want tuh see how strong I can be, then bring it on!" Birch flexed and got into a position that would allow him to easily charge at Abraham.

Abraham slowly backed up a few feet but kept a calm and professional tone. "Take an easy there, big fella. You misunderstand what's going on here. We had nothing to do with what happened at the gym. We came as soon as we heard what had happened and made sure they didn't get to you. The Organization already has a deal with you, and we'll honor our word. Keeping you alive is our number one priority. We certainly can't use you as a super-soldier if you're dead, now can we?

Oh, well, that was the *original* deal, but either way, we need you alive, Mr. Willow. We believe that those men were sent from another country to get your research."

Birch let out an aggressive exhale through his nostrils like a bull about to charge. "It seemed tuh be that way. They were from England, and they gave me uh background story about their reasons for being there and asking me for muh research. It all added up properly, but perhaps it was all just false information tuh try and get muh research. *Or* they're actors from The Organization!" Birch exclaimed as he kicked a table next to the bed across the room. Abraham jumped away as the table smashed into the wall where he had just been standing.

Having fallen to the floor, Abraham jumped up to his feet and brushed his lab coat off. "You have cost me my dignity, Mr. Willow. I promise you that those men weren't lying, and they're not actors or associated with The Organization in any way. You know what our mission is and how we feel about private and illegal scientists. You know exactly how we feel about self-made heroes and villains. We've been tracking those two for quite some time now, and everything they say is true."

"Is that so? What are their names?"

"You accuse me of lying? The two men that attacked your gym are Sir Thomas and Kronos Nephus. I'm sure they discussed their work with the manipulation of atoms on an individual scale, did they not? Then they talked about teleportation. I assure you that The Organization is deeply impressed with their inventions and scientific discoveries. However, we honestly don't care about any of that right now. Their weapons are our top priority. We need to confiscate their technology in order to maintain not only the public peace but to secure the safety of the entire world for the future. You saw what that gun did to your gym! Now imagine a whole foreign army equipped with similar weapons. They could literally reorganize the planet. They could even physically shape it into their image." Abraham took a deep breath. "Worst of all, they could wipe out anyone who stands in their way, and that's what scares me the most. They could take over with just one of those guns, which they have right now. If it falls into the wrong hands… there's no imagining what it could do."

Birch sat back down on the bed, which flexed downward and groaned under his weight. His anger cooled as it was replaced with a grave understanding of the situation. "That's absolutely terrible," he muttered as he gently shook his head, looking at the floor. "They could just wipe out everything and everyone. I'm afraid that weapon is already in the wrong hands, Abraham," Birch said as he looked up at him. "I understand now. It's not too late, though. There's still time. We have to stop them! We—"

"I'm afraid this isn't a 'we' situation, Mr. Willow. Our agents are just normal people, and the organization can't risk losing our ill-equipped soldiers to such a weapon. We have no idea what other technology or weapons they have. R.O.M.A.B.A. Industries is a powerful business… no, it's an empire. There is much to them that the public doesn't know about. I've seen some of their dark and hidden secrets, and so have you. Our men and women have families and lives to go home to at the end of the day."

"But I don't," Birch stated as he stared at the bland hospital floor once again. He let out a heavy sigh. "At least not anymore," he said quietly, his voice choking up. "The gym is gone. All of it… is gone." Birch slowly looked up at Abraham, all emotion gone. "That's why you're here, ain't it? I'm expendable, and I have nothin' tuh lose. Besides that, I already know everything regarding the situation, which makes it easier fuh ya. I assume you're hopin' that I can take care of them for you?"

Abraham shook his head in disagreement. "Wrong. Not for *me*, Mr. Willow. This is for your country. For the future. For all of humanity. For the world! We can't stop them, but you can. The Organization will be backing you up all the way, but we won't send out our own men and women. We'll assess the situation as well as supply you both financially and intel-wise. You have our full support, and I will work personally with you up until the battlefield. You understand that to attack them with any other weapon than you is to possibly wage war against England. We still don't know if those two are on their own or if they're working with parliament. We can't bomb a facility in England with American weaponry based on classified information. I hope you understand."

Birch took a deep breath and let out a heavy sigh once again. "I understand that I really don't want tuh do this, Abraham. But there's no other option. I know what weapons and science they have. I'll have tuh stop them by muhself if that's what it takes tuh save the world. I've nevuh seen myself as uh hero, but I know uh lot o' people are countin' on me, even if they don't know it. I already know where those two are. Their headquarters are stationed over in England, and I assume you can get me the exact coordinates."

"A team is working on that as we speak. However, we can't fly you over there just yet." Birch looked at Abraham in confusion. "They mentioned searching for others just like them, right?" Birch nodded his head. "We'll be tracking them as they travel across America searching for these other people. Our plan is to intercept them before they ruin anyone else's life. You and I will be in contact, and I'll let you know when we're going after them."

"Understood."

"We'll make sure your well-equipped for the mission. I have a team of some of the best and the brightest in the country working on a special suit and weapon for you to help even out the odds."

"Fine, but I know all of this doesn't come free, and I don't just mean money. What's the catch?"

"Again, you are mistaken. We *aren't* your enemy, Mr. Willow. *They* are. There is no catch. The only thing is that we'll take all the credit for the apprehension of these criminals, and we're taking their technology to lock up in safekeeping. If you can do this for us, you won't have to worry about our existing deal. This technology is honestly better than your cellulase ability, even as superhuman as it may seem. They're the technologically advanced future, and as strong and remarkable as you are, I'm afraid that you are now the barbarous past in the eyes of the organization."

"Barbarous past?" Birch asked, offended.

Abraham smirked. "Don't take that so personally, Mr. Willow. I'm not quite done yet. That's not the best part. Since we'll be preoccupied with the new technology, and our old deal is no longer existent, we'll leave you alone. You can finally live the peaceful life you've been longing for. Sure, you'll know we exist, as we always will, but you won't have to be looking over your shoulder, wondering if we're there. We'll even find you a hot woman. Maybe two if you'd like. Perhaps a fancy mansion with only the finest amenities. Whatever your big heart desires. But first, you need to stop these madmen. They're a danger to everyone."

Birch thought over how shady all of this was. He had actually hated The Organization from day one when they found him. A chance for a peaceful life was worth everything to him, though. More importantly, they had the funds with which he could rebuild The Heaviest Lifters gym. "Alright, whatever ya say. Uh peaceful life is all I need." Birch went to stand up again but winced in pain and immediately sat back down. He put a hand to his waist, which had suddenly flared in pain. "Gah, that hurts!"

"Oh, yes. That reminds me, Mr. Willow: you have a terrible system of tumors in your digestive tract."

"You mean-"

"Unfortunately, I do mean colon cancer. It might be a coincidence although cases have shown that chronic constipation increases the risk of developing stuff like that. Don't even worry about it, though. We'll take care of that for you as soon as you finish your mission. It shouldn't hinder you yet. Now rest up, Mr. Willow. We have a big journey ahead of us!" Abraham started to walk away but turned back to Birch. "Oh, and about the cost for this shoulder surgery, don't worry about it. Consider it a perk of working with us," he said with a smile. That's colored-in graphene, and that shit's expensive, by the way. Well, not the way we make it," Abraham said with a wink. "You'll understand once you take a look at your shoulder. Just unwrap it gently. That's a lot better than plastic surgery."

"Hold up, Abraham. What's graphene? I remember hearin' about that uh few years ago. It was uh popular topic for uh while but then it died down. And what do ya mean by 'colored-in' graphene?"

"It's made from the same material as graphite, but it differs in its atomic structure. It's a one-atom-thick layer of the stuff that is not only flexible but also one-hundred times stronger than steel. It could stop a bullet, and it moves perfectly with your organic figure. Graphene is normally transparent, but I had my team make it a metallic-grey color for you, so it looks like metal." Abraham started to walk away but turned back again. "Oh, and one last thing before I go. We spoke with Mr. Kellson. I assumed you never told him about us, and I didn't give away that information either. I admire his high intellect, however, and I reassured his concerns. Give him a call as soon as you can." With that said, the mysterious man was gone.

Birch looked at the door through which Abraham had left, but he slowly turned his gaze back to the hospital floor. At this point, his anxiety and dislike of medical facilities was nonexistent since his mind was preoccupied with more important thoughts. It was a lot to take in for Birch. Secret organizations, shoulder surgery, a teleporting man, the destruction of the gym, a death-ray gun, and colon cancer. All Birch ever wanted was to live alone in peace. Perhaps somewhere in the woods or mountains like a lumberjack. Just him and nature. Plants and animals were living organisms that did not judge him, and he admired their gentle nature. Although they were mostly calm around him due to a mixture of fear and awe. Birch had hoped that the gym would help him eventually get to this dream while also helping others, but that chance was gone now. Whether he liked it or not, his only opportunity to fix his ruined life was working alongside The Organization.

Unwrapping the medical wrap around his right shoulder, Birch closed his eyes before looking at what was there. As suspected, based on what Abraham had said, Birch was not entirely shocked to see his shoulder appearing as it did. Almost like a cyborg, eighty-five percent of it was made of graphene that evenly lined up to the thickness of his skin. The graphene plating traveled down about an inch, making up a little bit of his deltoid.

"Now you've really gone and done it," Birch muttered to himself as he shook his head in disbelief. He let out a depressing sigh. Now that all of his anger had dissipated, he was left with nothing but sorrow and hopelessness. "Only me. This could only happen tuh me," he remarked as he rubbed his left hand over the graphene plating. It was all one solid piece, cold and lifeless as his heart was slowly becoming. "That'll give ya one headache though if I shoulder charge ya," Birch said, watching the material bend slightly as he flexed his muscles. It was hard, yet it moved smoothly with his body. "Well, at least I got this. Any other sucker wouldn't have had uh secret agency performin' this surgery on 'em. They'd probably be amputated for all I know. I don't feel like I'm in too much pain either. They did uh really good job patching this up, which makes them all the more uh dangerous group."

Birch woke up about an hour later. He had fallen asleep, overwhelmed by everything and physically drained from his injuries and surgery, as well as the energy and immense strength he had exerted in breaking free of the California Crusader's magnetic cuffs. The colon cancer was not what scared him. He had known about it for some time now. He had never been medically diagnosed as having it, but Birch had been suspicious of it. After all, he had manipulated his digestive system and body. There would be consequences for that no matter what, whether it was cancerous or not. His research was a tool to getting a healthier lifestyle, but you had to know how to use it. It was a tool that could easily be misused, as well as one that would hurt you even if you used it right.

After a few minutes of Birch thinking to himself, a nurse walked in. She was tall with curly dyed hair that was not any single definable color. It looked like a mixture of brown and purple. Her skin was tan, and she had dark eyes surrounded by a lot of makeup. She started unwrapping the medical wraps around Birch's head when he winced in pain. The nurse started talking to Birch in an overly-enthusiastic voice that was high pitched and squeaky. "Sorry! Did that hurt? I didn't mean for that to hurt. My bad! Hold on, I'll be gentler." She started unwrapping the bandages even more slowly than she had been. It kind of annoyed Birch, as he was the kind of guy that would rip a bandaid off like it was nothing. "How are you feeling, Mr. Willow? You've been asleep for most of the day."

"Forgive muh sarcasm, but I was just diagnosed with cancer, I got shot in the shoulder, lost uh couple of layers of flesh and muscle, my whole life's work and business was destroyed, I was essentially kidnapped by The Organization, and now I'm stuck in the hospital, which is the place I hate more than anywhere else. How do you think I feel? Besides that, I have tuh go on this mission now, which you probably already know about."

"Oh, true. I forgive you, though. If I were in your position, I wouldn't be happy either. That's an absolutely horrible day, and I'm really sorry to hear all of that. And of course, I'm from The Organization. A regular nurse or doctor wouldn't be allowed to see your shoulder replacement. It's nothing too crazy, but it's not a hospital-norm either. I'm sorry to hear about all of that, though. We all have rough days, some just more than others. Hopefully, it'll all get better. Would you like something to eat? You haven't eaten anything you're entire time here. Pudding? Jello? Bread? A light fruit bowl?"

"I'll have the fruit bowl since it'll help me recover faster." The nurse went and dumped fruit from a can into a plastic bowl. Birch sat up to eat it with his left hand.

While Birch ate, the nurse threw out all of the bloody medical wraps before she took his empty bowl and put it on the side. "If you would please comply with me, Mr. Willow, I have some tests I need you to perform for me."

Birch tensed up. "What kind o' tests?"

"Relax, big guy. I'm not doing bloodwork or anything. We just want to make sure that the operation was successful, and that your right arm and shoulder are fully functional. So, I just need you to follow my instructions to move it a certain way and lift a few small weights. Well, small for you, at least."

Although he was relieved to know that the tests were not medical ones, Birch still did not want to be stuck at the hospital any longer. He reluctantly agreed, however, after sighing. For the next hour, the nurse instructed Birch through the tests. Squeezing weights, moving his arm this way and that way, lifting odd objects. It was supposed to be therapeutic, but Birch found it annoying and tedious. What he found even more aggravating was how fake the nurse was. He respected all people, but her voice seemed to be constantly full of lies, and all of her kindness was an artificial exaggeration that she forced out as part of her act. She was a person who would easily manipulate weak men to take advantage of them. She would take all that they have and all that they were. Sometimes even who they would be. He tried to block out her tales of her days of high school and college, but her voice penetrated right through his mental walls.

Given how healthy Birch's body was, as well as how medically capable the experts at The Organization were, not much therapy was needed to regain functionality. The results were excellent, and Birch was able to use his shoulder just as well as before. It was as if nothing had changed. Despite this, Birch put on a black sling to make sure no one would be suspicious of his recovery if they saw him. He peered through the window blinds and surveyed the outside parking lot. There were no news vans parked outside. If he was lucky, which was not the trend of the day, he could make it home without the media bothering him.

After an unfortunately prolonged conversation with the annoying nurse, Birch managed to quickly get discharged from the hospital through The Organization. Luckily for him, his custom-made convertible had been spared of the atomic destruction that had befallen the gym, and they had brought it over to the hospital for him to drive home. Using it, he drove through the back-roads of the town so that not a lot of people would see him. This meant not passing by what was left of the gym, but he was a bit glad because he did not feel ready to actually see the destruction for himself with his own eyes. After all that he had been through, he knew he would be unable to handle it.

By the time Birch got back to the farm, it was 2:30 p.m. Michael was waiting outside for Birch at the farm, worried and pacing around. Birch had called Michael before he started his therapeutic tests, asking him to take care of the farm animals for him and then wait until he arrived.

"I was beginning to think that you weren't coming back. I'm glad to see you're finally out of the hospital," Michael yelled at Birch, who was making his way down the dirt driveway. "I came over as soon as I got the call. All of the animals are taken care of, but I'm still a wreck."

The two men silently walked into Birch's house and sat down at a table in the kitchen. Birch removed his arm from the cast and removed the large coat The Organization had provided him with to hide his new shoulder. Michael gasped at the sight of Birch's shoulder. "Holy shit! Is that graphene?"

"Well, you figured that out real fast. I forget how smart you are sometimes. Anyway, it's about time I explain everything to you."

"You better! There's a lot of madness going on, and I have no clue as to what any of it is about."

For the next hour, Birch explained what happened with Kronos and Sir Thomas this morning, telling him all of the science they had discussed, though he could not remember every detail. "I know it sounds crazy, but that's exactly what happened, Michael." Birch gave him a minute to think about everything he had just said. "Anyway, that's not all I have tuh tell ya. A little while before we started the gym, we hosted the Macho Man Wrestling Challenge. Remember that?"

"Yes, I remember. It was July of 2008 or 2009. It was a really big crowd. We had it over at that one stadium. A lot of people went to that."

"Unfortunately so," Birch commented bitterly.

"Why do you say that?"

"Too many people went. It unintentionally drew some unwanted attention. After the show, uh man in uh business suit named Abraham approached me. He was with what he called 'The Organization', and they had been watchin' me for some time, as it was clear that I was biologically advanced." Birch took a pause, his face agitated. "Well, he claimed that this group worked with the American government. They were secretly hired and put together as uh company that focused on advanced weaponry and self-made vigilantes and such. According to him, the company had been made after the atomic bombings of WWII, and they were a big part of the Cold War. They had been trackin' down individuals, and I was on the list for the American sector. Abraham said that rather than bring me in, they wanted my help. I could help fight or capture the other wanted people on their list in return for uh high-paying position in The Organization. I declined politely, requestin' uh peaceful life, as I wasn't uh threat tuh society, and killin' was against my morals. Turns out, they had really been trackin' me well, because they knew that I was hoping to create a gym, which was my dream of making The Heaviest Lifters. They had me there. In exchange for the money tuh build the gym, I agreed tuh one day be uh personal mercenary for them."

"No. It can't be true. That goes against everything you stand for and believe in."

"It does, which is why I got out of that contract."

"How?"

"By offerin' something more useful than my monstrous body."

"Birch… you didn't-"

"I'm afraid I did, Michael. Our research. To them, the ability to digest cellulose was far more useful than just havin' me as uh member of The Organization, and I don't blame 'em for feelin' that way. I gave them the basic information and theories, promising that they would get the rest of the research when we had figured out how tuh get rid of and prevent the side effects. That's how I was able tuh build uh gym that was so much more than just uh gym. They supplied me."

"And you never thought about telling me that?" Michael asked with a violent shake of his body, feelings of betrayal stabbing him in every way. "The gym I've grown to love... the gym that I helped build up from the ground... was founded on filthy cash? It was made with borrowed money from a shady organization at the cost of my friend's soul? How could you keep something like that from me? And don't say it was to keep me safe, because not knowing that a secret government organization is constantly watching me is just as dangerous as knowing."

"You know I'm not like that, Michael. Of course, I thought about it. It haunted muh mind every second of every day, but it wasn't muh decision tuh make you constantly look over your shoulder. I didn't want tuh be responsible for takin' away your freedom like that. All I've ever wanted was uh peaceful life. Who was I tuh take that away from ya?" Birch shook his head in frustration at both Michael and himself. "Listen, I know how you're feeling, but we have uh bigger problem at hand. I'm telling ya all of this now because they were here today."

"Wait, at the gym attack?" Michael asked with a mixture of anger and shock. "So, were Sir Thomas and Dr. Nephus actually members of The Organization?"

"No. That's not what I was leadin' up to, although it's what I had initially thought as well. The Organization members were the ones who took care of me at the hospital. They got in, somehow, and fixed muh shoulder."

"How? It's not like they can just flash some kind of secret badge or anything. They might not even be a legitimate company, for all we know. You actually don't know anything about them."

"So, it might work like that fuh all we know. Look, I don't know how any of it works. The organization seems tuh have endless pockets and ties. All I know is that they want me tuh help them take down Dr. Nephus and Sir Thomas. In return, I get uh peaceful life and whatever I want. We could use it tuh rebuild the gym, and it'll be even better than before. I have more leverage over them than last time."

There was a cold look in Micahel's dark eyes. "*No*, Birch! This isn't what either of us wanted. The Heaviest Lifters wasn't founded on stuff like this! It's not just that, though. For all we know, this is one big setup to get your research or even you. You could be walking into a trap!" Michael hit his palms together for emphasis.

"I know, Michael, but I don't think I have any other choice. For one thing, if the people at the gym weren't uh setup by the organization, then we really are in danger. That means that Sir Thomas and Dr. Nephus really are muh enemies, as well as threats to all of humanity. Even if it's all just uh trick, I still have tuh go. It's the only way we'll ever have peace in our lives and be able tuh live without having tuh watch our backs all the time. I can't live normally if that weapon is still out there. My mind would never be at ease. It has tuh be destroyed, whether it's The Organization's or Dr. Nephus' weapon. I'll get rid of it either way."

"You're not a hero, Birch! Charleston Crusher is just a name. It doesn't make you any more special than anyone else. It's not your job to go after the bad guys and save the day. You're just a home town hero, and it's for being popular, not heroics. The government has people who are paid and trained to track people like them down. Let The Organization do it, for crying out loud! They could easily shoot down those two men if they wanted to. Except, they don't want to because they want to use those two as an excuse to get you right where they want you!"

"I know! That's all the more reason for me tuh go. I'll destroy them from the inside out if they're lying, and if not, then I have tuh go after those two. Not for heroics or fame. I have to do it for revenge. They just took away everything from me! Muh business. Muh life. The only part o' me that I actually liked. They have tuh pay for what they did, and I'm the only person who can charge them the bill. I'm sorry, Michael, but it seems like no matter what, I have tuh do something."

"I don't believe you," Michael sated coldly.

"About what?"

"About being sorry. You're not sorry at all, and you're certainly no Charleston Crusher either. After being a teacher for so many years, I'm ashamed that I never picked up on who you really were. You're not my friend."

Birch was taken aback by the harsh statements. "Micahel, how can you say that after all that we've been through together?"

"*Together*? Turns out that you've actually been on your own for a while now, haven't you? That's not the worst part, though. The worst part is that I've realized you're not humble and helpful like everyone says. You're proud and selfish. Terribly selfish, in fact. You accepted a deal from a shady group without consulting me. Then you sold your soul to them in exchange for money to build The Heaviest Lifters, which you've been using for the past ten years to make yourself feel better. It was never about helping others for their benefit. You helped others in order to give yourself a place in society because you're an outcast. Not only that but you secretly like all of the attention. Yet, that wasn't enough for you, was it? You craved more, and so you used my research for your own gain. Another thing you did behind my back, which means we aren't actually friends, Birch. After all these years, I finally get the truth, as well as a glimpse at the real you. Honestly, I'm glad Rose is dead so that she doesn't have to see any of this."

"You take that back," Birch threatened coldly as he grew physically angry, the light glinting off of his new shoulder.

"Exactly. The Birch the public knows would have agreed with me and apologized, but you're not Charleston Crusher. You're Birch Willow, and you always have been." Michael stood up. "Have fun using your blood-money to make The Heaviest Lifters Two, because I won't be there this time." Michael got up and stormed out of the house toward his car.

Birch stayed seated, and he sat thinking for a moment. He slowly stood up and walked over to a window at the front of the house. He watched as Michael left his life, and he was emotionless about it.

Less than a mile away from Birch's house, Michael was pulled over by a police officer, though he had not been violating any traffic laws. When he got out of the car, the officer revealed himself to be a member of The Organization, and he fatally shot Michael before driving off with his body.

www.ingramcontent.com/pod-product-compliance
Lightning Source LLC
LaVergne TN
LVHW011815060526
838200LV00053B/3796